CHARLES LAMBERT

Little Monsters

PICADOR

First published 2008 by Picador

First published in paperback 2009 by Picador
an imprint of Pan Macmillan Ltd
Pan Macmillan, 20 New Wharf Road, London N1 9RR
Basingstoke and Oxford
Associated companies throughout the world
www.panmacmillan.com

ISBN 978-0-330-45037-9

1 3 5 7 9 8 6 4 2

A CIP catalogue record for this book is available from the British Library.

Typeset by Intype Libra Ltd
Printed and bound in the UK by
CPI Mackays, Chatham ME5 8TD

For my mother and father

One

When I was thirteen, my father killed my mother. Three days after that, I was taken away from the hospital by two people I had never seen before and would never see again, a man and a woman who used my name each time they spoke to me – Are you warm enough, Carol? Have you got your case, Carol? Carol, come along with us now – as if they knew me, although they didn't tell me their names. I must have shown willing somehow. I expect I nodded and did what I was told. I was put into a car that smelt new and then, when I was sitting alone in the back, they told me I was going to stay with Aunt Margot, who ran a pub called the Mermaid. I suppose I'd known that I wouldn't be taken home, but I was still surprised, and shocked, as I would have been no matter what the destination. They spoke about my aunt as though I was supposed to know all about her. They laughed when the man said I'd be able to get tipsy for nothing. That was the joy, he said, of living in a pub.

When the car drew into the car park I could tell

someone was waiting just inside the back door from the way the net curtain was twitched to one side. There was nothing but dark beyond it; I couldn't see a face. Outside, a sign swung on the wall, with a painting of a dark pond and a plump, ungainly mermaid sitting on a flat white rock beside it, combing her hair. The expression on the mermaid's face – as if she was deep in thought – and the way her tail was curled round the rock almost made me smile.

Seconds later, my aunt stalked out. She was clutching a thick pink cardigan around her, and had slippers on, with clumps of white fur and no backs to them. I was wearing a summer dress bought the year before, slightly too small, tight under the arms and round the waist, which they'd given me that morning. It made me feel not only uncomfortable but foolish.

My aunt didn't ask the man and woman to come into the pub. She didn't speak to them except to say, with a sigh, as if she'd expected the worst and been satisfied: 'So you've made it, then. You've found us up here in the back of beyond.' She reached to take my case, then turned back towards the pub.

I stood beside the car, not sure what to do, until the man who had driven us coughed and gave my shoulder a gentle push from behind. 'Go on, love,' he said. 'Go on, Carol, love. Your auntie's waiting for you.'

But Aunt Margot was already walking away, the wind blowing her skirt about her legs so you could see how thin and bare they were, nothing like my mother's. When she was almost inside, she paused and turned, as if to make sure I was behind her. As if she was checking on a dog.

I followed her down a long corridor, through the bar and up some steps into a narrow hall and, at the end of it, a kitchen. A man was reading a newspaper, spread out on the table before him. He nodded at me when we came in and that was the first time I saw Jozef. 'That's your uncle,' my aunt said, jerking her head in his direction. 'Your uncle Joey.' She pulled the paper from under his hands and folded it into four while he sat and glanced at me with an odd expression, as though she had told him off and he was amused and mocking her. 'Sitting here reading this rubbish,' she said. 'I hope to God you've got the cellar ready. They'll be here soon with that spirits delivery.'

Uncle Joey had shiny black hair, cropped short at the back and sides, but longer at the front and hanging in a fringe over his right eye. He was wearing a sleeveless grey pullover tucked into his trousers. He stood and came across the kitchen to shake my hand, bending slightly from the waist in an odd little bow, not serious, perhaps intended to make me smile, although he didn't smile himself. 'It's all finished,' he said, not to me, though he didn't take his eyes off me. 'I thought to do it this morning, when you were standing for so long at the door.' And that was how I learnt my uncle was a foreigner.

He wasn't stern at all, I found out later, once I came to know him. He liked listening to the radio, when he could get away from the bar, listening to classical music, and working in the cellar, where he would stay for hours, in a small room with a neon strip-light at the far end beyond the kegs and crates of bottles. Aunt Margot said that kind of music was for people who didn't have anything better to do with their time, although she spent most mornings sitting at the kitchen table with the radio on, thumbing through magazines, in a dressing-gown and her backless slippers. Uncle Joey never answered when she made comments like that. He just went pale and muttered something in his own language, Polish, which none of us understood.

When Uncle Joey spoke English, you could see him concentrate to avoid making mistakes, even though his English was almost perfect, apart from his accent and its studied, over-careful quality. Sometimes he would use expressions he had heard on the radio, catchphrases, and customers would look at him for a moment, wondering if he was pulling their legs. He hated people to know he was foreign and that he had been forced to run away from the place where he was born, but as soon as he opened his mouth it was obvious he had come from somewhere else.

I know what refugees are like now. I have lived with refugees, and anyone who knew then what I know now would have understood at once that he was a refugee, with that way of being both grateful and resentful; grateful they have been taken in by others; resentful because they have no choice other than to be saved.

I think he understood I was a refugee as well, on the run from what had happened between my parents, and what I had seen and imagined and how it had all come to an end, although I didn't speak about that. Whenever my aunt was unpleasant to me, as she often was, or when I was teased by her son, my cousin Nicholas, my uncle would listen, biting his bottom lip, before stepping in to protect me with a warning word.

A few years later, Jozef said that I could make my life whatever I wanted, but I didn't believe him. I thought he was simply repeating words that other people had said to him, words of consolation. I sometimes think most consolation comes to that, repeating things we know are unlikely to be true, and will almost certainly never be true for us, because otherwise everything we have lived through will be meaningless.

Two

That first night my aunt said my bed wasn't aired properly. I'd have to sleep in my cousin's room on a camp bed. I was still wearing the vest and knickers I'd had on when I was taken away from my home. I hadn't unpacked my suitcase because I didn't know where to put my things. I didn't even know what was in it, whether my pyjamas were there or not, because it had been packed for me by the woman who'd brought me to the Mermaid. While we were waiting for the car, she'd told me she'd chosen the clothes she'd thought would be most suitable, although she never said for what. For an orphan, I suppose. 'You can go back later and get anything else you need,' she'd told me, when she put the case into the back of the car, and I hadn't said I would rather do without everything than go back into my house. I hadn't said, either, that it wasn't my case at all but one my mother had used for shoes when we went on holiday. I had nodded and looked away.

That first night Nicholas, my cousin, told me about the

mermaid. His bed was higher than mine and all I could see was the shape of his head and the outline of a shoulder as he leant over. He told me the story in a silly, creepy voice that frightened me, despite the noise from the pub downstairs and the light from the landing. The mermaid was the ghost of a witch, he said, who'd lived in the pub when it was still a house, hundreds of years ago, on her own with a cat. She'd been drowned in a pond near by, accused of stealing two children, twins, and boiling them to make soap. To make sure she was a witch they'd taken her to the pool and strapped her to a ducking stool – I didn't know what that was; Nicholas had to explain – and if she survived, he said, it would be taken as proof that she really was a witch and she would be taken away and burnt. But the woman who had lived in the house couldn't have been a witch because when the ducking stool came out of the water she was dead. And it was too late to do anything about it then, Nicholas said.

After the woman had drowned, the people in the village heard singing, low but loud enough to stop them sleeping. It seemed to be coming from the pond; they went together to see, and there was the woman, sitting on a rock with her clothes in shreds about her. They couldn't make out what she sang, but the priest said it was the language of the devil, which only those who had given their soul to him could understand. One morning, the man who'd first said she was a witch was found dead in his bed, with the sheets drenched and his lungs full of water. 'Even now you can hear her singing sometimes,' Nicholas said, 'during the night when everyone's in bed, and it means that someone's going to die.'

'Don't be stupid,' I said. 'You're trying to scare me.'

'No, I'm not. You'll see.'

I didn't answer. After a moment, he said: 'I'm going to join up. I've only got to wait till next year. I found a grenade in a field near here. I'll show it you, all right?'

'All right.' I lay there and waited until he had gone to sleep and the noise from downstairs had died away. My aunt and uncle came upstairs but didn't speak, and then the landing light was turned off and there was nothing but the cold light from the window and the gleam of the plastic models of fighter planes that hung on threads from the ceiling.

Three

That first morning, Uncle Joey made breakfast, the table cluttered with plates from the evening before. We ate toast he'd cut into triangles, with butter and marmalade spread thinly and evenly to the edge. Nobody spoke, which struck me as strange although I soon grew to think of it as normal. Aunt Margot didn't eat. She sat with the teapot beside her and drank cup after cup of tea without milk or sugar, chain-smoking, staring through the window with a peeved expression; now and again she pursed her lips.

When the rest of us had finished eating, and Uncle Joey was standing by the sink to wash the plates, I pushed my chair back from the table and stood up, expecting someone to tell me what to do. Nobody did, and I was about to sit down again when Aunt Margot said Nicholas would take me out for a walk. He didn't want to, but Aunt Margot said she'd leave me in his room unless he stopped playing up. Nicholas sighed and folded the magazine he'd been reading into four, pushing it into the leg pocket of his camouflage trousers, creasing it. I noticed this but didn't point it out because I was pleased; he would find out later and be annoyed, I thought, it would serve him right. 'Come on, then,' he said, as if it were the tenth time he'd called me.

The back of the Mermaid looked down on to the road between Leek and Buxton a thousand feet beneath us. There was no wind, and from where we stood I could hear the traffic all that way below. Nicholas said it would be a great place to organize an ambush, and I nodded, relieved. It sounded as though he had forgiven me for being there.

He scrambled on to the top of the guard rail surrounding the car park, holding his arms out for balance. He seemed solid when you first looked at him, well built for a boy of sixteen, then you saw that he was podgy, with his big round bottom and soft legs. I climbed up behind him and we walked like that, with the rocky slope on our left and the car park on our right, until Aunt Margot called from an upstairs window to stop playing silly buggers. We jumped down and ran behind the building until we were out of her sight. That was when Nicholas said he would show me the mermaid's pond. As he headed along the road beyond the pub, I lagged behind, dragging my feet. I wanted to slow him down, to let him know I had a mind of my own.

The land rose steeply to form a narrow ridge and, as I watched, Nicholas trotted up it suddenly and disappeared. I called his name, the first time I'd said 'Nicholas' out loud. It felt and sounded strange in my mouth, a foreign word. He didn't answer and I panicked. I clambered up the slope, slipping on the short grass once or twice and dirtying my knees. When I got to the top there was a shallow dip in the land and beyond it, sixty or seventy feet away, a second ridge. In the dip, which was wider in the middle, like an eye, there was a still, black pool, Nicholas kneeling at its edge. The air in the hollow felt cold as I slithered to join him, feeling my skirt ride up and the prickle of grass against the backs of my legs. My knickers will have green stains on them, I thought, but I didn't care; I'd been wearing them since my mother died. No one had thought to change my underwear or make sure I'd washed, no one, not even in the hospital. Already I had a rash round my bottom and between my legs, which burnt when I peed.

'This is where the mermaid was drowned?' I asked Nicholas. 'Yes,' he said. I peered into the water, hoping to see the bottom, but the surface was flat and closed. 'How deep is it?'

Nicholas shook his head. 'Nobody knows,' he said. He picked up a stone, dropped it in. It disappeared almost immediately. 'The army's sent divers down to try and reach the bottom,' he told me, 'but they can't because there isn't one. After a bit they don't know where they are. I've seen them. There was a diver once after a woman from the barracks down near Thorncliffe, one of the soldiers' wives, went missing and they thought she'd thrown herself in. When he came up he was bonkers. He said he'd seen the mermaid.'

'It can't be bottomless,' I said. 'It has to finish somewhere.'

'What do you know about it?' Nicholas asked, looking at me. His forehead was speckled with small red spots, shiny with grease. 'It always stays at the same level, even when it hasn't rained for weeks, even when the snow melts. That's how they know it's bottomless.'

'But how did the water get here in the first place?' I asked.

He shrugged, bent down to grab another stone and skimmed it across the surface. It jumped twice, sank. 'The same way as the hills did, stupid,' he said. 'It's always been here.' I looked back to where the road was behind the ridge, and my eye was caught by something in the sky that moved and shone. Nicholas saw me squinting. 'It's a glider,' he said. 'Our uncle Joey's mad about them.' He rolled his eyes: 'He's mad, full stop.'

'Why don't you call him Daddy?' I asked.

He glanced at me and gave a short laugh. 'He's not my dad,' he said. 'Any road, he isn't old enough to be my dad. My dad died in the war, in Africa, before I was born. He isn't my uncle either, come to that. He's nothing. He's a bloody Pole. They wouldn't even let him fight.' He stared at me; I could feel his eyes on me while I watched the shining thing in the sky. 'You ask him,' Nicholas said, and for a moment I thought he meant I should ask his father. 'You see if you can make him talk.'

I didn't know what a glider was. I suppose I imagined something natural at first, perhaps a bird, a large white bird, because what I saw was like a thread of light that gleamed and then vanished as the sun went behind a cloud. 'I can't hear anything,' I said, 'it isn't making any noise,' and Nicholas explained what a glider was as we climbed back towards the road. What I had seen was not a bird at all, but a sort of aeroplane with wide, spread wings, as smooth and silent as a toy.

Four

The room I was given to sleep in was at the back of the house, overlooking the valley, away from the noise of the pub. There was a window high in the wall and a cupboard full of cardboard boxes. A wine-bottle lamp, covered with raffia, stood on the chest of drawers by the bed. It had a yellow parchment shade with a burn inside it, where someone had knocked it too close to the bulb. There was no carpet, just bare wooden boards and the kind of oval rug you find in bathrooms, matted pink fake fur. My aunt put her hand beneath the bed cover and pulled out two hot-water bottles. 'It should be all right by now,' she said. Nicholas sniffed and left.

My case was open on the floor. 'You can sort that out yourself,' my aunt said, prodding at the lid with her foot and leaving me to it, pausing for a second before closing the door behind her.

Alone, I climbed on to the bed and tried to look out through the window to where I knew the pool must be.

I felt it slide away from the wall. Instantly my aunt was in the room again.

'I won't have it,' she said, as I jumped down. 'I won't have it, you ungrateful monkey. Moving everything around the minute my back's turned. I wouldn't have put the bed there if that wasn't its place.' I stared at my case because I didn't want her to see I was scared. She must have been waiting outside the door, I thought, to find out what I would do. I watched her kick the case to one side, the lid falling shut. 'I suppose you think it isn't good enough for you here,' she said. 'Well, you needn't think you can get up to your mother's tricks, just because I'm out of sight.' Not looking at her, itching to push my case back to where it had been before she kicked it, I shook my head. I wanted to ask her if I could have a bath because I was sore between my legs, but I was worried she would see my grass-stained knickers and be angry with me.

Anyway, it wasn't true that I thought the room wasn't good enough for me. I thought I deserved it, the poky bedroom without a proper window; I thought I deserved the offhand way she treated me. And I think now that I was silent about my knickers and the filthy state I was in for the same reason. I felt I'd brought it on myself. And then I wondered what my aunt had meant about my mother and her tricks. Later that day I thought about the soldier's wife, who had gone missing, and wondered if she had been like my mother, who had also gone missing, in her own way, even before she died.

I waited until my aunt had left the room again, then knelt beside the case to see what the woman had packed for me. I tried not to think about a stranger in my room, opening the drawers of my dressing-table and chest, looking inside the wardrobe trying to think what I might need. Inside the case I found three blouses, some vests and knickers, a pair of green woollen tights I never wore because they scratched when I sat down, some skirts, a kilt and two pairs of gym shorts, my favourite pullover, and another I hadn't even tried on because it had a pink and turquoise ribbon, which I hated, threaded through it just below the neck. Some socks, rolled into balls, and a pair of plimsolls. A toilet bag with toothbrush and toothpaste, nail scissors and some of the lemon-scented soap we kept for guests, still in its paper. She hadn't put in my school uniform, which surprised me until I remembered I'd have to start at a new school when the autumn term began. She'd forgotten my pencil case, mouth organ and teddy bear, a Spirograph I played with almost every day and all my books, except for one I'd just started reading when it happened. I'd left it beside my bed, with a bookmark at the end of the second chapter.

She had also put in my mother's hairbrush and comb, which made me cry, quite out of the blue, for the first time.

Five

The girl's the same age I was when I was taken to the Mermaid. Thirteen. Her name is Kakuna and she's a Kurd, I find out later, back at the camp. When she arrives, though, I'm at the beach with Flavio. It's almost three o'clock in the morning and I've been standing here for twenty minutes, waiting. He phoned half an hour ago – he'd seen my light on as he drove past the house – to tell me that a boat had been sighted, adrift, half a mile from the coast. I left Jozef sleeping and came at once.

'One of the big ones?' I ask him now, with a tremor of anticipation. Let them come, I think. Let them all come.

'No,' says Flavio. 'More likely a small commercial fishing-boat, probably Russian, though it's anyone's guess what port it left this time. The coastguards have tried to make radio contact, but no one is answering. It looks like the crew's hopped it. You can't blame them. They must have known they'd never land and get away. Besides, the boat's not worth much by all accounts.'

'Have there been any other landings?' I ask.

He shakes his head. 'There were radar traces an hour or two ago,' he says, shrugging and turning towards the water, which neither of us can see, except as blackness fifty or so feet from where we're standing. Nevertheless we look towards where the noise of the sea and the sharp smell of weed and ozone are coming from as if we expect to see the speedboats unloading their human cargo, their hulls light in the water as they skim across the Adriatic to the other coast.

That's when we spot her. Flavio cries out, more excited than alarmed, 'There's someone there!' Moments later, he wades in, his torch casting arcs of light across the waves. I see her lit by the jumping, flickering beam, struggling to her feet, with the water at chest level. She staggers towards Flavio, then, as the current catches her, is pulled back so only her face and an arm are visible. She shouts and I try to catch what she's saying, but it might be anything at all. *Get away, leave me alone, let me drown.*

I am standing in the shallows now, drawn into the water some distance behind Flavio, my own mouth open as I try to call above the pounding of the sea.

With an effort that must have used all her remaining strength, the girl breaks into a ragged crawl and, within seconds, reaches Flavio, just as I do. The three of us are together, beaten by the waves, one of the girl's hands weakly clutching my arm as Flavio grips her and lifts her from the water, against his chest.

*

This is when it all begins, of course, after the exhilaration of rescue, when the child is no longer a desperate buffeted thing you would risk your life to save, but someone to be won back into the world. Sometimes they have suitcases, vanity cases even, sometimes no more than one thing: a favourite pair of shoes, some object made of gold to be sold or bartered, a pistol in a sealed bag wrapped with tape, which is immediately confiscated, a doll, maybe, a Rubik's cube with one coloured square detached and missing, a plastic bag with letters in it. Never a document, of course. The last thing they need is an identity, reaching back like a running chain to their past.

Kakuna has a plastic model of a Pokémon, one of those Japanese cartoon characters, which she must have clutched in her hand all the time she was in the water. Later, at the camp, one of the volunteers tries to take it from her, gently, so that she can be washed, but Kakuna gives a stubborn little whimper and refuses to part with it. She only lets it go when she falls asleep on a chair and her fingers gradually unfurl. It's lying on the floor and I pick it up before anyone else can. I almost wake her to show her that it's slipped out of her hand, but she's breathing so peacefully I don't want to disturb her. I pop it into the pocket of my trousers, to keep it safe until she wakes.

At home I shower and change and begin to make breakfast for us both, because it's too late to go back to bed, and Jozef is already up and dressed. I tell him about Kakuna and her Pokémon. I think it might amuse him in a dark sort of way, the idea that a Kurdish child might cross the Mediterranean with a toy from a Japanese television cartoon in her hand, not knowing that its name, though warped and damaged, is English and means 'pocket monster'. Pocket-sized monster, I suppose. Little monster, the endearment we use to chastise a child. He listens, stirring sugar into his coffee, looking concerned and faintly puzzled at the word and I realize he doesn't know what a Pokémon is.

I pull it out to show him, watching him as he takes it in his hands as if to weigh it. I have to give it back to her, I think, filled with apprehension. It's all she has.

Six

When I was a child, there were so many questions I would have asked if someone had given me the chance, or I'd had the feeling they might be answered. How long would I stay at the Mermaid with Aunt Margot and Nicholas and Uncle Joey? For ever? Until my father came to fetch me? Would I be given another room or left in the one at the end of the corridor? When could I have a bath? What would I do with my dirty clothes? Where would I be going to school and when would it start? Would I be given pocket money?

The first few days at the Mermaid, each time I was about to speak, standing with my hands behind my back and my knees shaking – partly from the cold, partly from fear, and partly from resentment that I should have to ask her these questions – something would stop me: my aunt's expression, a sense that the moment wasn't right, that I would be better off waiting, that asking now would in any case not get me what I wanted. But my reluctance to ask wasn't only because my aunt was distant; it was also because an answer of any kind would confirm the truth of my situation – that I was no longer in my own home and would never return to it. How could I ask my aunt when my father would come if I knew, within myself, he never would? That he was in jail and might be hanged.

It wasn't the first time I'd stayed with her. We were eating our tea before the pub opened one evening when she reminded me that my mother and I had taken refuge with her once when I was six or seven. She said that her sister would have been better off if she'd stayed away from my father altogether instead of going back to him with her tail between her legs. She'd let herself be bought. A nice new coat, some curtains for the living room. That was her way of doing things: everything had to be nice, at any cost. She always had to have the best. She didn't care how she got it.

After my aunt had gone upstairs to get ready for work, I thought about what she'd said. I remembered the rough grey walls of a house and a boy, who must have been Nicholas, watching from a corner as my mother took me upstairs and put me to bed in a room overlooking the street. There was a large oak wardrobe with a mirrored door that wouldn't stay shut until my aunt jammed it in place with a piece of folded cardboard. Later, the cardboard fell out and the door swung open to reflect the room, making a creaking noise that scared me.

It was still light when I was put to bed. The adults must have wanted to talk without my hearing them. I lay there and looked at the wallpaper, beige and crimson stripes with a fleur-de-lis design, and the shiny black fireplace. After a while, as the room grew darker and I was beginning to worry why my mother hadn't been up to see if I was all right – because anything could have happened to me – the streetlights came on and the room was almost as bright as before. The curtains were open, and whenever a car passed the house I watched its headlights on the ceiling, swinging from left to right, from right to left, growing wider as they passed above the bed, then narrower again before they disappeared.

It was a double bed, and when my mother came she slept next to me in her petticoat, her clothes folded and placed on a chair. I could hear her crying, quietly so as not to wake me. I held my breath, excited that we had run away. Then she reached over and stroked my fringe back from my forehead and said in a low voice, so low I barely heard her, 'Oh, my darling child.' Such strange, uncalled-for words, I thought, and I have never forgotten the shame and the thrill of them. But I also remember feeling thrilled to see my father in the car outside my aunt's house, perhaps the following day, perhaps a day or two after that; he was waiting for us to come down the steps and climb in, my mother in front and me in the back. And when I was in my own room again, in my single bed, I stared up at the ceiling and missed the fan of lights, the excitement.

During those first few days at the Mermaid, I started to worry about my periods. I'd had my first a few months earlier and my mother had explained everything to me, so that I needn't be afraid, she said. She'd taken me to the chemist's and we'd spoken to the woman who worked there, who was an old friend of hers and called them 'monthlies' in a low voice. 'There's no going back now,' she said to me. I was embarrassed at first, then proud of myself, grown-up. The problem was that the woman who had packed my case hadn't put in my belt and towels and I was due to start any day. I would have to ask my aunt and I was afraid she'd be angry, although it seems sad now, as I think of it, that something we shared – being female – should have seemed so threatening.

As soon as I'd unpacked my case, I went into the bathroom. I locked the door behind me and took off my knickers, the elastic scraping my skin. Wincing, I sat on the edge of the bath, lifted my skirt and saw that the skin of my inner thighs was red and rough, like pinpricks. I tucked the hem of my skirt into the waistband and used a flannel to wash, but soap and water made the inflammation worse. I wondered what I could do to make the pain go away, then started crying because there was no one I could ask. That was when I felt most alone, I think, standing in my aunt's bathroom with my skirt hitched up, still wearing my socks and shoes as lukewarm water dribbled down my legs. I cried until the need to cry was over, temporarily, then dried myself as best I could on the towel and pulled on my knickers again because I had left the clean ones in my bedroom and didn't know what else to do.

By the time I'd finished there was water everywhere,

and I must have had mud on my shoes because the floor was dirty as well as wet. I looked around the bathroom for something to clean up the mess, but all I could see was a hand towel, yellow with embroidered flowers along one side, which looked new. Hurriedly – because I was sure Aunt Margot would knock on the door at any minute and want to know what I was doing – I knelt down and mopped up what I could, then tried to wash the towel, scrubbing one end of it with the other. That only made it worse. In the end, I squeezed out as much water as possible, twisting it until it looked like an old rag, soggy and grubby and striped with brown instead of yellow.

The bathroom overlooked the valley. I carried a stool to the window and tried to open it against the wind, pushing with all my strength, scared that the glass would shatter and cut me. When it swung back to strike the outside wall, I almost fell. I stood still for a moment, towel in hand, to regain my balance. Then I shook the towel open and threw it into the air, as far from the house as possible, praying the wind would carry it down to the valley and the road below. I watched it fall and float for a second, despite its weight, eddying on an upward current before it was dragged again. It finally settled on the slope perhaps fifty feet beyond the path at the back of the pub. I looked out towards the place that Nicholas had said would be good for an ambush.

Later that afternoon, before opening time, my aunt asked me if I'd seen the guest towel. I pretended I hadn't heard, my heart thumping, then jumped when she reached across to touch my arm. 'I put it on the rail by the basin,' she said. 'You haven't used it, have you?' I shook my head. 'It's buttercup yellow,' she said, 'with daisies embroidered all along the hem in white.'

I might have told the truth if I hadn't seen the towel, in my mind's eye, filthy and torn and hanging from a thorn beside the road below.

Seven

The first few days I kept myself to myself. It wasn't difficult. My aunt ignored me, Nicholas left me alone unless ordered not to, and my uncle disappeared after breakfast and went into the cellar, only coming up at opening time. I wandered around the house, avoiding whichever room my aunt was in, or sat on the floor in my bedroom, arranging and rearranging the things I had, folding my clothes and stacking them in piles. Nowhere was worth staying in for more than a few moments; nowhere held me. I thought at the time that it was the bareness, the shabbiness, the way the furniture was pushed up against the walls. But now I think it was because the pub took over everything. Boxes of crisps in the corner of the living room, which was never used except for storing things; crates filled with ginger beer and tonic water behind the kitchen door; even when the Mermaid was closed you could smell the sickening sweet mixture of beer and smoke. Before long my clothes were permeated with it, although I didn't realize this until I was outside and suddenly smelt myself, shocked.

None of us had a home. We lived and ate and slept around the borders of a public space that influenced everything we did; our lives were peripheral to its needs, its hours. It always puzzles me to read about pubs or hotels with a family atmosphere. How do they manage it? What do they know that we didn't? What we had was the opposite: a family with the atmosphere of a pub.

During the day my aunt wore her fluffy white slippers on her bare feet and an old dress, or sometimes a dressing-gown with a thin woollen cardigan pulled over it, no make-up, her hair held back from her face with a knotted scarf. It was hard to believe she was my mother's sister when she looked like that. My mother had always been ready for visitors, ready to go out, ready to be observed, admired. I had never seen her without lipstick and her hair done properly, her stockings on. I remember how upset she was one afternoon in the garden when she'd bitten into a pear and I had seen she had a single false tooth on a dental plate the colour of skin. 'My little secret's out,' she said, with a laugh, but she wasn't amused. One day my father had said that she was losing her looks, she had started to sag round the jaw. We were in the car, driving somewhere, perhaps during the school holidays when he would sometimes take us with him while he worked, leaving us in the car with a flask of tea and sandwiches as he tramped around building sites, waving towards the car every now and then as though to remind us we weren't forgotten. I wouldn't have remembered his words if she hadn't laughed, a cold little laugh. 'I'll never forgive you for that,' she said. She started sleeping with a scarf running under her chin and tied at the top of her head.

Aunt Margot stayed out of the bar at lunchtime, leaving the customers to Uncle Joey. Lunchtime trade was travelling salesmen, people from the gliding club a couple of miles away and sometimes tourists – attracted by the hand-painted sign outside that said 'Scampi and Chicken with Chips in a Basket' – who usually drove on when they found out the Mermaid didn't sell food during the day, only in the evening. Uncle Joey turned the radio on to the Third Programme, whistling quietly while he polished the beer taps. He didn't encourage the customers to talk but he was always polite, even when he didn't understand what someone said. In those cases, he would give a slow smile, his lips together, so that often nobody noticed he was bluffing. I started to hang around in the corridor near the bar, where I could see in but not be seen, except by Uncle Joey, who didn't react at first. Then sometimes, when a customer was talking to him, he would glance across and pull a little face, to show he was bored, which made me laugh. He had these funny expressions he used when he wanted to mimic or mock the customers; the mobile, pathetic face of a clown, his dark eyes always sad.

Aunt Margot stayed in the back, working on the accounts, she said, until mid-afternoon. Then she would disappear upstairs, into her room, only coming out when the pub was about to open for the evening.

The first time she walked downstairs I didn't recognize her. She had piled her hair on top of her head and sprayed it with lacquer. With the light of the landing behind her, it shone like candyfloss. She wore a lot of make-up, more than anyone wears today, green eyeshadow, thick mascara and pale pink lipstick. She had on what she called a cocktail dress, stiff shiny material that reached to her knees, with lacy white stockings beneath, but nothing on her feet. I found out later that she kept a pair of slippers behind the bar and a pair of white patent high heels by the flap that led to the other side, so she could put them on when she had to go out into the lounge and collect glasses, or join a customer for a drink. She often did that, sitting on a stool with her legs crossed at the thigh, letting a shoe swing from her foot. Uncle Joey never whistled when she was there, though there was always music – Matt Monro, Dean Martin. Her favourite singer was Mel Tormé.

She was always smiling as she worked, a tight, anxious smile that made the tendons in her neck stand out, unless a customer had told her something sad or shocking. Then she would pull a solemn face. 'Isn't that dreadful?' she always said. 'What a dreadful world we live in. It doesn't bear thinking about.'

I was listening from the corridor one evening and heard a man talk to her about my father, and it was then I realized that the story of what had happened to us must be in the newspapers. 'Now, what would make a man do that?' the customer said. 'Behave like that to his wife? With a little girl in the house as well. Prison's too good for him,' he said. He paused and drank; I heard the ice in his glass as I leant against the wall in the corridor, only feet away from them, holding my breath. 'I'd never treat the woman I loved like that,' he said slowly, in an oily voice, and I realized he was flirting with my aunt. 'I'd give her anything she wanted. I know how to treat a lady.'

'I'm sure you do,' my aunt said. 'I bet you know how to treat a lady.' I imagined the light in her stiff blonde hair as she shook her head. 'Isn't it dreadful?' she said. 'What a dreadful world we live in.'

Sometimes I think there is only one authentic loss, and the rest, the other deaths and departures, are echoes of it: we learn how to deal with loss just once, then apply what we have learnt until it becomes a sort of skill. But if this is true, it must be the nature of the first loss that determines how we handle later ones, and this is what frightens me. Because to lose your parents as I did is to know not only grief but shame. I love my mother because she wanted me to have a father, and died for that: she took me back to him when she could have run. But why should I have wanted to go back to him if I hadn't loved him? I love my father because he picked me up and swung me between his legs until I squealed and held me when I cried and brought me presents back from work and let me sit on his lap to drive the car and gave me whisker pie, rubbing his bristly cheeks against mine until I squealed. I love and hate them both with a fury that leaves me exhausted and sick with confusion. I am the key to it, I sometimes feel, as though what has been lost is me. Where am I? Where did she go, that little girl? Why did she let it happen and then disappear, to leave me with her life?

Eight

How much of what I remember really happened I can't say any longer. Even the first times I was asked to describe what I'd seen to the police, I had the sense that it was slipping away from me, that I was losing my hold on what I'd seen and heard. Yet I wanted so badly to tell the truth. I was the only witness, I knew that, and I was frightened by how elusive my memory was and how important it was for me to be sure I always told the same story, because if I didn't I might not be believed. Even during the first few days, the first few hours, I had begun to rearrange, to falsify, in order to defend myself.

The facts, though, are simple enough. I was in my bedroom, asleep, when I heard my parents shouting downstairs. I lay there in the dark, waiting for them to stop, as I always did when their rowing woke me, but this time the shouting got worse and when I heard my mother howl with rage I began to go downstairs. I was on the landing when I heard the first blow – like someone beating a carpet – and my mother's howling turn to a scream.

'*You bastard*,' she cried, '*I hate you, you bastard*.' I was shocked, because my mother never used bad language. I crouched, half squatting, half kneeling, and stared between the banister rails into the living room. All I could see was the fireplace and the corner of the sofa. There was another scream and a dull thump, and I saw my mother stagger across the space beyond the door, jerky like some figure drawn in a flick-book, and then my father came into view, his arms outstretched, as if he was trying to catch her before she hit the ground. She must have stumbled back and fallen across the arm of the sofa, because one of her legs kicked up in the air.

Other details, vivid and complete, *necessary* details, which deep down I know to be authentic, *because I was there*, I have since found out to be false. I remember my father's shirt being torn across the front, where my mother had grabbed and ripped it, I see it flapping as he dives across the room towards the sofa, I see his bare chest with a patch of hair at the centre in the shape of a diamond – but this was not the case because the shirt was intact, so I must have imagined it, perhaps to make my mother's role more active, perhaps to make her an accomplice in her death, as though to provoke the attacker were to reduce his guilt.

And then what happened? When there was no longer any noise I stood up and started to walk down the stairs and my father came into the hall and saw me freeze in front of him. He leapt the bottom few steps, making a groaning noise that scared me more than anything I'd heard or seen that night, and picked me up, hugged me to him, although I was too big for that. He was crying and his face was wet and ugly as he pulled my head into his chest and I could feel his heart beat at my cheek. 'I'm sorry,' he said, 'I'm sorry,' over and over again, and I said it back to him, the way people sometimes reply to 'Happy birthday' with those same words, 'Happy birthday,' because it is automatic, tit for tat, repayment in the same coin. 'I'm sorry too,' I said, as I slipped down out of his grasp and looked behind him towards the living-room door, waiting for my mother to appear. Already apologizing.

Nine

The first time Uncle Joey spoke to me properly, other than to ask me what I wanted on my toast or whether I was warm enough, was one morning when the two of us had been left alone in the kitchen and he caught me staring out of the window at the white plume left in the wake of an aeroplane. 'That's grand, isn't it?' he said.

I nodded.

'I wanted to be a pilot,' he said, 'when I was your age. You never saw planes then, almost never. They were special.'

I liked the way he talked, the simple phrases, the accent that seemed to give what he said importance, as though the words were made new by his using them.

'I've never been in a plane,' I said.

'Never? That's not good. I think we must do something about that.' He had been polishing his shoes and when they were done he smiled at me. 'I can clean yours for you,' he said. 'If you want.'

I was embarrassed by how much this offer touched me;

I almost burst into tears in front of him in the kitchen. I shook my head. 'Come on,' he said. 'It's no problem. I like cleaning shoes, you see. It gives me pleasure to see them look smart.' I sat down and took them off. My socks were dirty at the toes; I think we both pretended not to notice.

'The first time, I was a boy. I waited outside the gate of the air base near my town where the pilots were. They lived in a barracks near by, far from our house. I watched them go through the gate until they saw me. They made fun of me but I didn't care. Then, after a time, when they'd got used to me because I was always there, they said I could go in with them. It was the best day of my life. I helped them with things they had to do. After that it was easy. I was always there, every day, from morning until I had to go home for my tea. I didn't go to school any more, I didn't care for school.' He paused. 'There was a smell always at the air base, the smell of petrol. I loved it. I would have drunk it if I could,' he said, in a serious voice that made me want to smile. He held up the shoe he had finished, at arm's length to admire the shine, then put it down and picked up the other. 'These are good leather. Good, strong leather. They will last, but you have to clean them.'

'That's what Daddy says.' I gasped and caught my bottom lip with my teeth because I had promised myself I would never talk about my father.

Uncle Joey looked at me. 'Well, he's right. You have to look after leather.'

I felt that he had understood, and I was grateful to him

for not saying anything that would make it worse. I stood there, watching him brush my shoes, not knowing what else to do. When he had finished, he gave them to me. 'Put them on now because we must go outside,' he said. 'I want to show you something. Something you will like.'

He led me out of the house by the side entrance and round to the big cellar doors outside. I wondered why we hadn't gone down the stairs behind the bar, but then it struck me that Uncle Joey didn't want my aunt to see us. I felt both nervous and excited, in a way I never did with Nicholas. Everything in the Mermaid belonged to Nicholas in a way that was denied to me and my uncle, as though neither of us had any right to be there.

He lifted up the heavy flat door and waved me down the steps. For a second I thought he might swing the door shut behind me and close me in. He sensed my hesitation and slipped in front of me to go first, holding a hand up towards me when he was almost at the bottom. As soon as we were in the cellar he switched on the light and darted back up the steps to close the door. I was ashamed then that I'd felt scared of him and, even more, that I'd let him see. Now that we were together in the cellar, with no one else, I felt safer than I had since the night before my mother died.

The only light came from a single bulb near the ceiling. Uncle Joey walked towards the dark end of the cellar. As he disappeared into the blackness, I looked around me and saw casks of beer stacked one on top of another, crates of bottles, boxes. Then a second, brighter, light came on and Uncle Joey was visible again, standing in front of a glassed-in room, one hand resting against the door. He beckoned to me to approach. But I felt shy and wanted to leave – I might have done so if I hadn't been afraid it would hurt him. It was one of those moments when a child becomes capable of care, and aware of it. I was proud of myself as I walked across the cellar and let him lead me into the room, his arm outstretched in a flourish.

At the back of the room was a bookcase, with books, records and a gramophone on the bottom shelf, paints and pencils on the others. An easel was leaning against the wall and a stack of wood – each piece large and square, painted white – beside it. The back wall was covered with photographs of birds, taped on to the bare brick. Most looked as if they had been torn out of magazines and newspapers, some carelessly, with corners missing and ragged edges. There were so many they overlapped. I walked across to study them and saw that some had captions, in English and other languages I didn't know. I started to read the words I recognized under my breath. Golden eagle. Peregrine falcon. Albatross. They were mostly large birds, almost all in flight. Among the photos were drawings of wings and men wearing wings, complex technical diagrams, and sketches of what looked like primitive planes, mounted on bicycles. I saw a drawing of a seedpod, the kind that spins as it falls to the ground, and others of feathers, as finely hatched as engravings. I looked at everything, not knowing what to say, and all the time I was looking, Uncle Joey stood behind me without a word, letting me use my eyes. That was when I noticed he wasn't much taller than I was – when I felt his hand touch my arm lightly, and turned.

'Now look at this,' he said.

Behind him a long table was strewn with model planes made from balsa wood and tissue paper, resembling birds. Some were smaller than my outstretched hand; the biggest must have been three feet long. One of its wings had been covered with paper, but the wood of the other was bare.

'Do you like them?' he asked, his voice quiet.

I nodded.

'I am trying to understand how flight is made,' he said. He selected one of the smaller planes and held it up, then moved it towards me in a slow, gentle arc. He didn't make any noise as he did this, as Nicholas might have done with one of his plastic models; no sound of bombing, no ack-ack-ack. He made the small plane land on my hand.

'It's beautiful,' I said, as I lifted it, light and fragile as a small bird, to my face to see it better; I was too overwhelmed to look at my uncle, who seemed to know this and stepped back.

That was the day my aunt burst into my room, waving a filthy rag in front of her. I'd been holding the plane Uncle Joey had given me up to the light, but as she threw open the door I clasped it to me.

At first I didn't recognize the rag. 'You did this, didn't you?' She threw the towel on to the floor. 'You filthy little monkey,' she said, her voice breaking with tears. 'You filthy, filthy little monkey. You'll see. You think you're so special, you stuck-up dirty little madam.'

I reached down for the towel with one hand, shocked and sobbing in front of her for the first time and praying that she wouldn't see my new plane, now hidden behind my back in my other hand. 'I'm sorry,' I said.

'You're sorry!' she cried. 'You'll learn what sorry means before I've finished. My one nice thing!'

'Please,' I said. 'Oh, please, Aunt Margot, don't shout at me. I didn't mean to do anything wrong.'

She whipped the towel away from me. 'You lied to me,' she hissed, 'you deceitful little monster. You lied to me.'

I shook my head, one hand still cradling the plane.

'I'll show you what you're fit for!' she said, as she left my room. 'You'll see.'

I'd slipped the plane beneath my bed and was still on my knees when she reappeared, the floorcloth from the bucket under the bathroom washbasin in her hand. It smelt of Dettol, drains and vomit. I backed away, but she grabbed my hair behind my head and held me still with it, then pushed the cloth into my face, rubbing it against my nose and mouth. 'Let's see how you like that!' she said.

I fought back then, struggling to my feet, and pushed her away with all my strength. 'I hate you!' I shouted, when my mouth was free of the cloth, then flinched, appalled by what I'd said.

But my words seemed to satisfy her. She took a step back towards the door, holding the cloth as if she'd been wiping a shelf with it and been interrupted. She tossed her head, once, as if to say, 'So now we know where we stand,' then left.

Ten

Jozef and I go to the camp today to see what can be done. The newest arrivals are housed about two hundred yards from the coast in a disused army barracks, now called a welcoming centre. They resent it, as anyone would. They see the barbed-wire fences and locked gates as a way of keeping them in, and they're right not to trust us, however many times we tell them, through interpreters, that they *aren't* prisoners, we have their interests at heart, they're going to be looked after and released – that give-away word – as soon as the paperwork is done. Some of the younger men immediately make a run for it, wriggling under gaps in the fence or walking out through the gates, as bold as brass, while the bored conscripted soldiers, who might just as easily be them, share a joke or a cigarette.

A handful will be picked up after a casual request for documents in the street or a station bar, or because they draw attention to themselves by committing a crime: many of those who manage to get out in the confusion of the first few days become involved in petty theft, illegal street-trading, drug-dealing; some already have women in Italy, sisters, ex-girlfriends, and run them on the streets. The Albanians are known for that, and for reckless driving in powerful stolen cars. A few of the younger men and boys, the better-looking ones, become prostitutes themselves or are pimped by older men; of these, a dozen or so each year end up as murderers, hotly defending their act as self-defence, their looks already brutalized, turned inward.

The women are different. They withdraw, find sanctuary in passivity, their eyes unblinking, their grief emblematic. They move their few belongings from barracks to washroom to barracks to reception with a worn-down patience that makes me anxious and want to help. Because, of course, they are women like me, although I only think of that later, when I am calm enough to reflect. They are women touched by violence and damaged by it, as I have been.

I'd hoped to find Flavio at the camp, but they tell me he is at the police station and won't be in until after lunch. Today isn't my usual day and not all the faces I see in the office are familiar. Then Paola, who helped us find our house, walks in and I ask to see Kakuna, knowing full well we try to avoid attachment to individuals. But I haven't been able to sleep for worry, tossing and turning in bed as though I was back in the sea. I can't stop thinking of her waking up to find that her Pokémon has vanished. I have to give it back.

Paola sends Jozef and me to the rear of the camp. The boys and men gathered round the door move aside slowly, with an air that is not so much threatening as appraising, although I am old enough to be the mother of most. Inside the barracks, their mothers, sisters and wives are sitting together on the beds, arranged around the table in the centre. Some are peeling vegetables, others are sorting and folding donated clothes. We walk across, unnoticed or ignored. One of the women, old, with a scarf on her head and a goitre, pulls out a black and red lace-trimmed bra and holds it against herself, her feet picking out the steps of a stripper's dance, her wide hips swaying beneath the long, flowered skirt. The others laugh, and I ask myself what kind of charitable act it is to give a piece of lingerie that must have cost a week's wages to a refugee whose religion forbids her to show her face. Then I see one of the younger women throw a covetous glance at the bra as it goes back into the box with the other clothes.

Kakuna is crouched with some of the younger girls in a corner. As we walk towards them I realize how much I want her to look up and recognize me, but she doesn't seem to notice either Jozef or me until we are standing in the midst of them and they stop talking to stare. They wait for us to say something, as they always do – unless they have some complaint that must be made – because it is our country. Because it is our world.

I smile and feel my eyes move over them, aware that Jozef is behind me, aware of his strength. I greet them in Italian, wondering who will answer me, and a girl of about fifteen says, '*Ciao*,' and offers me her hand, a gesture so unexpected that at first I look down to see what she might be showing me. Then Jozef touches the small of my back and I shake her hand, momentarily abashed. I ask her her name and those of the others, waiting for her to reach Kakuna. She takes her time, as if she knows what I want and has decided to tease me. I listen carefully, although I know that I'll remember nothing; many of the words she reels off are unintelligible to me as names.

I listen until she comes to Kakuna. When she says the name, I smile, and it is clear to us all that something has happened, because the girl who knows everyone waits, as though it were my turn to speak. 'Hello,' I say, in English. One of the smaller girls behind me giggles and I hear her repeat the word in a whisper, but Kakuna says nothing. She looks at me without curiosity, apparently with no memory of me, until I reach into my pocket and pull out the small yellow toy she carried with her to Italy. 'Look,' I say, still in English, to reassure her that I am different from the others, someone who understands what it means to be different. 'I've brought you back your Pokémon.'

Eleven

A week before school began Aunt Margot took me into town to get my uniform. It was the first time I had been more than half a mile from the Mermaid since the day I had been left there with my suitcase.

At half past nine we waited in the car park for the market bus to come. I asked why we weren't going in the pub van, but she said Uncle Joey had better things to do than drive us all over the place, and I realized that, like my mother, she couldn't drive. I swore to myself then that I would learn as soon as I was seventeen; then I would always be able to get away.

'Here it comes,' my aunt said, pulling my arm.

It wasn't a normal bus, but a coach with crimson carpet on the seats, floor and walls, right up to the luggage rack, which was made of woven string on metal. The inside of the coach smelt of cigarettes.

The journey took almost an hour, with the bus stopping and waiting at farm gates as women hurried down rutted tracks in thick woollen coats with hats pinned to their hair. I watched them climb aboard, red-faced, greeting one another. One or two acknowledged my aunt, who nodded back but didn't smile. Some carried trays of eggs or jars; one had a cardboard box with holes punched into it. She sat just behind us; when I craned round to look, she smiled. 'Rabbits,' she said. She had two teeth, both in the top jaw, stained brown.

I watched from the window as we travelled down into the valley, past a low white building where, my aunt said, butter was made, through council estates, and into the centre of the town. The bus stopped at a war memorial in the middle of a square and the women got off with their bags and boxes. A group of boys, two or three years older than I was, sat on the steps of the monument in jeans and T-shirts. I glanced across at them, with the tormented mixture of attraction and disdain I see now in the children at the camp – sizing things up, testing the ground to see how much weight it will bear – but they were sniggering about the women who had got off the bus and hadn't noticed me.

My aunt pulled at my sleeve. 'Come on,' she said. 'We haven't got all day.' She was wearing a shiny black coat that came to just above her knees and black high heels but no stockings. She had pushed up her hair under a scarlet chiffon scarf, knotted behind her neck.

The shop was just off the high street and sold not only school uniforms but work clothes, mechanics' overalls, butchers' aprons, white coats for chemists and caps for waitresses. The old wooden counter had shallow, glass-fronted drawers and a brass strip along the far edge to measure cloth. The woman who worked there was short and square, with mannish side-parted hair and a fussy flounced lemon blouse. She read through the list my aunt gave her. 'Well, I think we've got almost everything,' she said, then smiled, not at my aunt but at me, as though she knew I was the one who counted. 'And what we haven't got,' she continued, 'we'll have to put our heads together and see what we can come up with.' She glanced then at my aunt, with apparent dislike. 'I'm assuming you'll be needing some nametags too. They're very particular about labelling at Eastwood.'

My aunt looked confused for a moment, then suggested that nametags could wait until we picked everything up at the weekend.

'That's leaving it a bit late,' the woman said. 'They'll require ordering.'

When the woman went into the back room of the shop to check her stock, my aunt sighed and lit a cigarette. 'This is a bloody mess, isn't it? We can't have you going around with *his* name. I suppose you'd better use our name.'

'Why can't I use my daddy's name?' I asked hotly, not thinking what I was saying. 'It isn't fair. It's my name too. Why should *I* have to change it?'

'Oh, yes,' she said, 'that'd be very nice, that would. Waltzing round school on your first day with the name of a bloody wife-murderer sewn into your knickers. As though we didn't have enough problems as it is.' She looked round the shop with irritation for an ashtray, then stubbed out the cigarette on the floor, grinding it with the toe of her shoe until it was crushed to shreds.

The woman reappeared from the stockroom with her arms full. 'Yes, you're in luck, young lady. I think we've got all that's needed. Come through here, my dear,' she said. She gestured to me to follow her. 'I think a little work with my tape's called for, don't you?'

She took me into the back, full of boxes on metal shelves. 'You look too big to be a first-year girl,' she said. I didn't know what to answer. I wasn't sure how much of my life, which had suddenly become a dark, secret thing, I was allowed to give away; even my name was dangerous, to be concealed.

'You're more a second-year girl by the look of you.'

'No,' I said, shy. 'I'll be in the third form.'

'So you're new to Eastwood. You'll be feeling a bit funny, I expect. Going to a new school.'

I sensed my aunt waiting. 'I'll be fine.'

'That's a good girl,' she said. 'No point fretting about what can't be changed, now, is there?'

She told me to take off my skirt, but I stood there without moving, afraid she would see the rash between my legs, which had spread to my knees. She gave an impatient smile. 'Don't stand there gawking. There's no need to be embarrassed. I've seen enough girls' legs in my time, my dear.' When I stepped out of my skirt, she gasped and took a small step back. 'Oh, my poor love,' she said.

'Please don't tell her,' I begged.

She reached in and eased her hand between my legs. 'Whatever have you done to yourself?' she said, and then: 'Has she done this?'

My aunt called through from the shop: 'What's taking you so long?'

'I think you'd better come in here.'

I heard my aunt sigh. I wanted to put on my own skirt – I didn't want her to see me exposed – but the woman stayed my hand. 'Oh, no, you don't,' she said, and then, to my aunt, who'd come to stand beside her: 'Just look at the state of this girl's legs.'

I felt ashamed, but my aunt didn't seem to care at first. She glanced at the rash, then turned away her head, exasperated. That was when I felt something wet between my thighs. 'You dirty little cat,' my aunt said, and I realized that she did care after all, and then that my period had started. I stepped into my skirt and fastened it; my aunt was furious. 'We'll be in on Saturday morning to pick everything up,' she said to the woman, who seemed to have lost the will to speak. 'Make sure it's ready. And the name on the tag's Foxe. With an *e*. Carol Foxe.'

That was how I took my mother's maiden name, which was also my aunt's. I have always thought of it as a woman's name, as though all the men in our lives – fathers and husbands – had been erased.

Twelve

Nicholas treated me well, in his way. He let me follow him round or sit in the corner of his room while he made his model aeroplanes. They weren't like Uncle Joey's. Nicholas bought them in kits, with all the parts attached in order of size to a central plastic spine; he would twist them off and put them in the box lid. He was always slapdash about assembling them; the windows of the cockpit would be daubed with glue, the ailerons would wobble. Some of the bigger aeroplanes he painted green, but generally he left the dull grey colour of the plastic. Once or twice he asked me to put the transfers on the wings, bull's-eyes in the colours of the flag, sequences of numbers. I enjoyed this – peeling the coloured symbols away from the shiny paper and positioning them on the model – but I took too long for Nicholas, who watched me with growing impatience, then snatched the stickers from me to do it himself. As soon as the planes were finished he hung them on cotton from the ceiling in a corner of the room and forgot about them.

Sometimes he talked to me while he worked on them. He told me about his plans.

He wanted to be a soldier, like his father. He wanted to go to Cyprus and bring it back under British control, where it belonged. He talked about guns and tanks, grenades and platoons, regimental colours and mascots, not caring if I understood, glancing up from his glue-stained fingers to the lid of the box and taking out another piece. He reeled off the names of weapons with what seemed to me professional accuracy: the flat, mechanical voice of a priest reciting the names of saints. He had pictures on his walls of Churchill and Hitler, Stalin and Roosevelt, and the Emperor of Japan. He had photographs of the atomic bomb and burnt-out buildings and people heaped like sticks. He opened a drawer and pulled out a cylinder of dull grey metal. 'Look at this,' he said. 'It's the casing of a German bomb. I found it down the hill. It's fantastic.'

We never went back to the pool but Nicholas took me to other places sometimes, when his mother ordered us out of the house. Once we walked to a wall of crumbling, jagged stone, about fifteen feet high – the remains of a small quarry. Nicholas liked to wear combat trousers and soldier's boots from the Army and Navy Stores and I watched his heavy legs as he climbed up the wall before me, sending a rain of small stones down on to my head. I pretended that nothing had happened, just closed my eyes and felt for the next handhold, reached out with my foot for purchase. I didn't want to give him the chance to think of me as younger, or a girl. The more I despised him for being dull and awkward, the more I needed his respect. After we'd reached the top we ran down the slope beyond it so fast that we both fell over, laughing, our fingers aching from the climb. 'You could get killed,' I said, 'when you're a soldier. Like your dad was.'

Nicholas used to watch me read with a sulky expression. 'What are you reading that for?' he'd ask, no matter what it was. Most of the time I read what I found in the house, romantic novels lying around on sideboards or pushed into a little glass-fronted bookcase my aunt called the display cabinet. Dog-eared and stinking of nicotine, they must have belonged to her, although she never said so, which suited me: I didn't have to thank her.

She found me once, though, in her bedroom, looking for one I hadn't read. She rested her cigarette in an ash-tray by the bed and opened the wardrobe. 'There's a box of them there,' she said, pointing into the corner with her foot. I knelt down, but waited until she had gone before I pulled out the box: I didn't want her to see that I was grateful. Sometimes I thought about the books I'd seen in the cellar and wondered what they were and why they were there. But Uncle Joey was keeping his distance again; I didn't know why, and I was hurt and puzzled.

Sometimes – out of desperation – I read the magazines Nicholas collected, with stories of mercenaries and des-criptions of torture that make me sick with the memory of them. Even then he seemed offended, as though I were using them in the wrong way. 'What are you reading that for?'

'Because it's interesting,' I'd say, although it wasn't true; I was reading them because I had nothing else to do, and was scared that if I were seen to be doing nothing, my aunt would notice me. I didn't want to be seen by her at all.

'They aren't meant for girls,' Nicholas would say, but that wasn't the problem. The truth was that he didn't read – not even his magazines, which he rolled up and pushed into pockets but rarely opened. It didn't take me long to realize I was brighter than Nicholas, faster at working things out, even though I was three years younger. I started to notice that he would repeat himself, or use the same words to describe different things, always the same few words. When he was watching television, he laughed at programmes for smaller children, like *Watch with Mother* and *Crackerjack*. When he stopped laughing his mouth hung open. 'Shut your mouth,' Aunt Margot used to say. 'Catching flies at your age.'

One day Nicholas asked me about my father. We'd been sent into the lounge bar and were sitting together at one of the tables. It was cold – the pub was always cold during the day – and everywhere smelt of cigarettes because my aunt hadn't emptied the ashtrays from the night before. I was trying to teach Nicholas to play cribbage with one of the sets from behind the bar, but he didn't understand the rules. Or didn't want to. He would move his matchstick the wrong number of holes, then lose his temper when I counted him back to the right place, explaining his mistake.

I was patient with him, but that only seemed to make him angrier. Perhaps that was why he asked me. To hurt me. Perhaps he wanted to see how much I cared. He wasn't entirely stupid.

'What's your dad like?' he asked.

At first I was too surprised to answer. Nobody had asked me about my father, or my mother, for that matter. Whole hours would pass without my thinking even once about them, so that when they did come into my head, recalled by something trivial, I was startled and confused. 'He's all right,' I said.

'He's a murderer,' said Nicholas, 'if that's all right.'

'Your dad was a murderer as well,' I retorted. 'That's what soldiers are. Professional murderers.'

Nicholas reached over, knocking the cribbage board off the table, and grabbed my hair. I squealed and seized his wrist with both hands but that only made his grip more determined. I thought he was going to pull it out by the roots, it hurt so much.

'You take that back.'

'What?' I gasped.

'What you just said about my dad.'

We heard a noise behind us.

'Let her go,' Uncle Joey told Nicholas, in his soft, quiet voice. And Nicholas did. I sat up, my eyes filled with tears, scalp smarting. I was afraid to touch it, to see what damage had been done.

'She said my dad was a murderer, like hers,' said Nicholas, enraged. 'My dad was a war hero.'

'You must never hurt a woman,' said Uncle Joey. 'A gentleman would never hurt a lady.'

That's what you think, I thought. That just shows how little you know.

I liked to watch my father shave. I liked the preparations: the way he tested the water in the basin with his finger, worked up the lather in the shaving-bowl. I liked to see him take apart the razor and unwrap the blade from the little square of paper, then rinse it and screw the whole thing together again. I liked the care and the sense of risk, which he exaggerated to tease me, pretending he had cut himself as he put down the razor beside the soap dish. I would sit on the side of the bath and watch him as he covered his face with the soap until he had a bushy white beard, then as the razor took off the beard in stripes, leaving his wet skin pink and shining underneath. When the water drained away, the inside of the basin would be flecked with his stubble, like specks of dirt, and he would splash the sides with his hands until the porcelain was clean again. Then he would ask me to stroke his cheek. He would say, 'Smooth as a baby's bottom.'

I knew my mother didn't approve of this, so I learnt to wait until she had gone downstairs, to avoid her as I sneaked in and out of the bathroom. I don't know why she minded so much. When I was older and she was dead, I began to think about these things. I supposed at one stage she was jealous. But now I don't know. Isn't jealousy wanting something for yourself? Isn't it possible to feel *ex*cluded without the desire to be *in*cluded? Because now, years older than she was when she died, I think that's what she must have felt. She didn't want to be part of that mundane intimacy; she simply wanted it not to exist. At such times she must have circled us both, skirting our affection, despising it – and perhaps despising me for having yielded so easily.

She was right about that. I let myself be cajoled by him because I allowed my need for him to overcome my sense of danger. If I had resisted, nothing would have happened and my mother would have lived. Because the last time she ran away, it was my doing that we went back to him. I was the one who wanted my father. I remember crying in a hotel room and my mother saying to me that she would never let him take me away from her.

Three weeks later she was dead. And I never saw my father again.

Thirteen

That afternoon, after we'd finished at the outfitter's, Aunt Margot left me by the bus stop, telling me not to move or I'd be for it, as though I had somewhere to run to. When she came back she gave me a paper bag. 'Let that be the last of it,' she said, but she didn't sound angry any longer, or at least not angry with me, just tired and faintly imploring, as though she had been arguing with someone else and expected, half against her will, that I would comfort her. I sat on the bus between her and the window and looked into the bag. There was some cream for my rash, a packet of sanitary towels and a belt for them. But how could this be the last of it? I wondered, when from that day on I would need towels every month. Perhaps she would expect me to pay next time – but how could I, if no one gave me money? Did I have any money? Did I have anything that was mine by right?

'Thank you,' I said. She didn't answer, just touched my arm with the tips of her fingers and I wanted her to hold me; if she had, I think we might have been friends – or not friends exactly, but fellow travellers, sharing a destination. Perhaps we would have recognized each other.

But she didn't hold me, and when I was sitting in the kitchen, later that day, feeling shivery with stomach-ache, she didn't ask me how I was. She just sat at the table and smoked her Park Drives, rubbing her legs with a hair-removal glove until they gleamed. I would have gone up to my room but the kitchen was warmer than anywhere else because the oven was on. My aunt had decided to make a stew. 'That'll do us for a couple of days,' she'd said, preparing the vegetables earlier. I'd offered to help, grudgingly, but she had pretended not to hear and kept on chopping onions and carrots and pushing them into the pan.

When Uncle Joey came in and saw me in the chair beside the cooker, he looked at my aunt, who ignored him, and then at me. 'Cup of tea?' he asked.

'Yes, please,' I said. My aunt didn't speak, just turned the glove round to use the other side.

When the kettle boiled, Uncle Joey filled the teapot and poured the rest into a hot-water bottle he took from the cupboard under the sink. He gave it to me. I stared at him, not understanding. 'This will help,' he said, miming where I should hold it, against my stomach. My aunt watched without expression, as though she was listening to something on the radio. Then her face changed and she looked at me as if she had never seen me before. As if she was thinking: What on earth's she doing here? Who let her in?

*

She didn't take me with her to collect my uniform, because one of the reps had offered her a lift and she didn't want to be fussed with kids. The rep laughed when she said this, standing by the car and pushing his hands deep into his trouser pockets so the cloth billowed out. He was wearing his hat, a trilby, on the back of his head; I hoped the wind would blow it away. But he lifted it as he opened the car door for my aunt, who giggled and said, 'Aren't you the gentleman?' Her skirt was shorter than usual; she smoothed it over her hips while the man watched.

The minute she'd left, I locked myself into the bathroom. The rash was almost gone. I pulled my knickers down and pressed my fingers gingerly against what had been the sorest part; the skin felt smooth and cool. I applied some more cream, just to be sure and because I liked the feel of it, then pulled my knickers back up, sat on the lavatory with the lid down and closed my eyes, imagining what it would be like at school. I was going to a girls' school, so I wouldn't be in the same place as Nicholas. Not that it would have mattered much: he had only two more terms to go. He would be leaving in June, before his O levels, to join the army. Still, having to go to school with Nicholas would have been more than I could bear; I would have been ashamed of him.

Sometimes I tried to imagine what I would do when people asked me my name. I was terrified I might forget and blurt out my real name, instead of Carol Foxe. But then I thought, Why shouldn't I use my own name? I haven't done anything wrong. I haven't murdered anyone. The books I was reading came into my head – my aunt's romantic novels, in which people killed and died for passion all the time – and I felt a sort of pride, as though what my parents had done made me special.

I went to look for Uncle Joey. He was checking the stock behind the bar. I watched him for a few moments before he turned round. 'How do you feel?' he asked, touching his stomach. 'Better?'

I nodded.

'You can help me if you want,' he said.

I nodded again, and he gave me a piece of paper and a biro.

'Call out the name,' he said, 'then I will tell you a number and you must write it down.'

'Canadian dry ginger ale,' I said.

He counted the bottles on the shelf. 'Seventeen,' he said, and I wrote '17'.

When we'd finished, I helped him tidy the bar before opening time. Saturday was different from during the week. People drove up from town to admire the view over the valley or stopped on their way to Buxton. There were children in the cars outside, and trays with bottles of lemonade and crisps packets balanced on the bonnets. Sometimes the mothers came into the pub with their husbands, but mostly they stayed outside, sitting in the cars with the doors open, talking to one another, making friends the way women do when left alone, while their children walked along the edge of the guard rail, looking into the valley far below.

The husbands would reappear now and then with another tray. When it was windy – as it usually was – some of them pretended to be blown away. They leant into the wind, tilting the trays towards their chests and pulling joke-anxious faces, so their families would be amused. My father used to do that: he would leave me in the car with my mother, who always seemed unhappy or bored, watching the door for him. Afterwards, as we drove home, he would swing on the steering-wheel so that the car veered towards the other lane, making us squeal with fright. One night, we killed a pheasant, which my father took home and hung in the porch. I don't remember what happened to it then. I suspect my mother threw it away when it began to smell, but perhaps she gave in and cooked it, and I was simply spared the ordeal of having to eat the thing. I remember that my father gave me the long bright tail feathers to keep.

Aunt Margot expected me to play with the children in the car park, as though I was part of what the pub had to offer, and that was when I knew I was ashamed of who I was, of who I'd become. It was worse, I thought, to be a publican's stepdaughter, or niece. I used to hang around near the door, waiting for her to return to the bar so I could sneak into the house. Nicholas would sit at an upstairs window, pretending to be a sniper, picking off the children one by one. 'Kill that one for me,' I said once, pointing to a fat boy in a buttoned-up coat. Nicholas looked at me, with surprise and admiration, and did what he was told.

When we had finished stocktaking and tidying up, Uncle Joey said we still had an hour before the pub opened. 'We can go now for a walk,' he said, then: 'I know. There is something I want you to see.' He smiled. 'I always have something to show you, Carol.' He said my name slowly, as though it were the only word that was foreign to him. I thought he would take me to the cellar, but he went into the hall to get our coats. 'Come on,' he said, as I took mine. 'We don't have so much time.'

We followed the road away from the valley, then turned off and crossed a field. Sheep barged into one another in their panic, fleeing as we walked towards them. We climbed over a dry-stone wall and my uncle pointed to some low buildings I'd not seen before: Nicholas had never brought me here. Half a dozen jeeps were parked outside one of the smaller buildings. We sat on the wall and, as we watched, some men emerged. Two walked across to the largest building and opened the doors, then wheeled out a small plane.

'It's an aeroplane,' I said.

'No,' said Uncle Joey. 'Look again. It's a glider.'

One of the other men climbed into the cockpit, while the first two crossed to the nearest jeep, which had a reel attached to the back. From this, one man unwound a heavy metal rope, which the other carried across and hitched beneath the nose of the glider.

'What are they going to do?' I asked.

But Uncle Joey put a finger to his lips. 'Watch,' he said. 'Use your eyes.'

The jeep drove off, pulling the glider behind it, bumping a little over the uneven ground. The speed picked up and then, as though someone had plucked it from above, the glider lifted into the air, leaving the wheels behind. I held my breath as it rose, rocking from side to side, buffeted and borne by the wind. Then the metal rope fell away and the glider climbed higher and higher into the sky, like a bird released.

'It's grand, isn't it?' said Uncle Joey.

'Have you ever been in one?' I asked.

'No.'

'Why not?'

'Money doesn't grow on trees.' He laughed. English sayings often made him laugh.

'Do you get any money for me?' I asked him suddenly.

'What do you mean?'

'I mean, does my father give you any money for me? To look after me?'

'Your father? No.'

'But isn't there anything left?' I persisted, turning to stare at him. 'What about the house we had? Surely there's something. I mean, nobody lives there now, do they? Now that we aren't there. What's happened to it all?'

He pointed into the sky, but I wasn't interested in the glider any longer. 'What's happened?' I repeated.

He shrugged, then stroked his chin slowly; he didn't

look uncomfortable, as I might have expected. That was why I never asked questions, I suppose, to avoid creating embarrassment for others. And that was why, when I finally did ask, I chose my uncle. After a moment he began to speak.

'When I was a child, a boy, I wanted to be a pilot. I came here for that, you know, to England. Polish pilots are famous. In the Battle of Britain we were among the most brave, the best. There is a monument to us, I think, in London. Our Polish allies, it is very famous.' He paused and shook his head. 'That, or I would become a mechanic. I knew everything about planes since I was a boy and always at the air base, seeing what they did. I was always beside them with a spanner, always the right spanner.' He smiled. 'You know this because already I've told you. You remember? But your Royal Air Force didn't want me. I was too young, they said. No. "No," I said. "I am seventeen, eighteen. I have walked across Europe to be here, to help. Look at my shoes. They have no soles. I am a pilot. I am a Polish pilot. Give me a plane to fly and I will shoot German pilots from the sky. I will bomb their German cities."' He stood up and brushed the seat of his trousers. 'But they were right. I was too young. And so I had nothing.'

'How old were you?'

'I was thirteen, like you, when I left my home,' he said. 'When the Germans came I was in the toilet, outside, because I had eaten something that made me go to the toilet many times that day, I don't know what. There was very little food then, so we ate everything there was, even food that was old and off, bad food we found in the street after the markets had finished, old vegetables. Some people ate rats, cooked in a pan, then drank the soup. All day I was in and out of the toilet, ten, twenty times. I made my mother laugh in the end. "There can't be anything left," she said. "You must be empty by now." I was sitting in the toilet and I heard them shouting in German, not my mother and father although they both spoke German – we all of us did – but the soldiers, the soldiers were shouting. I heard my sister crying, she was only three years old when they came, and then I heard my father say, "No, there is no one else," and I stood up and pulled up my trousers. I remember thinking, He's forgotten me, and I almost called out, "I'm in here." I wasn't surprised when they came. None of us was surprised because we knew that they would come. Every day we waited for them.'

'But why did they come?' I asked.

'My mother was half a Jew. My father was a Communist,' he said, sitting down again. 'Perhaps you do these things in school? No? So we knew they would come to us in the end. At first they took the people in the ghetto. They made the train go into the middle of the ghetto, to save time, right to the doors of the people's houses. The people there made the tracks, and they had to pay for them too, because the Germans told them to and they were scared, and perhaps they didn't believe what was happening, not really, because no one did, and then the trains came and they were taken away. I am surprised they didn't make us build the trains as well. "They will surely come for us," my father said then, though we were not in the ghetto because my father was not a Jew, but Polish. My mother was also a Communist, but that didn't matter. I mean, to them. They could only kill her once.'

'And they didn't find you?'

'I climbed up into the space above the cistern. There was a ledge beneath the tiles,' he said. He grinned suddenly. 'I was a monkey. I made myself very small and waited. One of them opened the door and looked in but he didn't see me. He pulled a face, I remember, because there was a very bad smell, of my shit, and he said, "Filthy Jews," because in those days the Germans did not shit, you know, they made beautiful perfume from their bottoms, and then he closed the door and I waited. I waited until it was dark before I climbed down. I didn't want to go back into the house, not even to get food, although I was hungry by then. Perhaps I was afraid, I don't remember now. I think I was scared that I would feel more alone inside the house. But then I had to change my trousers because I had dirtied them, there was no time to wipe my bottom when they came. I had shit inside my trousers.' I giggled when he said this. I couldn't help it: it was so odd to hear an adult use a word like that. Nothing else he'd said seemed as strange as the fact of that one word: shit. But he didn't hear me laugh, or didn't care, and carried on, his voice quieter than before.

'I took some clothes and some bread. I put them in a bag we used when we went to visit my grandmother's for the day. I used to carry it for my mother. Everything in the house was upside-down. They had broken the piano. My father kept some money under a loose brick in the pantry floor and I took that as well. I didn't want to at first. I thought, But if they come back?' He stopped talking then and stared up into the sky.

'Look,' he said, and this time I followed his finger and saw, almost directly above us, the tiny form of the glider. 'Soon it will come down. You see how the wind is bringing it round to face the landing area?'

'How long do they stay up?' I asked. My face was burning from the sun and the wind, and I was ashamed that I had laughed.

'As long as they can,' he said. And then: 'You mustn't think about money, Carol. Money is not important.'

I was born in 1948. When I was young, by which I mean the period before my mother died, the war seemed far away, although we were surrounded by its effects. I remember my mother talking about bombs and rationing and walking home in the pitch black after tea parties, feeling her way from lamp-post to lamp-post, making the war sound like an adventure, a game of hide-and-seek, except that sometimes her eyes would fill with tears, she wouldn't say why. I remember the taste of the pasteurized orange juice in its little bottle, which post-war children were given to prevent scurvy. But I didn't *feel* the war, except as history, and maybe not even that, as something mythical, with children's comics taking the place of sagas:

the only German words I had ever seen were *Schweinhund* and *Donner und Blitzen* in speech bubbles ballooning from the mouths of Nazis in *Rover* and the *Lion* – comics I wasn't supposed to read, as a girl, but did.

Now, though, as I grow older, it's as though the present is being tugged into that past, the way a wave tugs everything in on itself as it nears the coast, closer and closer as you push yourself through the water, not scared by the strength of it, finally succumbing and letting it take you into its eye of calm. Perhaps this is because three years were once a quarter of my life and now they are nothing, a handful of freelance editing contracts, a few grey hairs, a change of favourite restaurant or holiday resort. The time between 1945 and 1948 has shrunk to something inconsequential; I might as well have been born in the middle of it all. I talk about it sometimes, with Jozef and others, as though I had been there and remember as vividly as they do, as though the experiences I listen to were mine. The blackouts, dried-egg powder, whalemeat, the first news of the camps. I can smell it on my skin, in my clothes. There is no escape from it. Perhaps it is because we are besieged by other wars being waged all around us, in which we are deeply, hopelessly involved and can barely see the difference between then and now.

Fourteen

I was working in Rome when the first big ship came in. I had a freelance job with one of the international aid agencies, editing technical reports. I found the work relaxing, the way some women claim to enjoy ironing, the smoothing out of creases. What emerged at the end of the process was as far from the dirt of poverty as the bulletins from Croatia and Bosnia that we watched each evening – except that sometimes, despite our fatigued and habitually distracted gaze, an image would break through. As though the real thing had reached out through the screen, and hauled us in and would not let us go until it had finished.

It was one of the first big ships to arrive off the coast of Puglia. I don't remember where it came from, just that I sat and watched the news and reached across to touch Jozef's hand. The ship was the size of a cross-Channel ferry, and every inch was thick with people. Men, women, children, old and young, Kurds, Sri Lankans, Albanians staring straight into the cameras, shouting and waving shirts, flags, anything they could lay their hands on. They were filthy and starving and exhausted, weak with heat and thirst after days of danger and privation – but, alongside that, they were exhilarated to have arrived, with that edge to their happiness of desperation, perhaps even madness, which made them seem not only innumerably more than us, but also larger, more vivid and alive. I said to Jozef: 'They aren't afraid at all.' Their faces were far away from the cameras still, but you could see the beards, the unwashed straggling hair; you could smell them, their sweat and filth; foreigners from a dozen countries, alien not only to us but also to one another. And I was so excited for them, so thrilled and relieved, although I'd had no idea that they were out there, so many; no one could have known. I squeezed Jozef's hand until he grimaced playfully and pulled it away. They were so *visible*, I thought. They made me feel insignificant, as though I had slunk into the room and silently taken my place beside the hearth and accepted what little was available, like a thief in the night.

They were taken from the ship and carted to the football stadium, where they were left on the pitch because the stands were closed off, beneath the August sun. As soon as they were gathered together, the non-Albanians were taken away and the women and children separated from the men, which was normal practice but contrasted so sharply with the chaotic theatre of their arrival, a sea-bound city split off from the coast and launched, like a paper boat in the bath, to bob towards salvation.

Inside the stadium, we found out later, the situation had soon got out of hand. The younger men organized themselves into gangs. The Italian forces refused to enter, driving trucks as far as the entrances, depositing food and plastic bottles of water where hands could reach out to grab. Perhaps they realized – or their leaders did – that taking the women away had converted the men into reckless animals. Scores escaped through a broken gate to roam the old town, where they clashed with gangs of local youths. There were stabbings and attempted rapes. The cameras returned. On television and in the newspapers, the tone of the reports changed. The open faces of children and women were replaced by those of adolescent Albanians, their hair cropped short on top and left long behind the ears, speaking the Italian they had learnt from their televisions on the other side of the Adriatic. '*Stessa faccia*, *stessa razza*,' they said – 'Same face, same race' – as they were rounded up and returned to the stadium. A few days later, when it looked as though some of the older men might die for lack of water and heat exhaustion, the forces divided the exhausted refugees into smaller, more manageable groups. They were promised asylum and taken to different cities, allocated places to stay, given food. They must have been provided with clean clothes and allowed to wash with hot water and soap for the first time since their arrival. They must have begun to breathe again and wondered how soon they would be reunited with their women. They must have felt the return of hope.

The police arrived at night. They were being taken to Rome, they were told, for processing; it was cooler travelling at night. Most of them must have believed this because there was no struggle until the military planes banked and flew over the water. Then, finally, they understood, some sooner than others, that they were being taken back, looking down to see the lights disappear and the flat dark sea, more like an absence than anything else, as though there were no bottom to it. Even then, according to reports, they seemed to have accepted their fate. Perhaps they didn't want to hurt the soldiers escorting them. Same face, same race.

It was stifling hot in Rome. The streets were almost deserted, most of the bars and restaurants outside the centre closed, and I was obsessed by this story. It was clear to me that those behind the decision had taken advantage of the fact that Italy closes down for August, that no one who counted for anything was in the country. And the strategy had paid off: no one cared about this act of treachery, as I did. No one but Jozef. I couldn't work, I couldn't concentrate. I had a recurrent dream in which I was standing in a city I didn't recognize, looking for a lost child. I sat in front of the computer, staring at words, imagining what the men – boys, most of them – felt when they saw the lights of the land give way to the absolute black of the sea; I watched the television news and said repeatedly to Jozef: 'We must *do* something.'

'Well,' he said slowly, stroking Cocoa on the floor beside him, 'you could always go and help.'

'What could I do?' I asked.

'Sometimes very little, even nothing, can be useful to someone else,' he said. 'We could go down there and see, I suppose, if there is anything that might be done.'

Fifteen

Miss Randall told me to sit in the only empty place, in the third row. I had been escorted to the classroom by the headmistress, a stout woman with soft white hands, who couldn't take her eyes off me. I realized at once that she knew who I was and what had happened to me, and I wondered who'd told her until I saw a letter from my old school on her desk. I knew it hadn't been my aunt: she'd delivered me to the school earlier that morning, giving me a brief push towards the head's office before leaving, not even saying goodbye.

It's odd I remember Miss Randall's name so distinctly yet have no recollection what the headmistress was called. I don't even recall if she had a nickname. All I remember are her watery grey-green eyes, magnified by glasses, and that she called me 'poor girl' twice, but never asked me anything. How could she have known what I was going through?

The desk I'd been given was near the window, opposite the door. A single desk, which was a relief: I'd dreaded finding myself beside another girl. I walked across the room and sat down, still holding my satchel, empty except for a small English Gem dictionary and a pencil case my aunt had bought me from Woolworth's, with pens and crayons and the bits of transparent plastic I would need for geometry. In my old house there was a similar case, but made of leather; my father had given it to me for Christmas two years earlier, at the end of my first term at grammar school. The one my aunt had bought was orange plastic and was already splitting near the zip. I was ashamed of it.

I stared ahead, the eyes of the other girls on me. The upper row of windows was open and it was bitterly cold in the room: I shivered in my new uniform. When Miss Randall handed out books she stopped beside me and said, in a low voice, 'Don't worry. You'll soon warm up.' I looked at the textbooks she had given me. One of them, on British history, I'd studied at my old school.

Miss Randall walked back to the empty blackboard. I thought she was going to talk about me, and felt sick with apprehension, but she said, 'I'll expect those books to be covered with paper by tomorrow morning, girls. Sturdy brown wrapping paper would be most suitable. Failing that, wallpaper samples but, please, not that embossed stuff. We are not decorating a sitting room.' I wondered if there was any paper I could use in the pub. I'd ask Uncle Joey.

At morning break, after we'd drunk our milk at our desks and replaced the bottles in the crate, one by one according to our place in the row, we were let out into the playground. Three or four girls from my class gathered round to ask me questions in a brisk, hostile way. I wondered what to say, but my uncertainty lasted only a moment; I understood almost immediately that no one could ever scold me for not having told the truth, because the truth was the one thing I could never tell.

I said my parents had died in a car crash in Scotland. They'd been driving along a road high up on one side of a loch when an army motorbike had swerved in front of them. In order to avoid him, my father had driven the car into the loch and they had drowned. 'Why weren't you with them?' they asked me.

'Because I was recovering from an illness,' I said. 'They'd left me in a convalescent home in Bognor Regis. That's where I was when they broke the news.'

'Was it Loch Ness?'

'I don't know,' I said. 'They never told me the name of the loch. They thought it would upset me too much.'

'Did they find them?'

'No,' I said, 'they were never found.'

'So they might still be alive?'

'Oh, no,' I said. That was impossible, they were definitely dead and drowned. 'I expect they've been eaten by the fish,' I said. I don't know why, I don't know what possessed me to add that gruesome detail, other than that it just came to me, as did all the rest. The soldier on the motorbike had been drunk, I said, and now he was in prison for murder. He would probably be court-martialled and hanged because he was in uniform, which made it worse.

'What was wrong with you? What was the illness?' one wanted to know, suspicious.

I shook my head. 'Nobody knows,' I said. 'It came and then just cleared up in the end. It might have been my blood.' Then I said I was being forced to live with a woman who had once worked for my parents, as a cleaner, because there was no one else who could take me in. I told them my mother and father had been only children. That was why they hadn't wanted any other children, I said. Only me.

'So you haven't got any brothers or sisters?'

No, I said. I was totally alone in the world. I said I'd been made to call the cleaning woman my aunt although she was no relation. I had no relations. By this time the circle around me had grown and I saw that ten, maybe twelve girls were listening and believing everything I said, and that the rest of the playground was looking over to see what was going on.

When the bell rang and we had to go back to the classroom, one of the girls hung back to walk beside me. 'My name's Patricia,' she said, in an offhand way, not looking at me, then turning her head to stare directly into my eyes. 'You can be my friend, if you like.'

I shrugged. 'All right.'

We ate lunch in a building that must once have been an army shed, with wooden walls and a green roof. The tables were long and narrow, and Patricia and I sat near the end of the one presided over by someone in a nurse's uniform. 'That's Matron,' Patricia whispered. 'She's an evil old bag. You just watch out for her.'

We were given minced meat and fried-bread triangles. The part of the bread you could see was golden and shining with grease; the other half, buried in the sludge of mince, was grey and soft. I tried to cut through the hard part, but it splintered into pieces. I felt sick and pushed away the plate. Patricia nudged me. 'Eat it or you'll be in trouble.'

When I sprinkled salt on the meat, Matron called, 'You, girl.' I looked at Patricia, wondering whom she meant. With a gasp of exasperation, Matron stood up and walked round the table until she was behind me. She stopped, and I saw the faces of the girls opposite, agog with fear. Matron smelt of sweat and disinfectant; she reminded me of the rag my aunt had pushed into my face. I felt myself gag and I was afraid I really would be sick this time. Beneath the table, Patricia's hand tugged hopelessly at my skirt while Matron took me by the shoulders and twisted them back until I whimpered. 'Were you brought up in a fish-and-chip shop, girl?' she asked. I didn't understand what she meant. Did she know I was living at the Mermaid?

'No,' I said.

'No, *Matron*.'

'No, Matron,' I repeated, swallowing.

'Because in decent homes we put our condiments on

the *side* of the plate,' she said, with another twist, her hard thumbs probing the hollows of my collarbone.

'Yes, Matron,' I said.

One of the girls opposite explained, dragging the word out: 'She's an orphan, Matron.'

'Is she indeed? That's no excuse for being ill-bred.'

After lunch, in the toilets, when I'd thrown up and was trembling with nausea and rage, Patricia told me, 'She's like that because she's had her womb taken out. My mum's friend told her, from the hospital. She isn't a proper woman any more.' She glanced behind her, then reached a hand up her skirt and pulled out something wrapped in greaseproof paper.

'Come on,' she said. 'I'll show you a place we can go.'

I followed her round the toilets and along the back of a building until we came out behind the dining hall. Patricia grabbed my sleeve and ducked beneath a window. Beyond it was a wall that came up to my shoulder and behind that large grey dustbins, which Patricia squeezed between. I followed and found myself in a corner cluttered with boxes and plastic crates, protected on two sides by the brick wall and, on the third, by the bins. Patricia wrinkled her nose. 'It stinks,' she said. She unwrapped the paper and pulled out a slightly bent untipped cigarette and a match. 'There's only one so fingers crossed it doesn't get blown out.' As she spoke, she struck the match expertly against the wall and lit the cigarette. 'Mmm,' she said, inhaling deeply.

I decided that if Patricia offered me a turn, I'd refuse:

I'd never wanted to smoke – I'd always thought it was stupid, as my father had. 'Only uneducated people smoke,' he'd say, and I thought of my aunt and her Park Drives. But when Patricia held out the cigarette to me I took it. I didn't care. I kept the smoke in my mouth, too scared that I would cough to risk inhaling, then let it out in a thin white stream, like someone whistling. Patricia watched me judiciously, one hand on her hip, the other already reaching out to take the cigarette from me. 'Don't waste it,' she said, when I waited a moment before taking a second drag. 'Look, watch this.' She took the cigarette back and drew on it, making the smoke come out of her nose. 'You try,' she said.

When I think about those years, I am struck by how much detail I remember. Jozef connects it to my fondness for paintings in which each square inch of the canvas is treated with the same attention, each leaf and flower and distant tower given the same care as the face of the saint or Madonna, the dimpled hands of the child as it reaches up towards its mother or out towards the artist. 'Detail renders visible,' Jozef says, and of course he's right. Excess of detail, though, can have the opposite effect. If detail renders visible, too much detail can reduce visibility to indifference. It levels everything, cuts everything down to size.

Sixteen

My mother didn't want me to love my father too much. It scared her when I played up to him, as I sometimes did. Perhaps she felt excluded as her husband began to flirt with the child they'd made together, or perhaps she felt it gave him too much power. She must have known that he used our love to have his way with us – or with her, at least, because I don't think she needed to worry about me as a rival.

But perhaps for some women, love is always hazardous. I see them in the camp watching their daughters and younger sisters with the same wariness my mother showed when she watched me. They call them back, tell them to sit down and get on with what they're doing, find pointless tasks for them as distraction, as though their real business was, nevertheless, constant deep-rooted flirtation.

Like the scene I'm watching now. One of the Albanian women is washing her daughter's hair. As soon as she's finished she begins to make dozens of tight plaits and I think at first she's imitating some of the African girls in the camp, who keep their distance from the others because they are considered prostitutes. I see the plaiting as a gesture of rapprochement because, as Jozef always tells me, I have a bottomless capacity for sentiment, and feel my eyes dampen until, moving closer, I realize the mother is copying the style from a photograph of an Italian starlet in a magazine. As I stand there, a man walks over to talk to them and the woman watches not the man, who barely seems to have noticed the child, but her daughter, to see what she's doing. The girl, who couldn't be more than ten or eleven, laughs once, presumably at something the man has said, then lets out a yelp of pain as the woman tightens a plait and tugs at her scalp. The girl's eyes fill with tears. She slumps down into herself, neck buried between her shoulders, cowed, until the man goes away.

Kakuna is playing in the corner of the barracks with two smaller girls, one not much more than a toddler. She doesn't see me at first, which gives me the chance to observe them. I know that I want to be touched by the scene – and am – by the way she doles out the Dinky cars and dolls, the toys inside chocolate eggs that have to be assembled. There's no sign of her Pokémon and I wonder if she regards it as too precious. The other girls watch their small piles grow on the concrete floor until Kakuna has nothing more to give them. Then one notices me and whispers something to Kakuna, who turns in my direction as I smile and wave. I sense she's annoyed with me for having interrupted them, less from her face, which is impassive, than from a sudden rigidity in her body, a stiffening of the shoulders and upper back. And then I see her smile as though someone has told her to. Don't do that, I think. Don't make an effort.

I'm about to crouch beside them when a girl runs up to us and kicks at the toys, scattering them in a kind of fury. The little ones jump back and begin to cry. I wouldn't have recognized her if it hadn't been for the plaits that flail around her head. Kakuna waits while the girl screams at her, then pulls out a short small knife and stabs her in the leg, so quickly I think I must have imagined it, except for the emptiness that follows. The two younger girls are white-faced, frightened – as I am – into silence. Looking down at her leg and the rush of blood, the older girl squeals, then slaps Kakuna's face so hard her head snaps back. I hear my voice saying, '*No no no*,' and all four seem to notice me for the first time and turn towards me waiting for me to put right what has happened, as adults are supposed to. I grab Kakuna and the wounded girl and shake them, exactly as Margot did with me, as though all notions of guilt and innocence are irrelevant. Kakuna's bottom lip trembles; the other turns to me for help, her features twisted into a soundless cry. The smaller children are wailing now, rocking on their heels in the way they have learnt from their grandmothers, their hands in their hair.

When I put my arm round the shoulders of the girl

with the plaits, to help her walk, I see Kakuna nod, just once, her face expressionless, and I don't know what the nod means. At first, as I help the limping girl across the camp to be treated, I think Kakuna is saying: 'You see? You see whose side you're on, when it comes down to it? Don't lie to me.' And maybe she's right. The sight of her with the knife in her hand, the swiftness of the attack, has left me sick and shaken. But there's more to it than that. The thought that Kakuna might feel I've let her down confuses and troubles me.

Later, when I talk to Jozef, he says, 'Do you notice, though, how you're telling me all about it from Kakuna's point of view, as though you saw only her? She did this, she looked at me like this. You have placed her at the heart of it. You are like Milton, who loved Lucifer best, better even than God. You want it both ways, Carol. But you cannot pretend that she is immune to your sense of what is right and wrong because there is something about her that intrigues you. You will tell Flavio what you saw? That she stabbed the other girl?'

He smiles, his confidence in me – in my sense of right and wrong – unshaken, despite what he's heard. But with confidence in myself so deeply rocked, this infuriates me more than anything. And then to hear him talk of intrigue – is that what I feel? Intrigued? As though there is some small mystery to be understood? Too angry to answer, I storm out of the house and stand outside, with Cocoa beside me. When I sink to my haunches to stroke him, he places his front paws on my shoulders and licks my face until I relax and laugh.

I'm in bed, with Jozef breathing quietly beside me, forgiving and forgiven, when the thought comes to me: But what if she was giving me permission to help the other girl? When she looked at me, what if she was saying, 'We understand each other. Don't worry. I'll be all right, I'm strong. Look out for the weak.' What if she saw me, in some way, as her accomplice?

I think about the way she took the Pokémon from my hand three weeks ago, her fingers closing round it, lifting it to her chest. I didn't mean to stand there and watch, but I wanted some reward, some sign of thanks. And I received one. She smiled and said, 'My father.'

'Your father gave it to you?' I asked, and she nodded, then ran away to join the others. And I thought, So she speaks two words of English at least.

The stabbing turns out to have had nothing to do with the toys. Kakuna had promised to help the other girl concoct some potion to make her irresistible to Salvo, one of the conscientious objectors working in the camp, an Italian boy with blond hair and olive skin, for whom half the girls have fallen. So that explains the hair as well, I think, and the mother's anxiety. Kakuna had said she would gather some earth from where he'd stood that morning and they'd work it into mud with the girl's spit, then make a puppet in his likeness. But in the end Kakuna didn't do it: she told the girl not to be stupid, insulted her.

I find this out the next day, in Flavio's office. The wounded girl has told them, of course; Kakuna refuses to speak. When Flavio asks me what I saw, I'm vague. I tell him I was too far away, I noticed a sort of flash and then the blade was in the leg, I don't know how. I find myself shaking – I think imperceptibly – as I speak. I hear myself lying to protect a child I know nothing of, for whom I feel a sympathy that binds me to her.

All the way home, as I drive to the farmhouse Jozef and I rent outside Bari, I think about my silence, my eyes fixed on the road in front of me as though I'm afraid I'll lose my way.

Seventeen

Patricia took me home one afternoon. We had to skip the last double lesson or her mother would have been there. 'It's no good waiting till after school,' she said. 'My mum gets home before five and she'll be watching us all the time. It won't matter if we miss a lesson. It's only geography. We can drop it next year, for French. *Voulez-vous venir chez moi maintenant*?' We were in the corridor outside the hall where we had gym, which always smelt of the sweat of hundreds of girls, even during assembly.

'*Ça va*,' I said, following her into the changing room.

She pointed up to a window. 'That's the best one. *C'est la fenêtre plus bonne*.' That didn't sound right to me, but I watched her climb on to the bench at the bottom of the wall and pull herself up until her elbows were on the sill. 'It's easier than it looks,' she said, breathing hard. I stood beneath while she wriggled through, her shoulders, her waist and finally, with a flash of knickers, her legs, as she twisted round and was suddenly sitting above me. She looked back down, cheeks red, hair flopping into her eyes.

'*Pas de problème.*' A second later she jumped. I heard the thump of her feet on the ground as I reached up.

Her house was like the one I'd lived in with my parents; not identical, but similar enough to make me catch my breath as she took the key from behind a flower-pot and let us in. The stairs ran up the right-hand side of the hall, just as they had in my house, except here they were covered with a patterned crimson runner, the wood at each side left bare, whereas we'd had a fitted oatmeal carpet. I remember the man who came to lay it, youngish in blue overalls, and my mother watching him from the kitchen door, smoking a cigarette as he tacked it into place. 'You've done a lovely job,' she said, when he'd finished. 'And now I suppose you'd like me to make you a cup of tea.' She was teasing him, although I didn't know why, with that lilt in her voice she used with my father when she wanted him to take her somewhere in the car.

I must have stopped and stared because Patricia tugged me by the sleeve into the kitchen. 'Come on!' she said. 'There's bound to be something to drink in the fridge.'

We forget how strange it used to be, as children, to be left alone in the house. Even our bedrooms were unfamiliar when we knew no one else was around, when we could do anything we liked and not be seen. I sensed it then, this unauthorized freedom, as Patricia opened the fridge door, took out some lemonade then reached up to the cupboard to get the glasses, not knowing what to do with them after we'd finished, whether they should be washed and put away, or left as evidence. After a moment, she rinsed them under the tap and turned them upside-down to drain.

She showed me round the house – the kitchen, the dining and living rooms, her bedroom, her older brother's, her parents'. There was a patio at the back and a long wide garden with poplars at the end and flower-beds and patches of lawn and a path that wound towards the trees. 'My dad's gardening mad,' Patricia said. 'He's always out there, doing stuff.' She paused. 'Did your dad like gardening?' she said.

I shook my head. My father's only use for the garden was to grow flowers my mother could cut and arrange in vases, with fronds of fern and the stalks pushed into cubes of that spongy green stuff that squeaks when you cut it. But I didn't want to tell Patricia this; it was too painful to talk about my parents. And I didn't want to lie about them either, not to Patricia.

I watched her from the bedroom door as she bounced on the bed. The wall behind it was covered with photographs of singers, ripped from magazines: Cliff Richard mostly, Marty Wilde, Billy Fury, an enormous poster of Elvis Presley in blue jeans and a red shirt. Beneath the window, on a low table padded with white leatherette, there was a record player and a metal rack of singles. Patricia stacked some on to the player and started to dance. 'Come on,' she said, taking my hand. She pulled me towards her, then pushed me out, our school skirts swinging around our legs. We sang along, clinging to each other as we stumbled about the room, tripping over our feet, eventually falling on to the bed. We lay there, side by side, our hearts thumping, until the needle skidded and Patricia sat up. 'Oh, fuck,' she said. 'It's scratched.' She propped herself on one elbow, her cheeks hot and red. 'I'd let Cliff Richard do me, honestly I would. Would you?' I started to giggle. 'Well?' she insisted. 'Would you?'

'Yes,' I said, to please her.

'I'd let him kiss me between my legs,' she said, then clapped a hand over her mouth, horrified by what she'd said. I was still shocked to have heard her say 'fuck'.

Then the door opened downstairs and a woman shouted up. 'Is that you, Patricia? What on earth are you doing home at this time?'

Patricia grabbed my arm. 'Look, you just say you helped me home. I had a turn, tell her. It's my monthlies. That way she'll write a note for us both, just in case.' She stood up and pulled a face. 'I'm up here, Mum. Carol's come home with me. I don't feel very well.'

A large woman, with tight grey hair, came into the bedroom in a buttoned-up green coat. 'So you're this new girl I've heard so much about,' she said. 'Our Pat's taken a real fancy to you.'

Behind her, Patricia groaned. 'Mu-um,' she said.

Patricia wasn't the only one to want to make friends with me. I found myself sought after, which was a new experience. At my previous school, I'd blended in with everyone else, neither popular nor ostracized; more popular perhaps with the teachers than the pupils because

I was bright and conscientious. But here, for reasons that weren't then clear to me, I became the kind of girl to whom other girls are attracted. I was never alone, unless I sent them away, which I hardly ever did because I soon understood that I craved their company – which surprised me. They gathered around me as I went from classroom to classroom or into the playground, three or four, sometimes more; we moved in a pack, with me in the centre. I was aware of them, waiting. They'd stand around me, the way the others do with Kakuna, enthralled. I'd tell them a story about myself and they would be silent until I had finished. I never made mistakes, never confused my facts.

The teachers, on the other hand, regarded me with caution, almost suspicion, as though I'd brought with me an infection from another, more dangerous place. Only Miss Randall, who taught history, seemed to like me. That first term we did the Wars of the Roses and the Tudor monarchs. She was the one who told me that a man called Foxe had written about martyrs. 'So you see,' she said, 'you're famous.'

Eighteen

Ordinarily, I had no curiosity about the adult world. But Uncle Joey was different. During the last few days before school began, I'd hoped he would carry on telling me the story of what had happened to him as a child. I lay in bed and wondered what he must have done. Where do you go, at the age of thirteen, when you're hunted by Nazis and have no family or friends? Had he stayed in the town or left it, heading off into the countryside? I imagined the latter and envisaged an emptiness like the land around the pub. And then, as I lay awake in the semi-dark, listening to the noise from the pub downstairs, waiting for closing time and the light beneath the door to go off, I thought, What would I have done? I saw myself running through woods, breathless, hiding behind trees.

But Uncle Joey didn't tell me anything else, and after school began I saw less of him than I had done. During the day, when he had a few free hours and could talk to me, I wasn't there. By the time I was home, had changed out of my uniform, hung it up in my wardrobe and done my homework, he'd be busy in the pub, and Nicholas and I would be sent to the living room where we'd lie in front of the TV, surrounded by cardboard boxes of crisps and nuts.

After the pub opened the only adult I could talk to was Maudie, who came in from the farmhouse down the road, a mile or two beyond the pool, to cook scampi and chicken and put them into paper-lined straw baskets. I listened to her while she sat in the kitchen and read out recipes from books, sweating in her pink nylon overall; she was planning to go to catering college and had to learn as much as she could before she started so she wouldn't look daft. She liked me to test her by giving her the name of a dish and checking while she reeled off the ingredients in a sing-song voice: one pound of minced beef, four ounces of suet, one medium onion. Whenever she made a mistake, she said, 'Drat it,' and started again from the top. 'Nip through and fetch me a mild shandy. I'm that parched,' she'd say. 'You'd better ask your uncle, mind. And leave it if it's your auntie. She'll only dock it out of my wages. She's right mean is your aunt.' And then she'd look contrite.

'That's all right,' I'd tell her. 'You can say what you want about her.'

Nicholas and I became allies because of a girl called Nancy, who caught the school bus with us. She didn't take it the first few days. Then, one morning, we boarded it and there she was, dressed in a different uniform from mine – crimson and yellow, with a grey skirt. As Nicholas and I sat down, she wrinkled her nose, then pinched it between her fingers. 'What a pong!' she said. The other children, two small boys and an older girl, giggled. I sat opposite her, with Nicholas next to me, and watched to see what would happen next. 'I'm sorry for *you*,' she said to me then, her arms crossed. She pushed her glasses back up her nose.

'Why?' I asked.

'Well, if *you* don't know . . .'

Nicholas nudged me in the ribs; I could tell he wanted me to shut up, which annoyed me. Why didn't he defend himself?

'Are you a *friend* of his then?' Nancy asked and the older girl giggled again.

'Yes,' I said, I don't know why – perhaps just to see what she would do.

'You're welcome to him,' she said.

Nicholas tensed against me. His shoulders and legs were rigid, and he fidgeted, helpless. I didn't answer.

'You're not much better than he is,' she said next. 'You must be a bit *simple* too.' The older girl choked with laughter.

I turned to Nicholas, who was flushed with shame and staring ahead. 'What would a common country bumpkin like her know about intelligence?' I said loudly.

'You're a snob,' Nancy said.

'And you're a peasant.'

The older girl giggled, but none of the other children reacted, not even Nicholas.

'And that's enough of that,' the driver called back into the bus. 'I'll have none of that language. Not with nippers present. You're supposed to be young ladies, you lot are.'

Her lips pressed shut, Nancy swung out her leg in my direction, but she was too far away to do more than graze my skirt with her shoe. The second time she tried, I grabbed her foot and twisted until she squealed. I would have done more, I think, but Nicholas stopped me, resting a hand on my arm. 'It's all right,' he said, in a low voice.

I let go and craned forward. 'The next time you try anything like that,' I said, in a voice I barely recognized as my own, 'I'll smack you in your fat, stupid face.'

'You can't do that to me. I've got glasses,' she gasped, between tears.

'You'll see what I can do,' I said. 'I don't care about your glasses.'

When I got on the bus to go home that evening, she stared at her lap and didn't speak, not even when it stopped for Nicholas outside his school. The older girl, on the other hand, introduced herself to me. She was called Angela; she went to the same school as Nancy, a Catholic convent near the park.

'I thought you were Nancy's friend,' I said, merciless.

She flushed. 'I am.'

Nicholas told me during supper that Nancy had started teasing him after they'd played a game one afternoon and he hadn't known the answer to a question. All the others had, he said, but it wasn't fair because they'd never done it at his school. What was the question, I asked, but he couldn't remember. That was when she'd called him stupid, he said, then smelly and stinky. He had tried to answer her back, but she always got the better of him, with Angela laughing all the time. Just once, he told me, he'd slapped her on the side of the head and the driver had stopped the bus and threatened to turn him off it. 'Besides,' Nicholas said, 'you don't hit girls.'

'I do,' I said. 'If I have to.'

I asked Nicholas about Uncle Joey, but he knew less than I did. 'I tried to get him to tell me about the war,' he said, disgusted, 'but he didn't have a clue. He was useless. To talk to him you'd think it'd never even happened. He just says it's all over now and then shuts up. I know he didn't fight in it. Still, you'd think he'd have some idea – I don't know, about planes or something. About tanks.'

'And after the war?' I asked.

Nicholas told me about the first time he'd seen Uncle Joey, when his mother had been working as a barmaid in Coventry. She'd brought him into the back room of the pub, where she left Nicholas while she was at work. He was only small then, but Uncle Joey had shaken his hand, which no one had ever done before. After that, Nicholas saw a lot of him: Uncle Joey began to work in the pub, first in the cellar and then behind the bar. Later on, he moved into the flat above the pub. His mum had told Nicholas she was going to have to marry Joey or she'd never get her own pub. 'The brewery won't give pubs to widows,' she said, 'not even soldiers' widows. They force you into marriage,' she said. 'It's disgraceful.' He remembered her saying: 'Don't you mind him, you're still the man of the house.'

'Do you think she was in love with him?' I asked, thinking of her romantic novels, those boxes of books in her wardrobe. I tried to see Uncle Joey in that light, a dashing young pilot from the east – except that he had never been a pilot, and I didn't know what 'dashing' meant.

But Nicholas scoffed. 'Don't be soft. She loves my dad, she always will. She's told me that a million times. Just because he's dead makes no difference, she says. That's real love, that is. She says that one day he'll walk through the door just like he was then, before he went to Africa, she knows he will, and everything'll be back to normal. We'll be a proper family again.'

'He won't do that,' I said. 'He's dead. The dead don't come back.'

Nicholas looked upset. 'What do you know about the dead?' he demanded, and I wondered, for the first time, how much he'd been told about me. I would have asked, but then I might have had to explain that I knew a great deal more about death than he did, and I didn't want to do that.

Then, when I no longer expected it, Uncle Joey knocked on my bedroom door one morning – it must have been a Saturday not long before Christmas – and asked me if I'd like to go for a walk with him. He had something to show me, he said.

I dressed as quickly as I could and ran downstairs, but at first I couldn't find him. I checked the kitchen, then the public bar and the lounge, before finally running outside. The cellar door was open. I climbed down the ladder and heard music, very loud, a woman singing, coming from the workroom at the far end. 'Donizetti,' Uncle Joey said. 'Italian.' But that wasn't why he wanted me. He stepped aside as soon as I was near enough to touch and beckoned me towards him. 'I've finished it,' he said.

It was a new plane, bigger and finer than the previous models and even more like a bird. Wider than it was long, perhaps six feet across, it had wings that curved slightly upwards at the tips; they were broader than a plane's, like those of a kite. The body was as thin as my arm with a bubble for the cockpit – shaped like the round head of a gull – and a tail at the end. The skeleton of balsa was visible beneath the skin of rice paper; varnished and almost transparent, it had the dull gleam of polished bone or ivory.

'You can touch it,' Uncle Joey said quietly, a tremor in his voice. He pushed me towards it, gently, the palm of his hand against my shoulder.

I picked it up behind the cockpit and the plane seemed to lift into the air of its own accord. 'It's so light.'

'Well, yes. Otherwise it wouldn't work,' Uncle Joey said.

'You mean it'll really fly?' I asked, turning to see his face, which was flushed with excitement.

'I hope it will,' he said. 'Let's see.' He gestured to me to put the plane down, his hand sliding along my arm, then gave me an old windcheater that was hanging near the door, one that he wore to unload barrels in the rain. 'Put this on,' he said. 'It will keep you warm.'

We walked along the road to Buxton, carrying the plane between us. Uncle Joey asked if I'd seen the pool. 'Yes,' I said. 'Nicholas showed me. He told me about the witch.'

'He told you that? It is only a story, I am sure, about a poor woman,' said Uncle Joey, 'but I think it is a bad place all the same. There was a wood near me, when I was a boy, where people believed there lived a witch, but I never saw her. Nobody did. Perhaps there was an old woman who lived alone. But still the wood was a bad place where bad things happened.'

We must have walked half a mile beyond the pool when Uncle Joey struck off to where the land rose on our left. Between the road and the valley there was another escarpment – like the one that hid the pool, but higher, steeper – of ungrassed shale that shifted and crumbled under our feet. We scrambled up, careful not to drop the plane, and a few minutes later we were standing side by side with the valley beneath us. The wind was bitter, strong enough to blow me down to the main road below if I'd let it. I zipped the windcheater up to my chin, pulling the hood over my head, then leant back into the gale, my arms outstretched and my eyes closed. When I opened them again Uncle Joey had attached a thread from a spool to an eyelet under the plane. He unreeled the thread, as fine as fishing-line, until there was a heap of it on the ground. 'Now we must go back a little, then run with the wind,' he said, 'and we shall see what happens.' As he spoke, the plane lifted slightly from the ground. 'She is impatient,' he said.

I did as I was told, taking the tip of the wing and waiting until I could feel the air lift the plane before I ran forward, no more than ten or fifteen feet. Then, at a word from Uncle Joey, I pulled up sharply and let the plane go. We watched as it sank towards the ground, one wing dipping lower than the other. It grazed the shale with the tip of the left wing before righting itself and lifting, slowly at first, and then faster, until it was level with our eyes. Uncle Joey cried out – a strange sound, an intake of breath – as if some word had been forced back down his throat, and the model lifted again, jerkily, as though climbing a flight of stairs, and yet again, more smoothly, as though the stairs had themselves begun to move and carry it. It was over our heads now, maybe thirty feet away. We gazed into the sky as it swooped up and down, towards us and away, buffeted by a wind so solid we could barely speak. Uncle Joey pointed as the thread unravelled and was borne away. 'We have made a thing that flies,' he shouted. Then the plane hurtled towards the valley a hundred feet below us. And it was over.

Nineteen

My first afternoon in the camp, Flavio decided I would work as an interpreter for those who had some French or English but no Italian; then, if I wished, and if there was a call for it, I could teach English to the others. I thought he didn't know what else to do with me. Many hoped to pass through Italy to other countries, some of them to Britain or the United States; wherever they were going, Flavio said, English would help. I told him about Jozef, who hadn't come with me that day, wanting to offer his services beside my own, but Flavio shook his head.

'No, no, no,' he said. 'You cannot volunteer for others. When – what is his name? Jozef, so he is not Italian? – is ready he will come to speak to me himself.'

I realized then that I had wanted to be able to say to Jozef, 'You see, you must come, they need you to do this and this.' I smiled. 'Whatever you say,' I said, not altogether liking Flavio.

That was four years ago and I have never taught more than a few lessons to any group before it's broken up, my students dispersed. I stand in front of whoever comes and write the scraps I think they will need on the board and we set to work. We occupy a classroom with walls defaced by years of graffiti. I see the arrivals stare at them and wonder if they ask themselves the question I first asked myself: How can such a thing be permitted in a civilized state, such squalor and disrespect? The graffiti are sometimes sentimental, 'LUCA TI AMO', 'FRANCESCA SEI BELLA'. But the ones that catch my eye, the ones that shock, are, for want of a better term, political: 'VIVA HITLER. VIVA MUSSOLINI. EBREI AI FORNI'. There are some who pale as they read the words, and others who smile to themselves. The latter will question whatever is offered, as though its value has already been demeaned or it would not be offered.

The mothers send their sons to me to learn, less often their daughters. They know that children will be used as intermediaries, but prefer them to be male. I talk to the women and try to persuade them that their daughters must also live within the world, have dealings with it, that sometimes a daughter can obtain help for them more effectively than a son. I mention doctors, women doctors, women's problems. 'How can you send a man to shop for food or fabric?' I say. 'How can you expect your son to talk about what happens to us every month when we bleed?' This time I've persuaded a group of younger girls to attend my lessons and, with them, Kakuna. She didn't turn up at first but I recognized two or three girls I had seen her with in the yard and asked them where she was. They looked at one another, puzzled, even scared, as though they'd been accused. 'Kakuna? Where's Kakuna?' I asked. Then I said, 'Pokémon?' and they giggled.

'Tomorrow,' they said. 'Tomorrow Kakuna.'

I was surprised to find how shy I felt when she came in. She and half a dozen other girls sat near the back of the classroom in a semi-protective, semi-hostile huddle. They still wear the clothes they came with, or clothes they have given to one another, which make them look like Roma children – brightly coloured long skirts and headscarves, jewellery at wrists and neck or dangling from the hems. One laughs and shows a mouthful of gold teeth, and I wonder if she had her own extracted to make room for them. Kakuna, though, is dressed in pale blue jeans and a yellow T-shirt provided by social workers, and I am reminded once again that she is an orphan and that everything we know about her is what she has told us, which is almost nothing. And may not even be true.

During the lesson I walk over to the girls. I want them to repeat what we have practised together, in pairs, until they have learnt it by heart: simple phrases, the kind they will have to deal with for the rest of their lives: Who are you? Where are you from? How old are you? What do you do? Where do you live? Can you show me a document? I expect them to answer honestly, which creates a kind of hubbub as students ask me the English name for their homeland and I struggle to understand. 'No, no,' they say, shaking their heads, often but not always amused, 'not Afghanistan, not Macedonia,' repeating the same word they offered the first time, which, in the case of the youngest children, might be a village or a small provincial town. And I try again.

I think of Miss Randall as she walked among the ordered lines of desks, where we worked in silence, barely raising our heads to return her smile as she glided past; and how that smile was enough to make her seem sympathetic, perhaps because we expected no more from a teacher than discipline and guidance, because warmth was an unasked-for bonus. And I see myself, fifteen years older now than she must have been, kneeling among students as they call out my name: 'Carol, Carol, come here.' Flavio came in to look for me one morning, saw the empty teacher's desk and left. I had to struggle to my feet and run out into the corridor. 'Here I am,' I said absurdly.

With my group of girls, I stand at the edge and wait to be noticed, to see if I am welcome. I listen and hear my questions asked, all at once, but into a void; nobody is answering. 'No,' I say, 'it's better if you work in pairs.' They stare at me. 'Two and two and two,' I explain. 'One and one, together. You two,' I say, to the girls nearest me, touching their shoulders. They listen as I prompt the question. 'Now it's your turn,' I say encouragingly. 'Repeat.'

From the corner of my eye, I see Kakuna watch me with detached, unpitying attention. I feel a rush of irritation, and react. 'What's your name?' I say to her, my voice sharper than usual.

She smiles slowly, her lips together so that I don't see her teeth, and then, for the first time, speaks to me directly. 'No. What's *your* name?' she asks, her accent surprisingly good.

'Carol,' I say. 'My name is Carol.'

'Hello, Carol,' she says. 'Carol what?'

'Carol Foxe,' I reply.

Taunting and alert, she asks me other questions, not looking at the board, and I find myself answering because I want her to know about me, almost out of vanity. I am flattered by her attention and I sense, with an unexpected flutter of excitement, that she cares. And then, just as abruptly, I notice the rest of the class is silent and feel a flush of humiliation, as if I have been exposed.

That first evening, talking to Jozef, I mentioned that Flavio had refused my offer of his help.

'He was right to refuse,' said Jozef. I watched him cut the rind off some cheese, slip it under the table to Cocoa, and divide the cheese into pieces. I remember waiting for him to give me one and wondering, startled, as I heard the irritation in his voice, if he might not do so – which would be utterly unlike Jozef, who is never petty. 'You had no right to offer me to them or to anyone else. Why did you do that?'

'I suppose I thought you wanted to help,' I said. Cocoa sidled across to me, his nose against my leg, expecting more cheese rind. I stroked his ear until he pulled away to sniff my hand. Jozef picked up an apple and began to peel it and I thought, I'm being punished. No cheese, no apple.

'I don't think that's why you did it, though, not really,' he said, laying down his knife. He reached across the table and touched my wrist, the inside, his fingers damp with apple juice. 'I think you saw me as a way of persuading this priest of yours that you were serious. I would corroborate your desire to help, I would give you weight. You were afraid he might think you frivolous. I think he would have understood that. If he is worth anything as a priest, of course. I also think he may only have wanted you.'

I let Jozef stroke me while I thought about this. We have had so little practice when it comes to argument. I was determined not to be cross without reason, yet what he had said seemed demeaning to me. 'This priest of yours.' The 'yours' rankled.

'Maybe you're right,' I said. I looked up. 'Why do you talk about Flavio like that, as though you despised him? You've never even met him.'

Jozef divided the apple into two portions and put the plate between us. We looked at it, perhaps so that we would not look at each other, but neither of us ate.

'You are right, of course, I've never met this Flavio,' he said, with effort. 'He may be a good man for all I know. In any case, whether he is good or bad, I think that I shall not help you in your mission.' I heard, in the way he said 'mission', the same contempt I'd heard before.

'Why do you say it is my mission? Surely we both came

here for that, to do something,' I said, all at once close to tears. I didn't want the apple and cheese. My appetite had gone. 'That's why we've moved from Rome. What else are we doing here?'

'If it comes to that,' he said, 'if it comes to the good we can do, we may as well be anywhere. You know that as well as I. Besides, I am not here to do good.'

'But you are a good man,' I said, my eyes brimming. 'How can you say that?'

'To do good is not the same as to be good,' Jozef said peremptorily, then stood up and left the room, not closing the door behind him.

I sat and listened as he walked across the gravel towards the barn, where his work was, watching the sunlight in the room go out abruptly, the way it does here. When he didn't come back I cleared the table, throwing the uneaten cheese and apple through the kitchen window.

Twenty

After Christmas, Aunt Margot said I could bring people home if I had to. That was the word she used, without the slightest irony: home. But she wouldn't have me sleeping at other people's houses, she said, as though I hadn't got a bed of my own; she wouldn't give anyone that satisfaction. She must have seen this gesture as a concession, a reward for the help I'd been to Maudie with the fryer, for stacking the bottles of mixers under the bar each morning and sweeping the floor beneath the Christmas tree to get the needles out of the carpet – things I had really done for Uncle Joey, although she didn't know that.

For the first few months, I had mostly used silence as my weapon against Aunt Margot, but increasingly now I found myself answering back. I was constantly pushing, bickering, needing things: a light to read by in bed, money to pay for a school trip, more money for bright green ink and pens. I became adept at wearing my aunt down, sulking and whining in a way I'd never done with my mother. I'd follow her until she lashed out with her tongue and, appalled by my own defiance, I'd know I'd won – which didn't mean I'd get what I wanted but that I'd riled her. I was still scared of her, of what she might do, scared she would tell me things I didn't want to hear, as a witness not to my mother's death but to her life. But then I thought of the way she had treated me over the dirty towel and I wanted to hurt her, as she had hurt me, and my fear of what she might do was no longer enough to stop me from saying whatever sprang into my head. So when she told me I could bring friends home, perhaps imagining I'd be pleased, I said I didn't want my friends to see where I was forced to live, in a pub, with a barmaid looking after me. Not knowing where such cruelty had come from, I was, I think, as surprised as she must have been to hear myself say these words. She flushed and seemed lost for a reply, while I stood in front of her, shaking with tension, gloating.

'I won't have you talk to me like that,' she said after a moment.

'You can't stop me. You aren't my mother. You can't tell me what to do.'

'I can do what I like. I've got custody of you.'

'I'm not in prison,' I said.

She was washing up and slapped my face with her hand still in its wet rubber glove. I was more startled by the sound it made on my skin than by the pain, which came seconds later.

'My mother never hit me.' I stared at her, wishing her

dead. Then I felt my cheek burn and began to sob. 'I want to go away.'

'I don't care what your mother did,' Aunt Margot said. She peeled off her gloves and tossed them into the sink. 'Your mother's dead. And if you think I want you here, you've got another think coming. You're nothing but trouble, you are, you spoilt little monster, always giving yourself airs. Who do you think you are? I could tell you things about your precious mother that'd take her – and you – down a peg or two.' She paused for breath. 'So I'm just a barmaid, am I? Not like your mother! And what's so special, I want to know, about tarting yourself up to get a husband with money? What's so special about getting yourself pregnant so that he'll have to marry you?'

I was too shocked to speak.

She laughed, her head thrown back. 'You don't think *he* wanted you, do you? You were part of the plan, you were. Oh, we can't have the boss's secretary having a little bastard, can we? "Oh, no, darling, you'll have to marry me now, won't you? I know you love me, just put that ring on my bloody finger and we'll say no more. You wouldn't want me to tell everyone now, would you? You wouldn't want me to show everyone the bruises?"' She said all this in a voice almost identical to my mother's; even her face suddenly resembled her sister's, her eyebrows arched, her top lip pulled up a little from her teeth in a fastidious sneer. 'Your mother was a sight worse than a barmaid, I'll tell you that. Your mother was a bloody whore.'

I didn't for one second doubt the truth of what she'd said. It was as if I'd always known. I think I even felt relieved. So that explains it, I might have thought. That explains what happened. 'I hate you,' I said, under my breath but loud enough for her to hear.

'So you hate me, do you?' Aunt Margot said. 'Well, I can't help that. We're stuck with each other now and that's not my fault and it's not yours. So we'll just have to make the best of it.'

The first time I ran away was two or three weeks after Christmas. Patricia and I skipped the last two lessons and went to a matinée at the Palladium. We bought choc ices with money I had taken from the pub till and sat in the front row of the empty cinema to watch a film called *Whistle Down the Wind*, about three children who find a fugitive murderer in the barn and think he's Christ. And after the film had ended and we were standing in the alley behind the cinema I thought, Why *not* run away? Why not run away and hide somewhere, and be given food and clothing and be loved? Like the man in the film?

When Patricia asked me back to her house for tea, I said yes.

'Won't she be annoyed if you haven't told her first?' Patricia sounded surprised. We both knew who 'she' was.

'I don't care if she is,' I said, then thought again. I didn't want Patricia caught up in my plans, not then at least. 'I told her I might not be home this evening. She said it was all right. Just this once.'

Patricia hunched her shoulders against the rain and sucked hard on her cigarette, her lips drawn back into a grimace. She exhaled slowly. 'My mum always says I should bring you home. She thinks it's not right you should be living up there in the hills without any other girls your age. She says it's terrible.'

We were just out of the alley when she grabbed my arm. 'Watch it,' she hissed, jerking her head towards the other side of the road, tugging me back into the darkness. But it was too late. We'd been seen. Two boys sauntered across the road. They were older than we were, sixteen or seventeen. I didn't recognize them but Patricia called, 'What do you think you're after, Richard?' She spoke in a contemptuous, teasing way, dragging out his name.

The shorter of the two boys – though both were taller than us by at least six inches and broad, with donkey jackets over school blazers – came over. 'Have you been to the pictures then?' he asked, ignoring me as he pushed Patricia against the wall, just hard enough to indicate his right to do so, and held her there. 'You'll cop it if Mum finds out.' He sniffed. '*And* you've been smoking.' He turned to grin at the other boy, then said: 'If you give us some fags for later, I won't say anything. Not about the pictures or the smoking. *Pax*.'

He looked at me. 'I know who you are,' he said, neither friendly nor hostile, appraising me, my face, my uniform, my legs in their woollen stockings, my laced-up shoes. The other boy stood behind him, glancing back along the road. They had their caps in their hands, ready to put them on if a master appeared from the boys' school; not even folded, open. They're scared, I thought. They're more scared than I am.

'If you say one word to Mum, I'll tell her about that dirty magazine you've got hidden in your bedroom,' Patricia said, straightening up to force Richard back a step. 'With all those women in it.'

Richard laughed nervously.

'She's found your *Parade*,' the other boy said.

'It's filthy.' Patricia pulled a face.

'*Pax*,' Richard muttered. 'All right?'

'*Pax*,' I said, opening my mouth for the first time.

'Have you got any matches?' Patricia asked. Richard had an almost empty box of Swan Vestas. Together, huddled beside the exit door of the cinema, we shared the last two cigarettes in Patricia's packet.

It was funny to see Richard half an hour later at the other side of the table while his mother passed round paste and cucumber sandwiches. Mrs Austin was making a fuss of me, saying what pretty hair I had, that nice hair was a woman's crowning glory and if only Patricia would look after hers, which made us both giggle: Patricia spent hours on her fringe while I never did a thing to my hair except brush it and tie it back for games. She said I should eat up everything and get a bit more weight on me because that was what the boys liked, wasn't it, Richard? A girl with a bit of flesh on her bones? And Richard blushed and stared at his plate. Then there were chicken sandwiches and fruit cake that Mrs Austin had made, although she wasn't impressed by it. 'It's come out dry,' she said, cutting another slice and sliding it on to my plate when she thought I wasn't looking. 'You can put a bit of butter on it, if you like.' Whenever my teacup was empty she filled it, putting in the milk second and too much sugar, and I let her, revelling in it, shy but greedy at the same time, greedy for her affection. I decided that I would stay there that night, whatever anyone said. At least that night.

But when we were doing our homework after tea, Mrs Austin asked me straight out how I expected to get home to the Mermaid at that time of the evening. That was when I said in my most polite voice that I supposed I'd have to stay the night. 'And what will they think about that?' she asked.

'She won't mind,' I said. 'I told her I'd be staying.'

'Did you indeed?' She sounded more amused than angry. 'You'd better borrow a nightie in that case.'

She made me up a bed on the floor, a mattress that was just too short for me, but as soon as the light was off Patricia whispered: 'Come up here and get in with me so we can talk better. Otherwise they'll hear.' The bed was narrow but we lay on our backs, with our hands beneath our heads; our elbows banged together when we moved. 'Do you fancy Richie?'

'Is that what you call him?' I asked.

She straightened her arm over my face, and I felt her sleeve rub against my cheek. 'That's what the girls call him,' she said. 'I've heard them. "Richie, Richie, look at this, oh, Richie." They think he's gorgeous.' She paused. 'So *do* you?'

'What?'

'Think he's gorgeous?'

'No,' I said, although I half wished I did: Richie or someone – Doug, his friend, would do. I didn't fancy anyone. When other girls said they did, I wondered if it was true.

'That Doug's quite nice, isn't he?' Patricia said. 'I mean, he's all right. Did you see the way he kept pushing his hair back so that it'd stand up in the middle, only he hadn't put enough Brylcreem on? He plays football with Richard – Richie, I mean – but he's usually in goal.' She wriggled against me, her hipbone pushing into mine. The static electricity of our nighties was making them stick together. 'So he doesn't run around a lot. He just sort of stands there, waiting.' She giggled. Then, after a while, she asked: 'Have you ever kissed anyone? Properly, I mean?'

'No.'

'What's it like, do you think?'

'I don't know. All wet and sloppy, I suppose.'

'What? Like having a piece of wet fish in your face?' she said, and giggled again, low and throaty. 'I bet it isn't. Not if you use your tongue.' She lay there for a few moments, then twisted round and propped herself up on one elbow. 'Do you want to try?'

'All right,' I said. I lay there and watched the silhouette of her head come down until everything was black and all I could feel was her mouth on mine, the hardness of her teeth through her closed lips and then, as she opened her mouth, the hardness of her tongue, a different hardness. I let my own lips part a little until it was in my mouth. Seconds later, she pulled away and shivered, her face half turned towards me, although I couldn't make out her features.

'That was really strange,' she said. I nodded, unsure what she would see, my head against the pillow in the dark. 'What did you think?'

'Yes,' I said. 'It was strange.'

Patricia lay back. After a few moments she said thoughtfully, 'I expect it's different though, with a boy. It would have to be, really, wouldn't it? Otherwise, there'd be no point.'

We must have gone to sleep because soon after that we were woken by the phone ringing. I knew who it was before Mrs Austin came up and found us together in Patricia's bed. She turned on the bedside light and sat beside us.

'I think you've got some explaining to do, Carol,' she said, in such a gentle voice that I started to cry. She stroked my hair and, after a moment, I let her pull me towards her. She put her arms round me and held me until I'd stopped, then wiped my cheeks with her sleeve.

'How did they find me?' I asked.

'Miss Randall gave them our number. She knows what friends you are,' she said. 'And a good thing too. Otherwise they'd have called the police and who knows what might have happened?'

'What are you going to do with me?'

'We'll talk about that tomorrow,' Mrs Austin said. Then, in a sterner voice: 'And we'll talk about what you were doing at the pictures this afternoon as well, Patricia Austin, instead of being in school where you were supposed to be. You've been leading this poor girl astray.'

Patricia's body tensed. 'Who told you that?' she asked. 'I bet it was Richard. Why should he be able to tell tales and not me?'

'Never you mind who told me, young lady. The truth will out.'

'Please let me stay,' I said, my face pressed into Mrs Austin's cardigan. 'Please let me live with you.' As soon as the words were out of my mouth, I knew I should never have allowed myself even to think it. It only had to be said out loud for me to understand how impossible it was.

'Your aunt's been worried sick about you, my dear, and I'm not surprised,' Patricia's mother said, and she coaxed my head back with her hand until she could brush the hair from my face. 'You can't just run away, you know.'

'She only calls herself Carol's aunt,' Patricia said, behind me. 'She isn't really.'

Mrs Austin stiffened and pushed me from her. 'I don't know anything about all that,' she said, turning away from us both. She looked at my clothes, which I had folded and put on the table beside the record player, my skirt and blazer; my shirt was buttoned up and hung neatly on the back of a chair; my shoes were beneath it with the stockings rolled up inside them. I was never this tidy at home, at my aunt's house; I suppose I'd wanted to impress Mrs Austin. 'You'll be going to school tomorrow with Patricia,' she said.

'You mean I can stay here tonight?'

'Goodness gracious, love, it's almost midnight. You don't think I'd send you off into the night, do you? Of course you're staying here. Your aunt'll be picking you up after school tomorrow.' She glanced at Patricia and then, more generously, at me. 'So you make sure you don't get led astray.'

As things turned out, it wasn't my aunt who came to fetch me but Uncle Joey. Not that I cared by then. I'd already been told off, first by Miss Randall between one lesson and another, then by the headmistress during the lunch break. Miss Randall was gentler than the headmistress, who'd called me an ungrateful little monster, but what they said was the same. I was selfish and irresponsible, I had caused no end of worry, nothing could excuse what I had done. I could hear from their tone what they meant by 'nothing'. You may be the child of a murderer and a whore, I thought – that's what you want to say, so say it. I don't care. Say what Aunt Margot says. She's bound to have told you everything by now. Say what you want to say. You may have been orphaned through violent death and imprisonment and you may be forced to live off the charity of a woman who despises you, whom you despise, but that's no excuse. There is no excuse. Girls like you, bad girls from evil stock, have no excuses.

Even Patricia seemed scared of me. I caught her looking across at me that morning during French, as if she had been told something awful. Oh, please, I wanted to say, please don't believe it. It isn't true. When I saw her smile at me mid-afternoon, a conspirator's smile, I almost wept with relief.

Twenty-One

We are finishing breakfast when the telephone rings. I watch across the rim of my coffee cup while Jozef answers. He is about to pass the call to me, but pauses with a closed look on his face.

'What was that about?' I ask afterwards, apprehensive, stacking the plates and cups to take to the sink.

'There are some Turks in the camp with relatives in Poland,' he says. There's no need for him to explain that it was Flavio: we both know that. 'But the number they have doesn't work and they can't find an international operator. They need me to help them.'

'You haven't spoken Polish for years.'

Jozef shrugs. 'I'll come in with you this morning. We'll go together.'

'I'm honoured,' I say, standing by the sink, rinsing the crumbs from our breakfast plates. He looks at me sharply, with a pained expression, as though I wanted to hurt him. How strange, I think, that he should misunderstand me only when we talk about the camp, about Flavio. Perhaps he is jealous of Flavio, although he has no reason to be. Perhaps he is jealous of the camp.

Flavio is in his office when we arrive. He kisses me on both cheeks, as he always does, and shakes Jozef's hand, his eyes darting rapidly across our faces. I notice, as I always do, how fine Jozef is when compared to other men, pared down and clean, like driftwood. How can he doubt me?

The Turks who need help are standing near the window: a young couple with a girl, three or four years old, who clings to her father, pulling his jacket, too large for him, off his shoulder. They look hot: they are wearing far too many clothes for this time of year – it's still humid out and has barely begun to cool towards autumn. When Flavio gestures to him, the man speaks, in broken English, while the woman and child step back and listen. He gives me a soiled piece of paper that's been folded and unfolded too many times and is tearing along the creases. Why give it to me, I wonder, and not to Jozef? I pass it to Jozef, who takes it carefully and holds it in both hands, as if it is something precious.

'This is the number?' he asks, pointing to the paper, and the man nods.

'Yes, yes, the number. My cousin.' I can see they've decided to trust Jozef: the man's shoulders relax, and his wife seems to gain strength through him, holding the little girl's hand less tightly.

'And there is no reply?'

'No,' says the man, shaking his head, his wife behind him shaking hers.

'No,' repeats the little girl, in a bright, excited voice that makes us laugh.

'We have spoken to a Polish operator, I think,' Flavio says, in English, so that everyone can understand, 'but we can find no one there who speaks English.'

'And this is the address of your cousin?' Jozef asks the man.

The man spreads his hands. 'I hope,' he says. He pulls a face that reminds me of the one sad clowns pull, that parody of despair, the stubble on his cheeks darkening into furrows. Yet nothing could be more genuine.

Jozef turns to Flavio. 'You have the operator's number?'

Flavio sighs and picks up a sheet of paper. 'I have these,' he says. 'We have tried all of them. Sometimes there is no one and sometimes there is a woman, always the same woman, who starts to shout in Polish.' He grins suddenly, first at me and then at the little girl.

'But who gave you these numbers?' says Jozef. He sounds irritated.

'They are what we have for Poland,' Flavio says.

Jozef makes a disapproving click with his tongue, then picks up the phone and punches out the first number. Someone answers almost immediately because Jozef begins to speak.

I've always loved to listen to him speak a language I don't understand. We have been to Germany several times, though never to Poland, and I have made a deliberate effort not to learn German simply to have the pleasure of listening to Jozef. It's like watching a person perform with an instrument that in your own hands is wood and gut, at best silent, at worst discordant. I love the way his face registers meaning, his features play out what to me is merely the pantomime of communication. This is true of all unlearnt languages and of all speakers, I know, but Jozef makes it special. Or perhaps it is love that makes it special.

To our surprise, Jozef laughs, murmurs a few words, then puts down the phone. 'I have spoken to a convent of closed nuns, if that is the English way to say it. She came from my part of Poland. She recognized my accent. She said I sounded like an uncle of hers, who was dead.' He turns his body slightly, so that Flavio is excluded, because it is Flavio's fault this has happened. 'She was no help, of course. I shall try another.'

During the second call, the little girl sits on the floor and plays with her shoelaces. Flavio crouches beside her and gives her a pencil sharpener from the desk, in the form of a globe. '*Guarda*,' he says, spinning the globe with his thumb. The little girl takes it and does the same thing, not laughing – thoughtful, as though its movement is not a game but a problem to be solved. By the time Jozef finishes the call, she's bored with it. She puts the globe carefully back into Flavio's outstretched hand.

'The codes have changed in Poland,' Jozef says, writing on a scrap of paper. 'That's why there was no reply.

The number you were calling doesn't exist any longer. This is the new code.' He gives the man the paper. The man looks hungrily at Flavio, who passes him the telephone.

'Is this normal?' Jozef asks him, in Italian. 'Long-distance calls in the morning?'

'We are not only here to pray together, Jozef,' Flavio says.

I am walking back to the gate with Jozef when I hear a voice call, 'Carol.'

I turn round, and glow with pleasure to see Kakuna. She is standing on the far side of the compound, shielding her face from the sun with her hand. I wave but she doesn't wave back, just stands where she is, staring. 'Kakuna,' I shout back.

Jozef touches my arm. 'I'll see you later,' he says, but I barely hear him, I'm so thrilled. 'Kakuna,' I call again.

When I get home for lunch, I think: I won't say anything. I'll wait and let Jozef say what needs to be said. But he's busy in the barn and only comes out for a moment when he hears the car, to wave hello, then goes back in. I stand in the drive, not sure what to do, a little irritated that he hasn't walked over to speak to me, then decide – against my will – to go to him.

He doesn't hear me come in, though Cocoa does, getting up slowly from where he's lying and stretching, front legs first, head down between his paws. I reach out to stroke him and sit on a box. Watching Jozef at work in his own rich world, engrossed and unaware of my presence – as though I don't exist for him, have never existed – I think, with a sense of panic: I've left it too long. I'm losing him. An inexplicable anguish stifles me: I find myself gasping for breath as I watch him pace something out on the floor. Then he turns and smiles. He holds out his hands to me. 'I'm glad you're here,' he says. 'Come and see what I'm doing.'

Jozef has always been a maker of things and it's always excited me to see how what he makes affects him and the way he understands himself. And not only that: to see him realize that he may be judged by what he does and not found wanting, but replete, as people seek his objects out. That started when we'd left England, soon after our marriage, and people who visited us, friends and colleagues, would ask where this picture or that sculpture were from. 'Jozef painted it. Jozef made it,' I would say, unbearably proud of him. The first work, on paper, was delicate, nervous, in charcoal or blood-coloured pastel, but then he began to make figures out of clay, and wood, and, finally, bronze. There were shows, small ones at first, but successful. Everything Jozef does, even the hardest and least decorative thing, has something amenable in it, some handle that can be grasped. It is open work. It breathes.

Now Jozef takes my hand and leads me to the far end of the barn under the big lights. He has built a series of flexible structures, the height of a tall human being. They feel like rooms, but loosely woven, so air and light can pass without interruption from one to another. The walls are made from treated paper fixed to each side of a vertical frame, lacquered until it is almost as heavy and transparent as glass. Within the space created by the two layers, he has suspended leaves of painted paper, cut out and shaped, or other, more solid, forms, some human, though ghostlike, others not. I can see books, and words, and kitchen objects: a sieve, a bowl, a pair of scissors. And there are fragments of clothing, too, and what look like envelopes. The first impression is of passage; later, as you move from one space to the next, of loss; finally, perhaps, of oppression when you understand you, too, are being watched. When I say this to Jozef, he's delighted. 'That's just how it should be,' he says. 'You should feel watched by art. It's there not only to answer questions, you see, but to ask them too.'

I smile and nod, but I'm anxious as, looking more closely, I recognize the handwriting on one of the envelopes as mine. 'I sent that to you,' I say. 'When you were in prison.'

'Yes,' he replies slowly. 'This work is what we have made together, Carol. Like everything else I do, of course, but this time the material itself is us, who we are. It's visible to ourselves and to anyone else who looks, yet invisible as well, because what people make of it will depend not on us, but on them.'

Is this what I want? To be exposed? I'm about to speak, but Jozef is excited now. He takes my arm and leads me from panel to panel. 'Look,' he says eagerly, grinning and pointing at a scrap of cardboard. 'This is all that's left of the rent book we had in Exeter, in our first flat together. And there, look, do you see? A drawing I did of you when you were still a girl. When I was in love with you, and didn't know. But you can see from the drawing what I felt already. You can see from the line.'

'I think I prefer to be invisible,' I say, uncomfortable, knowing that this will disappoint him. 'This is all so private.'

Jozef shakes his head, impatient. 'You want to be invisible – to be private, as you would have it – because you think it makes you safe. But how will your voice be heard if no one can see you? How will you make yourself some place in which to speak, to act, if you hide away? And so you must allow yourself to be seen.'

Jozef waves his arms around and the walls of the rooms move slightly. This could fall down, I think, in a gust of wind. Does he intend the work to be so fragile? And what about you? I wonder. Where are you? Where is your past? Everything here is mine, or ours, our life together; there is nothing that is yours alone. But I'm afraid to ask.

'And now, of course, I have a problem. Now I have made the place in which we can be seen, I no longer need to search for us, so I have no other choice than to force us to be invisible again. And then, once more, I must find a place for us to be seen, to have our say. And not only us, of course. We're quite unimportant in the end. You see? What is that expression? Ah, yes. There is no rest for the wicked.'

He takes me by the shoulders and kisses the tip of my nose, something he hasn't done for years. 'Or anyone else,' he says.

Twenty-Two

I didn't know what Aunt Margot would do when we got back to the pub that evening, but I expected – even wanted – some reaction: to be told off, punished, deprived of something, hit. All she did, though, was look at me, then point towards the unheated living room. 'You can go in there. You'll have homework to do,' she said, turning back towards the bar. Now I think she was ashamed. She must have understood her part in what had happened. To say what she had said to a child and expect that child to accept it; to expect me to accept what she'd said about my mother, and with such violence. What kind of woman would do that?

The most obvious consequence of my night at Patricia's was the way I was treated at school. The following morning I found myself in the middle of a group of girls, most from my form but some from the classes above me too. They stopped me as I was walking along the corridor to the cloakrooms to leave my coat. 'What do you want?' I asked, looking along the corridor behind them to see if I could spot Patricia.

One of the older girls said, 'I bet you copped it last night when you got home.'

I shrugged.

'I bet you did,' she said and I heard admiration in her voice. I must have smiled, because she gave a hoot of laughter. 'I *bet* you did,' she repeated. Then the bell rang for assembly and they were gone, running towards the hall, and I was alone in the corridor, holding my coat, wondering what to think.

Later that day, when the two of us were smoking near the bins, Patricia asked, 'Where would you have gone if they hadn't called my mum? I mean, you couldn't have stayed with us, could you?'

'I'd have gone to France,' I said, without thinking, and immediately regretted it. The last thing I wanted was to lie to Patricia. But now I had to go on, or she'd never believe me again. 'I've got relatives there. That's why I'm working so hard on my French, so I can stay with them in the summer. I want to be able to talk to them properly.'

'I thought you said you didn't have any relatives,' she said. 'Not alive anyway.'

'They're only cousins. I've never even met them. That's why they didn't offer to look after me after the accident. I suppose they wanted to see what I was like first.'

'How come you've got cousins in France?' Patricia persisted. 'Your mum and dad were English, weren't they?'

'I'm not sure. They're on my mother's side. I think my grandmother lived in Paris.'

'But you haven't got a passport, have you? I thought you said you'd never been abroad.'

'If you get to the coast, you can sneak on to a ferry,' I said. 'It's easy. You walk on with other people, pretend you're part of a family. Nobody would think you were running away. Then you walk off at the other side and mingle. Nobody suspects you when you're our age.'

'How do you know?' Patricia asked, but she wasn't hostile, only curious.

I smiled and flicked the ash off my cigarette. 'I don't, really. I'm just saying what I'd have done. Perhaps I'd have been caught.'

'Are you going to try again?'

'I don't know. I might.'

When we were walking back to the classroom, Patricia took my arm. 'You won't tell anyone about what we did, will you? The other night?'

'What do you mean?' I said.

Patricia giggled. 'You know. What we did in bed. The kiss.'

'Of course I won't,' I said. It hadn't occurred to me to tell anyone. If she hadn't mentioned it, I might have forgotten. 'If you don't?'

Patricia pulled a face. 'I won't.'

Later that morning she told me Richie fancied me. 'He thinks you're really nice,' she said. 'I didn't ask him, honest. He just came out with it. He says he wants to take you to the pictures.'

'Well, you can tell him I don't want to go to the pictures,' I said. 'Not with him, anyway.' Patricia seemed pleased and reached for my hand.

We had gym that afternoon, and all I could think about, as we climbed ropes and stood in a shivering line to vault the horse into the arms of the sports teacher, was whether I wanted any boyfriend, let alone Richie. I wished I had someone to talk to and I remember feeling angry that Uncle Joey had been so silent in the van the afternoon before, and resenting him for his secrecy. Otherwise I might have talked to him.

Nicholas admired me for running away, although he didn't admit it until we were far away from the Mermaid. I think he was afraid his mother might hear. We'd walked across the fields to watch the gliders. It was cold and the sheep had lumps of ice dangling from their fleeces that banged together as they scattered. We were both wearing wellingtons but, even so, our socks were wet by the time we reached the gliding club. That was when Nicholas said he'd like to run away too. 'Why don't you?' I asked.

'I've got to look after my mum,' he said. 'That's what my dad would have wanted. Anyway, I don't need to now.'

'Why not?'

'Because I'll be going in any case this summer.' He

reached into the big breast pocket of his anorak and pulled out a crumpled brochure. 'Look.'

It was an application form for the army – Nicholas would be sixteen in April. Then, he said, he could go to Cyprus. 'Why Cyprus?' I asked.

'Because there are soldiers there, that's why.'

I remembered what he'd said earlier, about keeping Cyprus British, and wondered if he knew what he was doing. Before I could ask him, he tugged at my sleeve and pointed across the field. We watched, enthralled, while they wheeled a glider out from the hangar. It swept along the snow-covered runway and lifted, the cable falling back. We held our breath as it passed above our heads, black against the sun.

Nicholas unfolded the form and I saw he'd started to fill it in, the writing smeared where he had tried to rub things out. 'It's a bit complicated,' he said shyly, and I realized he wanted me to help him.

'I'll give you a hand if you like,' I said. And I was happy to. I was happy to think that Nicholas would be going to Cyprus, or Aden, or wherever; happy, even, that he might be killed and that would be the end of it.

I didn't care about Nicholas one way or the other. All I thought about was what his death would do to Aunt Margot, how sad she would be, and how she would deserve it. We walked back across the fields, our wet socks slopping around inside our boots, and went upstairs to Nicholas's bedroom to fill in the form.

Twenty-Three

When I was young, before what happened to my parents, I remember thinking I would never fall ill, never get old, never die. I didn't see how these things applied to me. Why shouldn't I live for ever? Why shouldn't I be the exception? Doesn't it all depend on chance in the end? On the flip of a coin? Why shouldn't I be the single head in an endless sequence of tails?

I stopped believing this long before the skin began to wrinkle round my eyes, my breasts and bottom to sag, before I began to eat sensibly and drink less. But sometimes, when I look at Kakuna and she is watching the older women struggle to their feet or sigh as they sink into a chair, I know she's thinking: I'll never be like that. I'll be the exception. She is scornful with certainty. And then I wonder if perhaps she will, if perhaps my intuition was right and I simply mistook the throw. It will be Kakuna's coin that comes up heads.

*

For today's lesson I have brought some maps and pass them out among the children. Each map has different names missing, and the children are supposed to ask one another for information to fill in the blanks, without letting their own be seen. Kakuna, though, is blatant. She grins at me as she places the two maps on the desk between her and her partner and points at the name she needs, her partner more diffident, watching to see what I will do. I study her grin, partly to see how long she can keep it up, but primarily to see how far I understand its purpose. What she wants is complicity, I think, but the grin might as easily express contempt. Perhaps she sees me as old and heading for death, like the women in the yard. At the end of the lesson I consider calling her over to me, but don't.

Flavio wants to talk to me about Jozef, although he won't come out with it and say so. He makes it clear that he has found out what Jozef does, name-dropping a gallery in Bari that had a small show of his work some years ago while we were still in Rome. I'm vague because I want to discourage this interest, which I don't trust; besides, it's the kind of attention that would irritate Jozef. When Salvo comes into the office, I ask him, to change the subject, if he's still being tormented by the girls, a question I wouldn't ask under normal circumstances. Perhaps because of this, because I am known for my discretion, Salvo blushes beneath his tan and hesitates before answering. 'Sometimes,' he says.

Flavio, who is sitting on the edge of the desk as usual,

legs crossed at the ankles, leans over and ruffles Salvo's hair, pushing it off his face. 'You wouldn't be happy if they stopped, Salvo, so don't pretend you would,' he says, with a laugh. 'You thrive on attention.' This is so true of Flavio and, to my knowledge, so little true of Salvo that I'm tempted to comment, but don't. Flavio is always teasing Salvo, as though he needs to establish rights over him in some way. Salvo says that a message was left earlier that afternoon: some people are coming to see if any children are suitable for adoption.

'I've never really understood what "suitable" means,' I say.

'You think we should hand them over to the first comer?' asks Flavio, his hand on Salvo's shoulder. 'To anyone who wants them? Here are some babies from all over the world. All colours, shapes and sizes. Like a bag of sweets.' He holds out his free hand. 'Come on. Take your pick.'

I shake my head, annoyed. 'Of course not. But the restrictions you have are mistaken, surely? Age, for example. Jozef would be excluded, do you realize that?' Flavio looks intrigued, and I wish I hadn't mentioned Jozef. 'I'd have thought it all came down to a question of vocation, and how can you establish rules for that?'

Smiling, Flavio strokes the edge of Salvo's ear with his thumb. 'Would you say you had a vocation for fatherhood?' he asks the young man.

Salvo stands up and moves towards the door. He smooths his jeans down his thighs to get rid of the wrinkles. I notice that his ear, where Flavio has been touching it, is red, a localized blush. He looks uncomfortable, as though the question was more intimate than he would like – as perhaps it is, in front of me at least. Then, with a flash, I see there is an understanding between them, from which I am excluded, and wonder why I have never noticed it before. How blind I am. 'I don't know,' he says. 'Maybe.'

Later, driving home, I forget about Flavio and Salvo and start to think about Jozef's age, which I almost never do, it upsets me so deeply. It always seems immaterial to him somehow, but I'm afraid I'll lose him. I imagine him as if he had been my father; I let myself see our love – which has never, I am convinced, had anything of father and daughter in it, which has always been the love of equals – as others must see it, as something pathological. As Flavio sees it, I suppose, or why would he be so fascinated? Why would he want to understand Jozef as he does, with his prying, unwanted questions? Yet perhaps his curiosity is justified. What does it mean, after all, to marry a man so much older? But, perhaps, when two people see eye to eye, a difference of twenty years is not so much.

And perhaps, I sometimes allow myself, almost luxuriously, to think, I will die first.

Twenty-Four

During the months before Nicholas went away he spent more and more time at the gliding club, leaving his satchel at the door and running off, still in his school uniform, coming back for tea an hour or two later, sometimes missing it altogether and scrounging chips off Maudie while his mother was in the bar. One afternoon he told us he'd been offered a Saturday job there. They needed someone to help the mechanics, he said, now they were using the winch to send up the gliders.

Aunt Margot shrugged. 'As long as you don't get into mischief,' she said. 'I suppose they'll be paying you something?'

Nicholas flushed, and I saw at once that he hadn't thought of being paid. I tried to imagine how Richie would behave if Mrs Austin spoke to him in the way that Aunt Margot spoke to Nicholas.

He took me with him sometimes, when he saw me hanging around the pub. He introduced me to the men there, who flirted with me. I stood and watched while

Donald, the mechanic in charge of the winch, showed Nicholas what to do. It wasn't difficult – I could have done it at once – but Nicholas struggled to understand, his round, painfully open face contorted with effort as Donald demonstrated the levers and the safety catch, explaining that he had to make sure the cable didn't twist as it coiled back on to the drum, guiding Nicholas's hand from lever to switch.

I liked to go to the big hangar and see the gliders. There were three, each with room for two people, one behind the other, in tiny bucket seats. They looked too heavy to fly, yet flimsy as well. When one of the men asked me if I wanted a spin and winked, I shook my head. I wasn't sure if he was joking, wasn't sure if I wanted to go up in a glider. I thought of Uncle Joey's model plane as it rode on the wind, then fell to the ground. What kept them aloft if the wind dropped?

I went down to the cellar one afternoon, after the gliding club, expecting to find Uncle Joey preparing the kegs for the evening. But he was in his workroom at the end. He had his back to me so I was quite near before he realized. I was close enough to touch him when he jumped and turned on his heels; I was as frightened as he was. 'Uncle Joey! You scared me,' I said, with a nervous giggle. He blushed so fiercely that later I asked myself whether that might have been the start of it.

'You're just in time,' he said. 'I need your advice.' I knew he'd been working on something larger than the model but I hadn't expected this. When he stood to one side, I saw a structure of wooden ribs, held parallel to one another by strips of wood and fixed with glue. 'I've used spruce,' he said, adding, with a shy smile, 'maybe from Poland. I like to think that it is Polish.' The whole thing must have been twenty feet long, maybe more, even twenty-five, and I was thrilled by the impossibility of it – building a plane in the cellar of a pub.

'Is there much space at the gliding club,' Uncle Joey asked me, 'in the place where they put the gliders?'

'In the big hangar, you mean? Yes,' I said. 'It's enormous. They've got three gliders in there already but there's easily room for another. Two, even.' Then I understood what he wanted: to move his plane there, put it together and make it fly. 'Do you think they'll let you?'

'I can ask.' He smiled again. 'Have you any time to give me?' He explained that I could help him cover the shell of the wing with specially cut sheets of plywood. I would have to be careful, he said, but he needn't have bothered. I knew that.

'Do you really think it'll fly?'

'Well, it should do,' he said. 'It won't be the first, you know. You've seen the ones at the club.' He patted the wing. 'I have to put something here, but I don't have space in the cellar. Something to make it fly better. I put a thing that projects here,' he moved his hand horizontally in front of the wings, 'to give control over pitch,' holding his hand at an angle and checking I knew what he meant before continuing, 'and also a little bit of extra lift. And then, at the back, a vertical rudder.' He grinned.

'You know, the first glider was made more than one century ago. And the first man to fly in a glider was a – what do you call him? A coachman? In 1853.'

'And someone is going to fly in this?' I asked. 'Someone's going to be able to go up in the air in it?'

He shook his head, then shrugged. 'This is a prototype. I have made some changes to the normal glider, you see, but I have no wind tunnel so it is difficult for me to know if they are good or bad. It is big enough, though, for one, for someone small like you. Or me perhaps.' He touched my shoulder. His eyes were sparkling, I remember even now, years later, and I wonder once more if that was the day we recognized each other, if somehow the decision was made then. 'In my head,' he said, turning back to the wing, 'they are good.'

When I came up from the cellar, I almost bumped into Aunt Margot as she stalked round the corner of the pub, her cardigan wrapped round her against the cold. She looked furious. 'Is he still messing about down there?' she said. I tried to walk past her, but she grabbed my arm and squeezed it, digging her nails into the flesh above my elbow. 'Don't you play the little madam with me,' she said. 'I asked you a question.'

I wrenched my arm away.

'And I suppose you've been making up to him?'

I stood there, staring at her, unblinking, until she was forced to look away, glancing along the road as if she'd heard a car. It was dark by now, almost opening time.

'Because if you haven't got anything else to do except

waste your time with him, I'll find you something useful to be getting on with in the bar, where people have to work for a living,' she said.

I didn't answer.

'You can make sure there are enough mixers for a start,' she continued. 'And give Maudie a hand with getting the scampi out of the fridge. There's always a rush on Saturdays.'

I was standing between her and the hatch leading down to the cellar so she had to push past me. I listened to her heels on the steps, then went into the pub because I didn't want to hear her talk to Uncle Joey; I hated her when she shouted at him, with her flat, ugly voice, but even more than that I hated him when he didn't answer, when he let her insult him, when he stood there and turned away his head, as though he was about to be hit. Sometimes she called him a stupid Pole. Once, when she thought no one could hear, she called him a coward. And you are, I thought, if you don't fight back, you are a coward. And I despised him for it.

And then I thought – my father would have hit her.

Twenty-Five

Patricia told me that the school had been in contact with her mother, to warn her I might be a harmful influence.

That must have been the headmistress, I thought. Those are the words she would use. 'Did your mother tell you what else they said?' I asked, because it was more than likely they'd told her everything, that I was the daughter of a murderer and only half an orphan.

But Patricia didn't know. 'She doesn't seem to think any different of you, anyway, whatever they said. She really likes you. She says I can bring you home when I want, as long as I'm sure your aunt knows.'

'Is that what she said? My aunt?'

'Well, that's what she calls herself, isn't it? Your aunt?'

Patricia sounded doubtful and I wanted so much to tell her the truth that I wondered momentarily if I could trust her. 'She's a liar.'

The next time I visited Mrs Austin didn't hug and kiss me at once, as she had before, but stood at a slight distance to look at me first, as though she wanted to decide how dangerous I was before she came any closer. I didn't know what to do, other than hope she knew nothing, that she still believed what I had told her. Finally she gave me a rueful smile. 'You will be stopping for tea?' she asked. 'I can't have you running off with an empty stomach.'

'I'm sorry,' I said. 'I can't. My uncle's picking me up at half past five. He's got to collect something in town. I only came round to say hello.'

Mrs Austin made a strange sound in her throat, almost a whimper. 'Come here, love,' she murmured, spreading her arms. 'Come over here and give me a hug.' I stumbled towards her, almost in tears, to let her hold me. Then there was a noise, and as I looked up the stairwell Richie ran down towards us.

He saw me and stopped in his tracks. 'I thought you were locked up.'

'Don't be silly.' His mother eased me away from her. 'Why don't the three of you go out into the garden for a bit of fresh air before it gets dark? I'll bring you out some cake.'

We stood in a huddle outside the kitchen door, not knowing what to say, although it occurred to me later that Patricia might have meant us to meet like that. Perhaps she had told her brother I'd be coming home with her that evening. I could smell aftershave, pine, and beneath it the sharper smell of alcohol, which surely wasn't normal. Then Richie said, 'That Nicholas is your cousin, isn't he? The one that wants to be a soldier?'

'Sort of. I mean, he says he is.'

'He's a bit of a spastic, isn't he? I shouldn't think he'd know which end of a rifle to hold. He'll probably shoot his foot off.'

Patricia snorted. 'And you're so special, I suppose?'

'I'm not going to get myself shot, if that's what you mean,' said Richie, speaking to her but looking at me. 'I've got better things to do, like be a speedway racer, for one, and win cups. Or go to Australia and get rich, for another.'

'He's right, though,' I said to Patricia. 'It is stupid to want to be a soldier. Nicholas is stupid.'

Patricia looked annoyed. 'And getting killed on a motorbike's clever, is it?' She turned to Richie. 'Anyway, what makes you think you're going to make any money in Australia? You only want to go because they pay your ticket for you. You're just idle.'

Richie ignored that. He pushed his hands deep into his trouser pockets. 'Have you ever been on a motorbike?' he asked me. I shook my head. 'Well, do you want me to give you a spin?' He spoke in a low voice so his mother wouldn't hear.

'What – now?' I glanced at Patricia, expecting her to look appalled, but she nodded keenly, as though she had proposed the idea herself. 'All right,' I said, my mouth dry with excitement.

Mrs Austin tapped on the kitchen window, holding up a plate and pointing to it. 'Cake,' she mouthed. But Richie said to Patricia, 'Tell her I'm taking Carol down to meet her uncle. OK?'

'You better had.' Patricia didn't sound put out that I was going off with her brother. 'Or she'll be in real trouble.'

He told me to hold on tight and I did. I clasped my hands together, feeling his belt buckle bite into my wrist, and dug my knees into his legs. My satchel banged against my back as he took the bike slowly along the road that led up the hill into town, then swung left and accelerated. Five minutes later we were in open country. My skirt whipped round my legs, my thighs were purple and goose-pimpled with cold, but I didn't care, just clung on tighter, thrilled to the bone as I saw the road beneath us smooth and shiny as glass. I turned my head to the right and saw, far away at the top of the hill, a building that might have been the Mermaid, but the force of the wind made me gasp for breath and I moved back behind Richie's head. His hair blew into my face. The skin on my cheeks and forehead felt tight and my lips were taut against my teeth. I started to hum some silly tune and then sang, loud as I could, the words snatched away by the wind.

Richie slowed, pulled into the verge and stopped. He kicked the stand down and dismounted, his foot leaving a dirty mark on my thigh as he brought his leg over the tank. Seconds later, as I got off, I felt so wobbly I almost fell. I looked at my wrist and saw the imprint of his buckle, the smear of dirt on my leg. 'Look,' I said, holding out my arm, 'You can see your belt.' He took my wrist in his hand, then let it go. At that moment, he reminded me of Nicholas, which gave me confidence. I had some cigarettes in my satchel. To make him feel better, I offered him one. He leant against the bike, crossing his legs at the ankles, his donkey jacket unbuttoned. Neither of us spoke for a minute or two. Then, when our cigarettes were almost finished, he asked, not looking at me but at the road: 'Did Patricia tell you anything about me? About what I said to her?'

'Such as?' I was only teasing – I'd already decided I'd agree to anything he suggested. I liked the way he'd dared to take me out like that, I'd liked the feel of his donkey jacket against my cheek when I bent my head to protect it from the wind. His shyness appealed to me and made me feel safe. Besides, if I went out with Richie I would have the use of his motorbike: I would be free of the Mermaid, able to come and go whenever I wanted. Perhaps he would teach me how to ride, if we went into the country where no one would see us. Then I could sit in front, with Richie behind.

We got back just as my uncle was parking beside the war memorial. I slipped off the bike and ran across to him, excited, not turning to wave at Richie, who told me later that he had watched me running and that I was beautiful, words so unexpected that I kissed him, rapidly, on the mouth, for the first time. But that was days later.

Twenty-Six

I try to work but I can't settle. When my screensaver appears for the third time in half an hour, I walk out to the barn and tell Jozef that I'm going to the camp. He barely nods, engrossed in what he's doing.

I stop at a news kiosk on the way and buy some Pokémon stickers, deciding not to give them to Kakuna in front of the others because it will make them jealous and resentful of her, and I want to protect her from that. Girls come and go as their families are settled, but Kakuna remains. The girl she stabbed was taken away weeks ago and I have almost forgotten about the incident, so when I do remember I am as shocked as though it were happening again. It's like that when I see her, each time as strong as the first, with that same dumb thrill I experienced when she was pulled from the water and on to the beach – that thrill of recognition. Sometimes I catch her near the fence, when she thinks she's unobserved, and she seems to be cowering, yet not afraid, almost as though she weren't cowering but waiting to strike. And I think, once again with that sense of exhilaration, You're dangerous. Because wasn't I dangerous at her age? I wanted to be.

I park the car and walk through the gates, and the first thing I notice is a pair of volunteers hurrying out of one barracks and into another with that air of self-importance the unpaid tend to wear. How few of the women who work here have children, I think. We must have love to spare; or perhaps we prefer to spread it thin.

Then I spot Kakuna with a group of girls who also come to my English lessons, so I hurry across before anyone else can see me – I'm not supposed to be here today – and crouch in their midst. I always speak English to them now, which amuses them. Kakuna has improved so dramatically that I ask myself how much she spoke when she arrived. How much would a Kurdish girl know? When I ask her about her own country she doesn't reply, although generally she answers my teacherly, purposefully bland questions with her own blandness, encouraged by the nature of language learning and maybe language itself, where everything essential is washed away.

This is when I decide to ask them to my house for tea. 'Not today,' I say, 'because I have nothing ready and must check with Flavio.' I do a headcount: five, so they will fit in the car. 'This must be our secret,' I say, and lift my finger to my lips. 'You must promise me you won't tell anyone. This is a treat.'

'What's "treat"?' they want to know.

'A different, special thing,' I say.

Twenty-Seven

Patricia was pleased and not pleased, in more or less equal measure, that I was 'really going out', as she put it, with Richie. On the one hand, she saw it as something that reflected well not only on me and Richie but on her too; she bragged about us to the other girls in our year, only a handful of whom had boyfriends then, who considered her a source of wonder and information. On the other, the idea that I should devote time to Richie I could otherwise have spent with her threw her, made her confused and uncomfortable, as though this was not, after all, what she had planned.

The first time Richie came to school to meet me, waiting outside the gates on his motorbike with his coat collar up and a cigarette cupped in his hand, the three of us stood together, not knowing what to say, while other girls sidled past, curious and staring openly. It was obvious to me that Patricia wanted to stay with us, but was too embarrassed to ask. I understood her perfectly, her loneliness, her pride; despite that, all I wanted was to get on the bike and drive away. After a few moments, she hitched her satchel on to her shoulder and said, 'Right, I'm off home. See you tomorrow, then, I suppose.'

Richie offered me what was left of his cigarette, holding it with the filter towards me and the burning tip inwards to his palm. I shook my head, not because I might be seen but because it would only slow things down. It would soon be dark and I hadn't told anyone I'd be late. I should have waited for the school bus to pass and told Nicholas that Richie would bring me back to the pub, but I was on the bike before Patricia had even reached the corner, my legs against the leather, my hands on the metal bar behind my bottom.

'Where do you want to go?' he asked.

'Anywhere,' I said.

'We could go to the park?' I saw him in profile, his hair curling away from his forehead, his ear, as small and pink as mine, some blackheads on the side of his nose. He sounded nervous, which pleased me. I didn't feel nervous at all.

'Anywhere you want,' I said.

When I got back the pub had been open for hours. Richie wanted to come in with me or for us to go somewhere quiet outside. But I told him I'd see him the next day, after school, if he wanted. It was late, I said, fending him off with that sense of sexual economy women seem to be born with; the need to save something for later, for just-in-case. Besides, my lips were chafed and sore with kissing. He reversed the bike while I stood at the edge of the road, shivering now that I was still, yet hot as well, flushed and feverish with excitement, impatient for him to go so that I could be alone and understand what was happening to me – by which I didn't mean Richie, or not only Richie, but all of it: the sense of cold speed in the dark, the taste of smoke on someone else's breath. I watched the back light disappear down the hill, then walked across the car park. I knew I'd be told off whatever I did, but I hated the idea of sneaking in like a thief. Besides, I thought that if I walked through the public bar, rather than the side door, Aunt Margot would be too intimidated by the customers to shout at me. My face was burning as I walked into the heat of the almost empty room, undoing my coat.

She was on the customers' side, sitting on one of the stools and leaning towards the man beside her, one elbow on the bar. She was wearing a pale blue dress stretched taut across her bottom, a thread of silver running through the material that glinted in the dimmed lights of the pub, her bra straps showing as she bent forward. Her hair was white blonde and raked up from her neck into a lacquered roll. Seeing her like that reminded me of when I'd heard her talk about my father with one of the customers. 'What a dreadful world we live in,' she'd said. She reached for a cigarette and let the man light it, her fingernails on his wrist, then blew out the smoke slowly over his head. I noticed the way he looked at her breasts as she arched her head back, her throat stretched in front of him.

Then he became aware that I was standing there.

'Look what the cat's dragged in,' he said. 'You've got a refugee from St Trinian's.'

I walked past them, pretending not to have heard, feeling his eyes on me as I lifted the counter to go through. I was almost on the safe side of the bar when he chuckled and said, 'You've had a bit of an accident.'

At first I didn't know what he meant. I turned back and saw my aunt staring at me as she swivelled, one thin white stiletto heel catching in the foot-rest of the stool and twisting her shoe off. She stumbled against the man, who grasped her bare arm hard enough to leave marks. But she pushed him away – 'Leave me alone, you big ape' – and I could tell how drunk she was from her voice. She caught me by the skirt and pulled it towards her, twisting it round until I could see what the man had seen: a dark stain on the back. I gasped. My period had started. Aunt Margot knew at once what it was. 'You dirty little beast,' she slurred. 'You should be ashamed of yourself.'

'I want to see my father,' I said. 'Why won't you let me see him?'

'Well, you can't, can you?'

'I want to see him.'

'And why would you want to see him?' she asked. 'If ever a man deserves to be in jail, he does. A man who murders his own wife is no man as far as I'm concerned.' She struggled back on to the stool, then jabbed her cigarette in my direction. 'You let him do it, so there's no point pulling that face. You stood there and watched. You know what I'm talking about.'

The last time my mother ran away from home we didn't go to my aunt's but to a hotel. It was on the coast – I don't remember where – but you couldn't tell that from our room, which overlooked the car park and kitchen bins. When I asked her why we couldn't have a view of the sea, she didn't answer, and it wasn't until the following day, when I pestered her to buy me a pair of shoes I'd seen and she snapped at me and tugged me away from the window, that I realized we didn't have enough money for luxuries. We only saw the sea when we walked along the windswept promenade together, my mother holding my hand until I pulled it free to lean on the railings while she walked off. After a dozen paces, she'd wait, not turning, until I caught her up.

It was out of season. The hotel lounge was freezing and the dining room almost empty; we ate in silence, our cutlery rattling against the plates. Even the pier was closed. Sulking and resentful, I followed my mother up a hill to a mini-golf course advertised in a bus shelter, but the gates were padlocked and a handwritten sign said: 'See you in May!'

'I hate it here,' I said.

My mother sighed. 'It won't be for long,' she told me. 'Bear with me.'

We'd been there for three, maybe four days when I started to sob in our bedroom after lunch. My mother had hardly spoken to me since breakfast. I was bored and frightened, I didn't know what was expected of me, or what would happen next; even worse, I didn't know how to find out, what words to say. When she asked me what was wrong, I refused to answer, just rolled over on to my half of the bed and buried my face in the pillow. She walked across from the window and sat beside me, stroking my back. 'Speak to me, darling,' she begged, in a low voice. 'Tell me what's wrong.'

Finally, struggling for breath, I muttered, 'Daddy.'

She pulled me up and hugged me, holding my face against her blouse. 'I'll never let him take you away from me,' she said. 'Never.'

But that wasn't what I'd meant: I wouldn't have minded if he had. I pushed her away, as hard as I could, wanting to hurt her. 'I miss him,' I cried.

She didn't understand me at first; perhaps she didn't want to. 'We can't go back,' she said. 'You don't know what it's like. Your father's a monster.'

'Please,' I begged, 'I hate it here. I want to go home.'

Twenty-Eight

Before the lesson I watch Kakuna. I am standing near the classroom door with Flavio, who wants me to translate a letter received from someone in Cleveland, America, an Armenian woman who has lost contact with her sister, it seems, and imagines she might have been smuggled into Italy across the Adriatic, perhaps in the last few months. She says she will pray for us. At the bottom of the letter there is a sticker of the Virgin Mary, the kind that children put on their exercise books, except that theirs are the Lion King or Roger Rabbit or some saucer-eyed girl from a Japanese cartoon. There is a photograph as well, of a group of young women, all with headscarves and each indistinguishable from the others, standing, smiling and squinting in front of what looks like a combine harvester. The woman from Cleveland has ringed one figure in crayon and drawn an arrow, beside which she has written: 'My loved sister. Please, your help.'

Kakuna is crouched on the floor with two smaller girls I've never seen before, who must have arrived in the last few days. She is playing with some toys and I recognize the Pokémon she was clutching in her hand the night she arrived, which she won't let the others touch. She is teasing them in a way I already think of as hers, with an edge of barely restrained aggression, as though she'd do more than tease them if she could. Yet it's obvious they adore her.

'Isn't she too old to be playing with that kind of thing?' I realize as I speak that this has been troubling me for some time. 'I don't know,' Flavio says. 'That rather depends on how old she is.'

'What do you mean? I thought she was thirteen. Isn't that what she told us?' I hear my voice rise, almost hysterical, and am startled.

'Yes. That's what she told us.' Flavio folds the letter and slides it back into its envelope. 'It's what she wants us to believe. It isn't necessarily true. You know what they're like, Carol. Some of them think it's safer to say they're younger than they are; others pretend to be older, on the grounds that adults have more rights. Either way, what we get isn't necessarily, or even generally, the truth. In her case,' he indicates Kakuna with a glance, 'we don't even know what her name is.'

'She can't have lied about that?'

'I don't see why not,' says Flavio. 'Whatever you might suppose, as far as I can find out, Kakuna's certainly not a Kurdish name. Nobody's ever heard of it. Besides, haven't you noticed the way the other girls snigger when you call her, as though they'd been let into some secret? Something funny's going on. We'll be the last to know, of course. As usual.'

I shake my head. Later, though, in the lesson, I say her name, *Kakuna*, with as much emphasis as I dare, to see what the others do, but note nothing unusual in their response, no glancing around, no giggling. Only Kakuna looks at me, with her little smile, her hands resting side by side on the desk in front of her, the fingers slightly curved; an ageless gesture. What beautiful eyes you have, I think, so dark, so liquid, and immediately I'm uncomfortable, as though I've been caught committing some disgraceful act.

Last night I had one of those dreams that are humiliating in their simplicity, as though a slow-witted child is being addressed. It was dark and I was out of my depth in black cold water. I struggled to keep my head above the surface as the weight of my clothes dragged me down, and then I saw a woman far away, on a beach, and raised my arm to wave. '*Carol*,' I cried, '*Carol*,' desperate now, the water filling my mouth and choking me. But she couldn't have heard me because she started to walk away. I watched her disappear, then woke up coughing, with Jozef beside me, concerned, his face as open as a boy's, and I couldn't tell him what I'd seen; some inner censor blocked me. 'I've had a nightmare,' I said, 'that's all. I don't remember what about. Go back to sleep.'

Over breakfast, I tell Jozef I've invited some of the children for an afternoon. 'To get them away from the camp,' I add hurriedly, before he can ask me why – although, I realize at once, he never would, and I feel ashamed of myself for doubting him.

Twenty-Nine

It was thanks to Nicholas that we got permission to put the wings of the glider in the big hangar, right at the back, where no one would notice them. And me, of course. I spoke to Nicholas, who then spoke to Donald and the others. I think he liked the responsibility it gave him; he wouldn't have done it just for Uncle Joey. In the end, though, I suspect it was Donald who arranged it, to curry favour with me.

Uncle Joey and I went together, one Saturday morning when Aunt Margot had gone to town with a rep, as she often did. It was cold, but the snow had thawed, and there were two or three newborn lambs, I remember, that made us laugh. I started to tell him about Richie, repeating the sort of stories that one boy tells another and that Richie, despite this, had told me, because what else would we have talked about? I must have sounded excited, though, excited about something else that lay beneath what I was saying and made me blush, because after he had listened quietly for a while, Uncle Joey began to ask questions I hadn't expected. How well do you know Richie? How old is he? What does he think to do when he leaves school? The kind of questions one would naturally ask a fourteen-year-old girl with an older boyfriend, except that Uncle Joey was the wrong person to be asking them. I answered at first, but I wasn't happy. I became evasive, then silent.

I waited outside with Donald while Uncle Joey talked to the manager of the club. Donald put down his tool-bag and sat beside me on the wall. 'So, he's your uncle, is he?' he asked, gesturing towards the office with his thumb. 'The mad professor,' he said.

I wondered what Nicholas had told him. 'He isn't mad.'

Donald lit a cigarette and I asked for one, to see what he would do. 'And what will your uncle say to that? If I give you a cigarette?' he teased.

My heart was beating fast. 'He won't mind,' I said. 'Nobody cares what I do.'

Donald hesitated, then grinned and reached into the breast pocket of his shirt. It was tartan and made of flannel, the kind the men who delivered the beer used to wear, except that Donald's smelt of oil, or Donald did. 'Well, don't say I didn't warn you,' he said. He took the packet out, pushed it open from the bottom – they were Piccadilly, which I'd never tried before – and watched me while I chose a cigarette. His hands were big and rough, with scratches near the knuckles and ragged skin round the nails. My fingers were tiny beside his. I could feel his eyes on my hand and then, more cautiously, on my face, and I felt the thrill of excitement I felt with Richie, and a power as well, as though I had made something happen. When I put the cigarette into my mouth and lifted my head for it to be lit, looking through my lashes at Donald, I saw beads of sweat along his upper lip.

Later that week, after school, Nicholas and I helped Uncle Joey take the first wing to the hangar. The hard part was getting it out of the cellar and into the car park, Uncle Joey showing us how to hold it, calling from below as we pulled it up through the hatch, and guiding it with his head and shoulders. Carrying it across the fields to the gliding club was easier, but not much. It was light enough, but cumbersome because of its length and because we couldn't see where we were treading, with the wing between us like a bridge. The ground was rough and I was worried I might fall over and graze my knees. I wished I'd changed into jeans instead of keeping on my skirt, but there hadn't been time for that: it would soon be dark. Uncle Joey shouted once, at Nicholas, when he jumped from the top of a wall and let the wing slip from his hand. It might have ripped if I hadn't managed to jump down too, almost twisting my ankle.

'You can't tell me what to do,' Nicholas said.

Donald showed us where to put the wing, his eyes on my legs. He'd never seen me in a skirt before and I felt shy, even though it was only my school skirt, wishing once more that I'd changed. He brushed against me and

I moved away, not frightened, just enough to establish distance.

'Fancy a smoke after?' he whispered. I shook my head, but didn't speak. Nicholas was watching us.

Uncle Joey came across and offered Donald a half-bottle of whisky he'd brought from the pub. 'For your help,' he said.

I pretended not to watch as Donald unscrewed the top and took a mouthful, then gasped and beamed with pleasure, replaced the cap and slipped the bottle into his back pocket – a little performance just for us. 'That's a nice bit of stuff,' he said, winking at Nicholas, who looked bashful, and I thought, suddenly, Nicholas has given him whisky before, certain that I was right. That would explain why Donald was so patient with him, I thought. Nicholas was so useless that anyone else would have lost their temper.

When Uncle Joey and I left to go back to the pub, Nicholas stayed at the club. Because it was just the two of us, I thought Uncle Joey would talk to me about the glider, but he didn't. He said nothing until we'd been walking for about a quarter of an hour. He'd stepped behind me to make room for a car, so I couldn't see him when he said I shouldn't ask about my father, that asking questions would do no good.

'What do you mean?' I asked, hot in the face, as if I'd done something to be ashamed of.

'I heard you ask about your father,' he said, 'that night

you came home late and you weren't well, and I was worried for you.'

'I was well enough,' I said angrily, because I'd been hurt by his silence. I'd thought I could trust him to help. But he had let her get away with it.

'I cannot talk in front of her, you know that,' he said. He sounded impatient with me, as though I was the one who had let him down. 'And then she is always there listening, to hear what we say. She thinks we talk behind her back.' He caught up with me then and touched my elbow. I stared ahead but I could still see him, walking at my side; I could see the concern in his face. I was practically as tall as him, I remember – almost as tall then as I am now. We do talk behind her back, I thought. We do it all the time.

'What do you mean?' I asked, my words coming out in a rush. 'About my father? Why won't anyone tell me anything? Do you know where he is?'

'He's in prison, Carol, you know this.'

'But why can't I see him?' I was about to start crying and I saw, through the corner of my eye, my uncle bite his lip. I felt his hand on my arm.

'He doesn't want to see you,' he said slowly. 'They called one day, maybe two months ago, and spoke to Margot, the people who brought you here, or people like them, I'm not sure which. From the police. From the government. They had a message from him for you, written, you understand, but they thought it was right that you don't receive this message. It would be cruel. They wanted me also to listen to what they said because I am your uncle, you see, it was my duty. They have decided that your father was ill, very ill, that you would be made to suffer. It would be too cruel to you. The letter was filled with anger, with hate. Terrible things about your mother. About other people. Terrible things that surely cannot be true. You could not read such a letter. It would do no good.'

We had stopped walking by this time. Uncle Joey put his arm round my shoulders and held me to him while I cried, my face pushed into his jacket. I cried until my throat hurt. 'What else did he say?' I asked eventually, when I could speak without choking.

'He loves you,' Uncle Joey said. 'He says this many times. He loves you very much, but you cannot see him. It is not the police that stop you, it is not I nor your aunt, it is your father. He will not permit that. He feels very, very bad for what he did to you, and what he did to your mother, that she is dead by his hand. He will never forgive himself. He says you must forget him. You can do nothing for him. He would die for you if it would help, he said.' He held my head and lifted it away from his shoulder, brushing the tears from my cheeks with his thumb. 'Can you do that? Can you forget your father? Because it is this that he wants from you. That you forget him.'

'But how can I?' I wailed. 'How can I?'

'Perhaps one day he will change and he will have the courage to see you and say what he has done to your face, what damage he has done. And then you will forgive him perhaps. Perhaps you will also have the courage.'

He hugged me tight until I had stopped crying, then gave me his handkerchief. 'You are a brave girl,' he whispered, as I wiped my eyes. 'And now we must go home.'

Thirty

'Are you sure you can handle five of them?' Flavio asks, when I tell him about my plan for the afternoon outing. I think he's making gentle fun of me, as he sometimes does. Normally I enjoy it, but this time I'm annoyed.

'Are you suggesting I'm too soft?' I laugh, wanting to let him see that I'm irritated, but also afraid he might simply forbid me. Perhaps it's not permitted to take these children away from the camp. In one sense, they are still illegal immigrants, still in the process of being *welcomed*, as the function of the camp has it. Then Salvo glances up from his desk, where he is tidying papers in what seems to me an entirely unfocused way, as though it is merely an excuse to stay in the office to listen. He grins at us both and I understand that Flavio has been joking; when it comes to Flavio and Flavio's moods, Salvo is never wrong.

'On the contrary,' Flavio sounds amused, 'it's Jozef I worry about. An artist of his calibre needs tranquillity. Isn't that what people say? That's what Salvo always says, isn't it?' He turns to Salvo, who blushes and bangs his fistful of loose sheets into a block against the desk. 'When you go off somewhere to write your mysterious poetry and don't want anyone around?'

'An artist of Jozef's calibre doesn't need tranquillity as much as stimulus,' I say, embarrassed for Salvo. 'You shouldn't worry about him, in any case. He can look after himself. Besides, he's perfectly at home with children.' I don't say that he hasn't mentioned the subject since I brought it up two days ago and that I feel this as a sort of reproach. Besides, it is disingenuous of me to claim that he is at home with children, since what he does with children now is what he did with me when I was a girl. He treats them with cautious respect, which either unnerves them or makes them love him and reciprocate. You can see how surprised the second type are, less by him – because he is entirely natural with them: that is his secret – than by their own new-found capacity to return respect. I have seen this happen, though not often, and it is like watching a child grow up before your eyes.

But most children slide from unease into a sort of wary hostility, responding to his carefully considered, uncomfortably *adult* questions as noncommittally as they can, gradually worming away from him, sniggering from a distance if they find allies among the other children there. Jozef, however, is blithely unaware of this, since he has eyes only for those who recognize him, and respond. The others disappear from his sight, more than ever now he's older and has no time for anything not to his purpose. And I have to admit I'm worried Kakuna might not appreciate Jozef, that she might disappoint me. I couldn't bear to see his eyes slide off her for someone else, some other child.

They are quiet in the car; three in the back, then Kakuna and Magda, a smaller girl and Kakuna's constant ally, in the front beside me. Kakuna has one hand resting lightly on Magda's knee and the other round her Pokémon. I'd thought of bringing Cocoa with me, anxious that entertainment might be needed. But now their silence reassures me. It seems to be focused entirely outwards, their faces turned to the unwinding roadside, and I realize this is the first time they have seen Italy since the day they were taken from the boat and brought to the camp. This is the first glimpse they've had of the land of milk and honey that hasn't been provided by the screen of a television or the pages of a magazine.

'We'll soon be there,' I say, because I have decided that today is an English day, and even though no one speaks the faces turn towards me, smile, and I am happy, convinced I am doing the right thing. I glance at the seat next to me and see that Kakuna is tugging Magda in to whisper something in her ear as we turn off the road and down the drive.

Cocoa is waiting. He bounds up to the car, his large paws scratching at the window, and I sense rather than see the girls in the back flinch. 'He's a good dog,' I say hurriedly, catching at his collar as I open the door and gesture for them to get out. 'Good dog, good Cocoa,'

I say, and take a long step back, pulling him with me, because they are wary, unused to him, perhaps unused to dogs that serve no other purpose than companionship.

They climb down from the car and stand in a row, keeping an eye on Cocoa but also glancing round to get some idea of where they are. The youngest one edges behind the others, her fingers twisted into the hem of a pullover that is too big for her so that it loops up over her hip as she lifts her hand, like a heavy skirt. They look so utterly lost I want to cry, but I smile, hold Cocoa, wait for them to relax. They watch me to see what to do, and they seem so small outside the camp, as though the scale of their world were there, with its fences and soldiers.

Kakuna doesn't look scared. She takes a step forward and puts out her hand, palm up, for Cocoa to lick and I see that she is used to dogs; she knows exactly what to do. Cocoa crouches, playfully, front legs pressed against the ground, rump in the air. She makes a low *chuck-chuck* through pursed lips, with Magda holding her arm. She will be all right with Jozef, I think, relieved.

I should have thought about what I would do with them once we were home, but all I have planned is their lunch. The kitchen table is covered with chicken sandwiches cut into quarters and piled under damp teacloths, the way they do in bars, to keep them fresh; there are plastic bowls with crisps and salted peanuts, and small iced cakes I baked myself, arranged in a spiral beneath a wire-net dome to keep the flies off. I have made a cocktail from pineapple juice and lemonade, with orange and apple floating in it. I want the day to be special, but now, as we walk towards the house together, it occurs to me that all I have done is provide these children with food, as though it were food they needed. And it strikes me, too, that even the food I have prepared is wrong, frivolous and quietly insulting. I have turned out something cheap, trite and unimaginative – something Aunt Margot might have prepared for me, if we had ever celebrated anything together. But, of course, we never did.

What would my mother have done? I wonder, because I have no memory of an occasion like this in my past, when we were a family, two parents and a child, although surely there must have been birthday parties, at least, when I was smaller. And for the first time in years the thought of my mother brings tears to my eyes, although I don't know why, because what comes into my head is bitter, and only partly true. My mother, I think, would have hired caterers.

Thirty-One

Letters began to arrive from Nicholas. They had sent him to a barracks near Preston for his training; after that, he bragged, he'd be going abroad, he couldn't say where. I thought about his talk of Cyprus and wondered if he even knew where it was.

The day he left, we took him into town to catch the coach. Aunt Margot took a snap of him, then kissed him goodbye, stroking his cheek with one hand, her glove in the other, and his face changed and I saw that he finally understood he was going; as though, until then, everything had been a game but he hadn't known it at the time and had thought it was real, his racing up and down the hills with his arms outstretched, ack-acking as Germans were picked off one by one from the skies. He had been playing at soldiers for years and now, in his new suit, with his khaki holdall on the pavement beside him, the playing was over. He took Uncle Joey's hand and stared at it, so as not to look up, I suppose, and wouldn't let it go until Uncle Joey slowly pulled it away from him, then gripped his shoulder to compensate. He didn't shake my hand, or kiss me; he even refused to meet my eyes until the very last moment, when the coach drew off and he pushed his round face against the glass and stared directly at me, accusingly, as though I should have stopped him leaving; as though I had been the one to make him go.

On the way back to the Mermaid, I asked if I could move into Nicholas's room now he'd left. Aunt Margot reached round from her seat in the front of the car to slap my leg. 'He hasn't been gone half an hour,' she said.

I didn't see much more of the first letters than the envelopes, which I picked up from the doormat and took to my aunt, sitting in her usual place in the kitchen. 'Look,' I'd say, 'a letter from Nicholas.' She would open it and pull out a single sheet of lined blue paper, which she'd read without expression, cigarette in hand. When I asked her how he was, she gave a short, unamused laugh but didn't answer.

A new letter would arrive every couple of days or so and eventually, when I had almost stopped reading the name on the envelope, because it was always my aunt's, I saw that one was addressed to me. I slipped it into the waistband of my skirt and said nothing to my aunt: I didn't particularly care that Nicholas had written to me; I cared that I could deprive her of something she would regard as hers.

I went upstairs and locked myself into the bathroom, where I sat on the side of the bath, reading the letter quickly, surprised to find myself excited; it was so long since anyone had written to me. It was the usual paper, with a ragged edge along the top where Nicholas had ripped it off the pad. His handwriting was round and babyish, rising and sinking around the pale blue lines of the paper, and some of the ink had run. I didn't realize immediately that he had been crying as he wrote. Then, as I read, it was obvious.

Dear Carol
I hope this finds you well. I espect you are doing well at school and going out with your boyfreind a lot on his motorbike because it is spring. It is very cold here and we havnt got proper blankets and I am always cold at night but they say it makes us tough and if we complain we are not soldeirs we are no better than girls. Ditto for mess. The food is filth, but I am not hungry because when I come back the other lads hit me until I am sick and now I have no appitite I just eat bread. They say I have to learn to be a soldeir. I told the sergant and he said I was a crybaby. The other lads touch me and make me stay in the toilet and clean it after they have gone and not to use a brush. Will you write to me and say you are my girlfreind? I know it wont be true but it will help me. Don't say I asked you for gods sake or I will never live it down. They say I am a pansy.

Yours sincerley
Nicholas

That afternoon, when I was waiting for Richie to meet me outside school, I showed the letter to Patricia. She read it quickly, then giggled. 'He's really thick, isn't he?' she said. 'I always thought he was a bit dim, but I didn't think he was this bad. He can't spell for toffee.' I took the letter back, ashamed for Nicholas, furious that I hadn't kept it to myself. Patricia must have seen this, because her expression changed. 'What are you going to do, then? Are you going to do what he wants? Are you going to pretend to be his girlfriend?'

I hadn't decided. All I had thought up to then was *poor Nicholas*. But Patricia's giggling had made up my mind. 'Yes,' I said. 'But you mustn't tell anyone.'

'Not even Richie?'

'Don't be stupid. Especially not Richie.'

Patricia pulled a face. 'It isn't fair, though, is it? You'll have two boyfriends then.' I think she was only half joking.

Later, I let Richie put his hand inside my knickers for the first time and tried to imagine it was Nicholas. I let his fingers grope between my legs while he rolled on top of me, my overcoat beneath us. I could feel his penis, stiff, through his trousers and wondered if I should try to touch it in return, but I didn't because I didn't want to do anything that might encourage or discourage him. Nicholas will never do this, I thought, not to anyone, and I felt almost sick with sadness because I was certain it was true.

Richie's mouth was near my ear and all I could hear

was his breathing. His lips, much softer than they looked, were hot against my neck; I could feel his teeth on my skin as they clamped down. I tried to sit up, to stop him giving me a love bite just beneath my chin, where everyone would see it, but his clumsy fidgeting weight held me down. 'Stop it,' I said into his hair, in a thin voice I could barely hear myself.

We were in the park, between some laurel bushes and a potting shed, and it was cold with the damp grass beneath my coat and the smell of compost, of rotting leaves, in my nostrils and, alongside that, the smell of something Richie had put on his hair and the taste of it in my mouth, something sweet and alcoholic, which made me feel light-headed. I twisted my head round for air. All I wanted was for him to take his hair out of my face, to let me stand and get away. I didn't mind his hand in my knickers; it was being marked that I hated.

Later that evening I sat in my bedroom with my homework open before me and tried to write a letter for Nicholas, but couldn't. I couldn't see him, however hard I tried; it was as though I'd never known him. I touched my neck where Richie had bitten me but there was nothing to feel; it was only there in the mirror, a livid red stain the size of his mouth. I picked up my biro and wrote: 'Do you remember the love bite you gave me?' then scribbled the words out. Twenty minutes later, I started to thumb through my aunt's romantic novels for inspiration; soon I had written half a page. Surely that was enough. I was about to sign it – Carol – when I thought that perhaps the lads would know who Carol was. When I heard the noise of the fryer in the kitchen downstairs, the clatter as fat was shaken off the pan, I wrote Maudie's name instead. Love and kisses, Maudie. Nicholas had always been fond of Maudie.

The next day, at break, I showed Patricia the letter. After reading the first two lines, she started to smile. 'What's this bit, then? "I feel your lips on mine and my aching heart beats faster." You're so pathetic, Carol, honestly. You don't think that's what you put in a love letter, do you? To a soldier? They'll kill him if they read this, they will. I bet you.' She folded the page down the middle and gave it back to me. 'I could do better than that,' she said. 'With my eyes closed.'

'Go on, then,' I said.

'Let me have his address.'

I wrote it out for her on a piece of paper from my exercise book. But as soon as she had put it in her satchel, I felt anxious. 'You'll let me see it?' I said.

'See what?'

'The letter. You'll let me see what you write? Before you send it?'

Patricia giggled. 'Don't you worry,' she said. 'I'll make sure he gets a really passionate love letter, a billy-doo.' She said the word 'passionate' again, more slowly, drawing it out like a woman in a film. 'I'll give him something to think about.'

'You won't make things worse for him, will you?' I asked.

But Patricia was looking at my neck. She reached over and pulled at my collar. 'What's this, then? Is it a love bite? Did our Richie give you that?' She sniffed. 'You're a fine one to try telling me what to do, Miss Love Bite. You'd better not let Mum see it or you'll both be in trouble.'

Thirty-Two

Kakuna watches me peel and slice yellow peaches into the fruit cup I've made for them. She's the only one with me in the kitchen; Jozef is showing the other girls around the house, not knowing what else to do with them, it seems. But Kakuna hung back, saying, in her slow, clipped English, 'Please, no, I want to stay with Carol,' and I was touched, because she has almost never used my name before. I wonder sometimes what she calls me to herself, when she thinks of me – supposing she does. But I was disappointed, too, that she didn't go upstairs with the others, because I want her to make friends with Jozef more than anything. And, absurdly, I'm hurt she said 'please,' as though I might have denied her this simple request – to watch me slice fruit into a jug.

She leans against the sink, as far away from me, I feel, as the kitchen permits.

'Did you have a dog?' I ask her. 'When you were at home?'

She nods.

'Like Cocoa?' I say.

She looks puzzled. 'His name is Cocoa,' I say, gesturing with my knife towards the door to the yard. 'Was your dog like mine?'

She considers this. She lifts her hair away from her neck, slowly, an adult gesture, then lets it fall to her shoulders once more. She has fine hair, I notice, so black it seems almost blue.

'We had three dogs, very big, bigger than your dog,' she says. 'Like *lupi*.'

'Wolves,' I say. '*Lupi* are wolves in English.'

'Yes. Like wolves.'

'What were their names?'

'Dog, Dog and Dog,' she says, after a moment, with such a tragic face I don't dare smile.

'That must have been awfully confusing for you,' I murmur, not really wanting to be understood. Then, in a louder voice, to tease her: 'And your name is Girl.'

She stares at me, as if surprised. 'If I want it is,' she said. 'And you are Woman,' she adds, turning away, without amusement.

'And you were good with them, I expect,' I say, perturbed, wanting to win her back. 'I saw how good you were with Cocoa outside. I think you like dogs. Do you?' I put down the knife and wipe my sticky hands on a cloth, then take the jug and pour a glass for her. She still hasn't answered my question. I sense that I'm pleading and feel irritated with myself. 'Would you like to try some?' I ask.

'Tell me if it's sweet enough. If it isn't, I can put some sugar in. See what you think.'

She walks across but doesn't take the glass. Instead, with a sly, upwards glance at me, she picks up the knife I've been using, my favourite, and holds it in her hand, laying the wooden handle across her palm, looking at it thoughtfully as if to estimate its weight. I watch to see what she'll do, afraid to think what it might be, afraid for myself. Then she puts the knife down, and I hear myself breathe out. She's good with knives as well, I think, and the phrase reminds me of something I've heard before, I don't know what. She must have grown up with them. Knives and dogs, and who knows what else?

'I don't like sugar,' she says. 'Sugar makes fat.' She strokes her stomach and all at once I see her as much older than she is. I remember what Flavio said, that we know so little about her.

'Do you have any brothers?' I ask. 'Or sisters?'

She shakes her head, then seems to reconsider. 'I had one brother, but he is dead. The army killed him. They took him from the house.'

'Were you there when it happened? Did you see?'

'Yes. He was very strong, very *coraggioso*.'

'Brave,' I said. '*Coraggioso* is "brave" in English. Why did they take him away?'

She looks at me without expression, then shrugs.

How could she know? 'What was his name?' I ask.

'Memo. Also my uncle was Memo.'

I have a vision of Kakuna's family, grouped for a

photograph. I see her brother, tall and slim like her, her parents, Uncle Memo standing to one side, other relatives, cousins, aunts. The men with moustaches, the women with scarves over their heads, a backdrop of painted mountains. They are dressed in their finest clothes.

'Where is your uncle now?'

'Dead,' she says. She opens her hands as if to offer me what they contain. 'All my family is dead. I am alone.'

I can't resist. She lets me hold her, and stroke her hair, and murmur my sorrow into it. She doesn't hug me in return, but I don't expect her to. That would be too much to ask.

When Jozef comes downstairs with the other children, Magda's small hand in his, we move apart, but must look guilty because he asks me, one eyebrow raised, 'And what have you two been up to?'

'We've been talking about Cocoa,' I say, in my teacher's voice. Magda lets go of his hand and runs across to Kakuna, talking to her in a breathless, excited way, while Jozef and the other three walk to the table.

'Are you hungry?' I ask, my voice overloud, rubbing my hand on my stomach to imitate hunger – the gesture Kakuna used with me only moments ago. They nod.

'Let's eat outside,' Jozef said. 'It's warm enough. I'll set the table.' He seems to consider each of the children in turn before settling on Kakuna and Magda. 'Can you two help me?' he asks, and it is a genuine question, which makes me feel for the first time that he has stopped disapproving of their visit. 'Two big strong girls like you.' Magda titters behind her hand, then stops and glances at Kakuna, beginning again when Kakuna nods her approval, quite openly, as if we count for nothing.

'And you three can help me carry everything out,' I say to the others. 'It will be fun to eat outside, with Cocoa.'

By the time the table is prepared, I have made myself a chance to ask Jozef what he thinks of the girls. He smiles. 'They are children,' he says. 'They are not so very special, you know, no more special than other children. You worry too much.'

'Worry?' I hear my voice rising. 'They're refugees, Jozef. If you, of all people, don't understand, what hope is there?' How cruel I'm being, I think, he doesn't deserve this. Outside, Cocoa barks, an odd high yelp, and I move towards the kitchen door to see what's going on.

But Jozef stops me. He takes my hand and cradles it in his, slowly stroking the palm. 'Do you think they might not love you?' he says. 'Is that what frightens you? And if they don't? Why should they love you after all? Because you have given them food to eat, a table to sit at? Because you teach them a language they may never use? Because in the end you may be someone they will remember, in many years' time, when they hear English spoken in the street and your voice comes back to them? And that would be the best of it, of what you might hope for. That they might remember you with warmth.'

I pull my hand away. 'You needn't do this, Jozef,' I say. Cocoa yelps again. 'Just listen to that dog.'

'Do what?'

'Take me down a peg emotionally.' Furious, I choose an expression he might not know, to throw him off guard and give myself the upper hand. 'I don't need to be looked after, you know, and protected. I'm not broody.'

He picks up some plates and stands before me, waiting, perhaps, for me to take them from him and carry them into the garden, perhaps for some other gesture that might relieve the tension. 'I didn't think you were brooding,' he says, shaking his head, hurt. 'Why should you brood?'

'I didn't say "brooding",' I snap, angry with him now that he has failed to understand, has fallen into my trap. I stalk past him and into the garden, empty-handed.

The girls are clustered round Cocoa, who is lying beside the table.

'What on earth's wrong with him?' I ask, and they fall back, glancing towards Kakuna as I push them away and kneel. Kakuna crouches next to me and picks up one of his front paws with both hands, twisting it round to show me as Cocoa yelps and jerks to free himself.

'See,' she says. There is blood and dirt and what might be bone, something white and gleaming, but I'm not sure; my eyes start to water and I can't see a thing.

'What's happened?' I ask, hearing the hysteria in my voice. I cry out, 'Jozef!' and wait, kneeling in the gravel, for him to come. 'Jozef!' I call again.

Thirty-Three

Patricia didn't show me the letters she wrote to Nicholas, not after the first, which was short and to the point. She'd written it on lined pink paper and sprinkled it with some of her mother's Parma-violet toilet water and drawn a row of hearts along the bottom. But the words she'd used were words I had never seen written down before, except on toilet walls. She said she couldn't wait for him to fuck her, that she wanted to kiss his dick and play with his balls. She said her love-bud was waiting for him. I read it with hot cheeks and a feeling of horror mixed with excitement that she could have written such a thing. 'It's so dirty,' I said, folding it into four. 'It's disgusting.'

She shrugged in a don't-carish way, but seemed uncomfortable. 'It's just the way boys talk,' she said. 'You know what they're like. You've heard them as well as I have. When they think we aren't listening. I looked at that magazine of Richie's for some of it.' She shuddered. '*Love-bud.*' She had signed it 'Maudie.'

'You can't send this,' I said.

'Well, that's what he wanted, isn't it?' She snatched the letter from me. 'They won't think he's a pansy now, will they? Not when they read this.'

'You can't send it,' I said again, but she put it away in her satchel. I'll do what I want, her body said.

Five days later, I received my second letter from Nicholas.

Dear Carol

I hope this finds you well. I have got a girlfreind now, her name is Maudie and I have told the other lads about her. They didnt beleive me at first but then I showed one of them her letter, his name is Jhonny and he is from Cleveland, he has been up Blackpool Tower and is a boxer, and now he thinks I am grate and wants a girlfreind like Maudie too. He says he wants to meet her freinds. What do you think? It is still very cold here, they make us march miles in the rain and the food is filth but I am eating it now because there is nothing else and I am hungry. My mum hasnt sent me anything even though Ive asked her evry time. Could you ask her to send me somthing? Biscits like rich tea or neece would be all right. I want to let the other lads see the letter, then they will leave me alone for good, but Jhonny says they will only keep it so I havnt. Thank you, Carol, your a brick. I have writen to Maudie at her address. Then she will write to me agin I hope.

Yours sincerley

Nicholas

I stood by the kitchen door that evening and watched while Maudie dipped the battered scampi into the fat, her dimpled arms and face dripping with sweat. I tried to imagine her with Nicholas, doing the things that Patricia had said, as though the letter really had come from her. She noticed me after a moment – 'Hello, my love,' she said, 'what are you doing there, hanging round the door like a little lost sheep?' – and offered me a piece of scampi hot from the fat.

'No,' I said, shaking my head, embarrassed for her, as though she had been found out, as though I knew her secret. She dropped it back with the rest and blew on her fingers to cool them down.

'It's a pity we can't send some scampi to Nicholas,' I said. 'He's starving. He says she isn't sending him anything.'

Maudie glanced behind me, towards the door into the bar, then pursed her lips. 'Some people don't deserve to have children,' she said.

The next morning, at break, I spoke to Patricia. 'I've had another letter from Nicholas. He says he's heard from Maudie.'

Patricia pretended not to understand what I was talking about. 'I don't know any Maudie,' she said, in a snooty voice.

'Oh, come on, Patricia. I know you sent that letter. He's shown it to one of the other soldiers in the barracks and now they're leaving him alone.'

She grinned and grabbed my hand, squeezed it in hers. 'I told you it'd work. That's what boys want. All that dirty stuff. I don't know why, it makes me sick just to write it down, honestly.'

'Is that what your Richie wants, do you think?' I asked.

'Richie's not a boy. He's my *brother*,' Patricia said, with a grimace. She let go of my hand and pulled at my collar. 'You can still see that love bite on your neck, you saucy cat.'

'Have you had a letter back from him?'

She swung her hips. 'I may have done. What's it worth if I show you?'

I gave her a piece of pork crackling out of a packet I had taken from behind the bar that morning, before leaving the pub. 'Go on,' I said.

She pulled a sheet of crumpled paper from her pocket. 'Here you are,' she said. 'You read it.'

It was the same paper he'd used to write to me. But all it said, apart from 'Dear Maudie' at the beginning and 'Nicholas' at the end was I LOVE YOU written over and over again in wobbly capitals.

'I told you he was pathetic,' Patricia said. 'Can you imagine a boy of his age writing a letter like that? At least he's spelt it right.'

'He thinks you don't exist, I suppose. I mean, he thinks you're me.'

'Does he? Well, I'll have to tell him the truth, won't I?'

'You can't do that,' I said, shocked. 'He'll be worse off than ever if they find out he's lying.'

Patricia shrugged. 'He deserves it. I thought I'd get something a bit more exciting than just "I love you". It's so soppy. You'd think he really is a pansy if that's all he can bother to write.'

'Write to him again,' I said. 'I know. Say something horrible about me in it. That way perhaps he'll guess.'

'Like what? That you're covered in love bites and steal things from the bar?' She took another scrap of pork crackling. 'Your aunt would give you such a slapping if she knew.'

This made us giggle. 'And I'd slap her back,' I said. 'Right across the face, as hard as I could.'

'I'd do more than that if I were you.'

'What would you do?' I said.

Patricia thought for a moment. 'I'd put some pepper in her knickers. That'd give her something to think about.' We giggled even more.

'No,' I said, 'you know what she'd hate most? If someone cut off her hair. I'd sneak into her bedroom while she was asleep and cut her fringe off with a pair of scissors. Then I'd tie a bow round it and put it on her bedside table, like some old voodoo doll. She's too ancient for a fringe anyway, it makes her look stupid.'

'You know what I'd do,' Patricia said, lowering her voice. 'I'd tell her that her darling soldier son was a pansy.'

Thirty-Four

Cocoa's paw has been cut wide open, a clean cut right across the pad that seems to have been done with a knife, according to our vet: a penknife, perhaps, or peeling knife. 'But that's impossible,' I tell her. 'No one would hurt a dog like that for nothing.'

'Well, I'd assumed it must have been an accident,' she says, and I wonder why that hadn't occurred to me at once.

'Of course,' I agree.

'Perhaps a knife fell from the table,' she says. 'You were eating outside, weren't you? And you know what dogs are like, especially with children. They're never still for an instant. Or it might have been a piece of broken glass.' She cleans the wound as she speaks, pressing the sides together to staunch the bleeding. 'Whatever,' she says, 'there's no real harm done. This will heal in no time. I'll put some stitches in and bandage it. You'd better try to keep him in for a few days, to stop it getting too dirty. And I'll put him on a course of antibiotics, because you never know . . . But he'll soon be back to his normal exuberant self, won't you, Cocoa? Won't you, beautiful?'

I half listen to her, standing by the metal table and stroking Cocoa's haunches while she works. I turn my head away as she puts in the stitches, although I am not squeamish. It's the idea that someone might have done this to him deliberately that disturbs me. This is what Jozef thinks, I know. As soon as he saw the cut, his eyes flashed along the row of children, then halted on Kakuna. How dare you accuse her? I thought.

When he said he would look after the girls while I took Cocoa to the vet, I hesitated. 'I ought to stay with them,' I said, although even then their faces had become unreadable to me.

'No, no,' he insisted, 'it's better that you go. It will take no more than half an hour. Go to her house, you are friends, she will deal with it at once.' He fetched some clean sacking from his studio and laid it on the seat beside me as I started the car. I couldn't bring myself to look at anyone. Now I find myself thinking about the way Kakuna played with my paring knife in the kitchen, how she weighed it in her hand. Maybe Jozef is right.

When I get back from the vet, with Cocoa's paw bound in bandage and a sort of webbing sock, I watch the girls run down the drive to meet me. I watch Kakuna's face as I open the car door and lift the dog from the front seat and carry him into the house, wondering where Jozef is, resenting his absence. But as she reaches up to touch his head, her eyes glistening with tears, my heart goes out to her. 'Don't worry, my dear,' I say, in a low voice only she can hear. 'He'll soon be well again.' She leans her cheek against my arm, her fingers buried in the thicker fur behind his neck and I know she would never injure Cocoa, not willingly.

Later that day, Jozef and I are alone in the kitchen. We've barely spoken since I took the girls back to the camp. I feel that neither of us wants to admit what we thought, but were too ashamed to say. I walk across to Cocoa's basket and crouch to stroke him. He lies half sleeping with his head between his paws, one whole, the other in its fraying sock.

'Poor love,' I say. I glance at Jozef, who is drying a plate. 'The vet says it might have been a piece of broken glass.'

'It might have been?' His expression is wry. 'Is that what she thinks? That is very perceptive of her. And might it not also have been a knife?'

'Well, of course it could.' I stand up. 'Did you look for a knife after I had gone? It would still have been on the ground somewhere, wouldn't it? Did you find anything? Perhaps it was one of the knives you had taken out before.'

'There was no knife on the ground,' he says slowly. 'Naturally I looked. Nor piece of broken glass, if you prefer to think that was what it was.'

'Why on earth are you taking that tone?' I ask, annoyed.

Jozef gives a short laugh. 'Do you hear nothing strange in what you are saying? You do not think, perhaps, that you are trying not to see what is staring you in the face?'

'I don't know what you mean.' I flinch as he walks across to me and takes hold of my elbows. I have never flinched before at his touch. Appalled by myself, I want to brush him off.

'Of course you know,' he says urgently. 'You see that child in your classroom every day and yet you see another child, not her. You see some child from a book you have read and found touching, some poor unwanted refugee whose heart is good. Carol. You see yourself.'

I find myself shaking, I'm so furious with him. And I resent his using my name like that, as though I need to be brought to my senses by being reminded of who I am. 'How can you say such things?' I say. 'How can you be so cruel, not just to her but to me as well?'

'You told me once she had stabbed another girl,' he insists.

'That was in anger.'

'Which makes it acceptable?'

'Which makes it different.'

He lets me go.

'Find me the knife you used today to slice the fruit,' he says. 'The small knife with the wooden handle that you always use.'

I look around the kitchen, as though I'll see it lying on a worktop, wherever I might have left it. Of course, it isn't here. We've spent the last two hours tidying everything away. There had been no knife, I know that. We both know it.

'This is absurd,' I say.

'Why is it absurd? Do you think perhaps she may have taken your knife to the camp? Is it absurd that she may have your knife and use it? Perhaps to stab another child? Perhaps to cut herself? Some children do that, you know, to suffer or make others suffer. She is not a happy child, that's plain. There is much that is hidden inside her. She might be capable of that.'

'Why do you hate her so much?' I hear myself ask, aghast, because I have suddenly found the words to express a thought I would never have known without Jozef's insistence. 'Why can't you leave her alone? What harm has she ever done to you?'

'Please, Carol,' Jozef says, but his voice is not consoling, only stern. 'You are talking nonsense now, which you will regret. You are too close to this child to see what is plain to everyone else. You must step back.'

'How can you be too close to another person?' I ask, angry yet pleading. 'Can't you see you're talking nonsense? Can't you see how much she needs me? Needs us? She has no one, Jozef. No one. You know that all her family are dead? Her brother was murdered by the army. Can't you understand what that means?' I pause. 'Because if *you* can't, Jozef, how can anyone else be expected to? Haven't you been there too?'

Jozef stares at me. 'You are damaging yourself,' he says coldly.

You're jealous of her. It comes to me with the force of a revelation – I'm not damaging myself. I'm damaging you.

I only discover the knife when I run my hand behind the back seat of the car on an impulse, not really expecting to find it. I almost cut my thumb as I pull it out, not wanting it to be my knife, wishing I had never looked. One of them must have put it there while I drove them back to the camp. Kakuna was in the front of the car with me. But they were alone in the car while I opened the gate. She could have passed it to one of the others to hide. They would have done that for her: they are all a little scared of her. In rapid succession, I see them as innocent then guilty, guilty then innocent. There is no escape from these thoughts, I realize, and I wonder now what Jozef meant when he said I couldn't see Kakuna, as though caring were a form of blindness. It seems to me that I see her all too well; I see her for what she is, both guilty and innocent, and that is what I want to help and cherish. My caring for Kakuna and my doubts about what has happened are distinct, I discover, and incommensurable; I can see her as responsible, yet not blame her.

There is no moon visible tonight and the sky is overcast; tomorrow looks like rain. The only light on the sea before me comes from the headlights of the car. As I turn them off, I can see nothing; the water, which has no colour in any case, is abruptly black. I sit here with the car doors open and listen, holding my breath, to the waves from which she came.

Thirty-Five

When the days began to lengthen that summer, I would beg Richie to collect me from school on his motorbike and normally he agreed. Sometimes, though, we'd walk to the park instead, holding hands, until he pulled me behind a tree and started kissing. I let him do nearly everything he wanted, but we never did *it*, as he would say. I would always say no, but gently, as though next time my answer might be different. He never used the words that Patricia had written in her letter to Nicholas, despite what she said. He never tried to force me either, perhaps because I accommodated him as far as I could in other ways, allowing his hand between my legs and inside my blouse while his face nuzzled my neck.

Other days, he'd drive me straight back to the pub and we'd go down into the cellar to see Uncle Joey. Richie liked it in the workshop – I thought sometimes he preferred my uncle's company to mine. He liked Uncle Joey's operatic music too, even when he pretended not to, wrinkling his nose and asking for Adam Faith and Marty Wilde.

Uncle Joey watched him with amusement as he combed his hair and sang 'What Do You Want.' 'I see you love your hair very much,' he said once.

Richie was indignant. 'I don't,' he said. 'That's pansy stuff.'

Sometimes Aunt Margot would come down the steps and shout at us from the far end of the cellar, as though we were separated from her by a moat. 'Haven't you got anything else to do?' she'd ask, then turn her gaze to Uncle Joey. 'And you're no better than a kid yourself, leading them on, a man your age.' Finally, she would smirk at Richie. 'Now, you mind you behave yourself,' she would say. 'I know what you boys are like.'

By the time school broke up for the summer holidays, Uncle Joey's glider was ready to be assembled. It took us almost a week to put it together; the whole hangar smelt of freshly planed wood and the special glue we used, which had to be heated and painted on with a brush. When it was done I stood back and clapped with delight. I'd never seen anything so perfect. It was different from the gliders the club used; smaller and lighter, more elegant. The others looked elegant only in flight.

Donald walked across and stared at it, unconvinced. 'You'll never get two grown men in that,' he said.

'It isn't designed for two grown men.' My uncle pointed at the cockpit. 'Look, there is only one seat.'

Donald shook his head. 'Well, that's no good, is it?

They'll never let you take it up from here. There's got to be two people and one of them's got to have a licence to fly and all.' He winked at me. 'And you haven't got one of them either, I don't suppose.'

But Uncle Joey was running his hand along the underside of the fuselage, murmuring to himself, as if he was alone. I couldn't tell what he was saying so I moved closer. That was when I heard he wasn't speaking, but singing. 'What's that, Uncle Joey?' I asked. 'What are you singing?' He stopped immediately and I was sorry I'd interrupted him. I had never heard him sing before.

'It's a song I learnt when I was your age, more or less,' he said. 'When I was a child in Poland.' And he stroked the side of the plane again, the way one might stroke a horse's flank, as though it were alive and would respond.

Does he still know that song? I wonder. Perhaps that is what I catch him singing in his sleep, his voice so absorbed, so low, it's impossible to distinguish the words however close I get. Perhaps he is singing a song that someone taught him, his eyes tight shut to keep me away. Perhaps he isn't sleeping but only pretending, his face turned into the pillow like a child's so that the muffled words belong to him and no one else; pretending to be invisible because he has closed out the rest of the world.

Thirty-Six

This morning Kakuna is waiting for me outside the classroom.

'Hello,' I say.

But she isn't interested in this. 'Cocoa?' she asks impatiently. 'How is Cocoa? His foot?'

I feel my body ease, the way it does when I slide into a hot, scented bath after hard work, each muscle loosening. Of course I've been right to trust her. I lift the dark hair from her cheek and hook it behind her ear to see her face more clearly. I want to miss nothing. 'He's much better. Would you like to come and see him this afternoon?'

'Yes,' she says.

I want to lift her up and kiss her; I desire this so strongly I feel myself blush. 'We'll have to see what they say.' I nod in the direction of the office.

'You must ask?' She continues, in Italian: 'Other people just leave when they want. It isn't difficult.'

'I know,' I say, in English. 'But I must ask for permission. If I don't, they might not allow me to come here any more and give lessons. And that would make me very sad.'

By this time the others have arrived. I unlock the classroom door and let them in, smiling to see how they jostle for the seats at the back, pleased when Kakuna chooses one near my desk. I notice that Magda isn't there and ask the class if anyone has seen her. One of the newer girls glances at Kakuna but doesn't speak.

'Kakuna?' I ask.

'She isn't good today.'

'She isn't well?' I correct. 'What's wrong with her?'

'She isn't well,' Kakuna repeats.

'All right,' I say. 'After the lesson, we'll go and see how she is.' I turn to the class. 'Today I want to talk about animals. Can anyone tell me the names of any animals?'

One of the boys calls out, '*Topolino*.'

'And what's *topolino* in English?' I ask. 'Does anybody know?'

Kakuna shouts: 'Mickey Mouse.' A few of the others laugh. She flushes and stares at me. Her eyes say, 'Make them shut up.'

'Thank you, Kakuna, you're right. Mickey Mouse is a very famous mouse.' I write 'mouse' on the board.

After the lesson we go to look for Magda. I assumed she'd be with the older women, but they haven't seen her. Kakuna doesn't seem to want to be with me: I feel I'm dragging her. Eventually I give up and we walk together to Flavio's office. He's sitting behind his desk, opening letters with a wry expression.

'My bishop's not too thrilled about these anti-immigration demos in the papers. He seems to think it's our fault, that we should be more discreet, keep our heads down – dare I say it? – stay at home where we belong. Three letters in as many days! Not to speak of demands from the bank and food bills and – would you believe it?' he cries, waving a handful of coloured brochures. 'All this advertising for trips to Lourdes and the monastery of Padre Pio, as though we weren't in the same business, dishing out hope and more hope, and miracles as well if we're lucky. At least we aren't selling saucepans too. Perhaps we should organize some day trips for the idle faithful, a glance round a couple of churches, a nice set lunch and then down to the hard sell, like our rivals here, before they've finished their cake and coffee,' he says, then notices Kakuna, who is standing uneasily by the door seemingly about to run away. 'How was the picnic?'

'We had a lovely time,' I say. 'Didn't we, Kakuna?'

She nods, but doesn't speak.

'That's what I wanted to ask you about, actually,' I say. 'You see, my dog had a little accident while the girls were there and I was wondering if Kakuna could come out this afternoon, just for an hour or so, to see how he is.'

'An accident?'

'Nothing, really. He cut his paw on something outside. It looked worse than it was.'

Flavio seems uncomfortable. 'Kakuna,' he says, 'could

you wait outside for a moment? I'd like to talk to Carol about something private.' Kakuna glances at me. When I nod, she leaves the office.

'Well?' I ask, in a sharper tone than I intend.

'This won't do, you know,' he says. 'You can't have favourites, Carol. It isn't fair on the others. I had that little Romanian girl in this morning, the one who's always playing with Kakuna, crying her eyes out, saying she was scared of something – she wouldn't tell me what – and she wanted to go home.'

'I don't see what that has to do with Kakuna,' I say slowly, my voice as low as I can make it without whispering. 'I'm simply trying to make her life a little less grim, not making a favourite of her, as you say. You aren't suggesting that Magda's scared of Kakuna, surely?'

Flavio laughs and lifts his hands, palms up, a characteristic, vaguely biblical gesture that means he's open, innocent of guile. 'Of course not, Carol. That's the furthest thing from my mind. Although the way you spring to her defence does tend to confirm what I was saying, don't you think? About favouritism?' He walks across and strokes my shoulder, in what must be intended as a reconciliatory gesture. I have to stop myself slapping his hand away.

'You seem to have mixed me up with Salvo,' I snap.

He steps back, visibly startled. 'Salvo?'

I shake my head, annoyed with myself.

'This isn't like you, Carol,' he says.

And that's another mannerism of yours, I think: using

the other person's name to cajole them into acquiescence, to make them feel recognized. The way Jozef does.

'You're normally so sensible,' he adds.

'So, can I take her or not?' I ask. 'As far as I can see, people are coming in and out of the camp all the time. Isn't that what your bishop is complaining about, the fact that it's more like a colander than a refugee camp?'

Flavio sighs. 'I tell you what. Let's pretend you haven't asked. You know perfectly well what I think, Carol, and I'm surprised you can't see my point. But that's clearly how it is. If you insist on taking her out, I'd rather not know.'

'If you wish,' I say, but I'm still too annoyed with him to leave it at that. 'Though, I must say, I think that's a rather cowardly position to take.'

Flavio shrugs, obviously displeased. Kakuna was right. It would have been wiser not to ask. This conversation has done neither of us any good. I'm on my way out when he says: 'Oh, Carol, before you go.'

'Yes?'

'You couldn't just ask Kakuna if she knows what might have upset Magda, could you?'

'Of course,' I say. I don't want to fight with Flavio, after all. 'We looked for her, actually, before coming here. I thought she'd be with the women, but they haven't seen her.'

'That's odd,' he says. 'She must be hiding somewhere. Don't worry, we'll root her out.'

*

In the car, Kakuna is strangely agitated, jumping up and down in her seat as we drive through the town, pointing excitedly at other cars, people, shops, talking incessantly, mainly in Italian, which she finds easier; perhaps because it makes us more equal as well – in Italian, we are both foreign. Sometimes she mutters a few words of Turkish, which I recognize but don't understand, and sometimes, in a sing-song way, what must be her own language, as though she were chattering to another person in the car. 'Look,' she says, pointing towards a fat woman on a bicycle, a toddler perched on the handlebars. '*Guarda*,' she cries, as we drive past a group of six or seven boys playing with bows and arrows beside the road. They must have heard her, because they stop to wave and whistle. She whistles in reply, two fingers in her mouth, then falls back into the seat to hide. She is behaving like a child for the first time, and I feel privileged to have seen it. This child is who she is.

We are driving past a petrol station when Kakuna squeals with delight and tugs at my arm so hard I almost lose control of the wheel. 'Look, look,' she says. Slowing down, I turn my head in the direction of her hand and see an open trailer parked behind the pumps.

'What is it?' I ask, pulling on to the forecourt. 'What have you seen?'

As soon as the car stops, Kakuna leaps out and runs across to the trailer and I notice how skinny she is, her thin legs in handed-down jeans, her sharp high shoulders. I can see what attracted her attention now: two camels tethered side by side in the trailer. I lock the car and follow her, watching as she clambers up the wheel, worried she might fall.

The camels turn their heads in our direction, attracted by Kakuna's clicking fingers and the cooing noise she's making as she reaches to touch the shoulder of the nearest animal. I've never been so close to a camel before and find their massive yellow teeth off-putting, but Kakuna is perfectly at home as she slips her Pokémon into her pocket and stretches across the side of the truck, her fingers scratching the coarse pelt that seems barely to cover the bones beneath. They're scrawny, their matted coats like coconut. They stink of fetid straw and old blankets.

'They're camels,' I say. 'I wonder what they're doing here.' I see a young woman walking towards us with a roll of posters beneath her arm. She's wearing an electric blue miniskirt and jacket, fishnet tights and a blue top hat, with a short whip tucked into her belt. 'Look,' I say, touching Kakuna's arm. 'They must belong to a circus.'

The woman smiles and speaks. Her Italian's good, but it's clear that she, too, is a foreigner; she sounds eastern European, Russian perhaps. I wonder how many languages she has and, for a moment, feel all the magic of the circus, its rootlessness and promiscuity. 'The little girl should come and work for us,' she says. 'She is good with animals.' She looks at us more closely, her eyes examining our clothes. 'She is your daughter?'

'No, no,' I say. 'She is a friend.'

The woman strokes Kakuna's hair away from her face; I'm surprised Kakuna lets her. 'You are a very pretty girl,' she says. 'Where do you come from?'

Kakuna smiles at her, and I'm surprised a second time. 'I'm Italian.'

The woman laughs. 'Of course you are,' she says, grinning at me. 'We are all Italian today.' One of her front teeth is chipped, I noticed; it makes her more attractive. Before we walk away, she gives us a flyer for Circo Paradiso.

We're in the car again, driving to the house, when I ask Kakuna about Magda. She turns away from me and stares out through the window. I ask again. Finally, she replies, 'She didn't want to see you. She thinks you'll be angry.'

'Why should I be angry with Magda?'

'I can't say.'

I'm silent for a moment.

'Did Magda hurt Cocoa? Is that why she thinks I might be angry with her?'

Still staring through the window, so that I can't see her face, Kakuna nods, slowly at first and then with vigour. So that's it, I think, with relief. All along, she's been protecting Magda. The smaller girl was afraid of Cocoa, I remember; she'd tried to hide behind Kakuna. How idiotic of me not to have guessed at once. Now I shall be able to tell Jozef what really happened – that Kakuna is innocent – and he will understand. His face will lighten and open up again. Now the violence he is inflicting on me, and on the girl, who needs us both so badly, will end.

Thirty-Seven

Jozef must have heard the car pull up, but chooses to remain in the barn. Kakuna and I stand in the drive, waiting for Cocoa who always rushes to greet me; when he doesn't appear my first thought is that Jozef has kept him in. The exhilaration Kakuna had shown earlier had fizzled out abruptly during the last part of the journey, after she'd told me about Magda, and I suppose she feels guilty because she has betrayed her friend. Now her whole body is stiff and turned inwards somehow, each hand grasping the opposite elbow, her chin pushed down into her chest; what I can see of her face is closed and sullen. When I reach to take her arm, she shrugs me off, preferring not to speak, letting her small, hard frame communicate for her, except that I am at a loss to read it. What have I done? I think, for her to shut me out like this?

'Let's go and see what Jozef's doing,' I suggest. I'll drag him into the light, I think, and make him see that he was wrong. And at this point, unexpectedly, I feel cheerful, as though I've already won.

Kakuna follows, two or three paces behind me, dragging her feet in the gravel as we walk across the yard. There's still no sign of Cocoa. I'm about to call but a moment's fear that he might not come prevents me.

Jozef is at the far end of the barn, hidden behind the endless folding panels of his installation, with Cocoa lying beside him on a blanket Jozef has brought from the house, his head between his front paws, the webbing sock intact. At first I think Jozef is asleep, because he's sitting in an old armchair he rarely uses, his hands between his knees and his head hanging down so that we can't see his face. But then he looks up, his eyes red and damp, and I understand at once that he has been crying and feel my heart leap into my throat. He sees Kakuna with me and gives a small wry grimace, as though he has been expecting this and isn't disappointed, except that, of course, he would prefer me to be alone and to surprise him. Then he stands up and walks across, as slowly as an old man, his hands outstretched as though he and I were alone.

'I have some bad news,' he says, and my immediate thought is of Cocoa. I start towards the dog, but Jozef catches my arm and I smell whisky on his breath.

'No, not Cocoa.' He's too close to me, his breath in my face, and I feel so sorry for him, suddenly; I don't know why. Because he has been drinking? Because I left him alone and now I'm back with Kakuna? 'After you had gone this morning, I had a letter from England, or we did, rather, a letter addressed to us both, from that place where

Margot lived. That home. I opened it without you. Forgive me. I should have waited, I know.'

'Margot?' I ask stupidly, thinking, Margot, what Margot? I have an urge to cover Kakuna's ears with my hands, to protect her from whatever Jozef might say, which can only be bad.

'She died two weeks ago, of cervical cancer. They had no address. They say she always refused to give them one, saying she had no relations. They looked through her belongings and found our names and address in her purse and wrote. Someone who works in the office at the home remembered you had visited. You were her only visitor, the letter says, in the years she spent there. So she was right. There was no one else. They want to send everything she has left to you.'

'Oh, no,' I say, horrified. 'I don't want anything of hers.' But what I want to ask is: Why do you care? Why have you been drinking and crying, after what happened? What right does she have to your grief? How much else don't I know about you?

'There is nothing of any value,' he says. 'At least, that is what they say. By their standards, I imagine. They say there are letters, many clothes, of course, those books she used to read.'

'I want the letters,' I say urgently. 'The rest they can give away. Some charity will take them, I expect.'

'Don't be harsh with her.' His voice is soft. 'She cannot hurt you now. What use would her letters be to you?'

'I'm harsh with her for the past,' I say. 'For what she's

done to me, and to you for that matter, in the past. Must we always forgive?'

'Oh, yes,' he says. 'Always forgive.'

'But you refused even to see her,' I cry. 'When I went that time, you wouldn't come.'

'I had nothing to say to her. That has nothing to do with forgiving.'

'There were a thousand things you should have said to her.'

I want to strike out and hurt him, shatter his acceptance and the sense I have that he is revelling in the opportunity to be good that her death has provided. I want to make him hate her, as he has done in the past, because I know – no one better – how deeply he's loathed the woman, her coarseness, her hectoring. I know how frequently, how effortlessly, she offended him. Now, standing in the barn, I remember one evening when she humiliated him in front of customers, the usual gang of unaccompanied men, by pretending not to understand him when he spoke, making him repeat himself; how she continued long after the customers had stopped laughing and begun to look at one another with discomfort, and at Jozef with a sort of sympathy. I am angry enough to remind him of this, and am about to do so when Kakuna runs across to Cocoa, flinging her arms round his neck as tightly as she can and covering his head with kisses.

The last time I spoke to Margot she was living in sheltered accommodation, in the town where I went to school, five miles from the Mermaid. Her room overlooked the park where Richie and I used to walk and kiss, but everything was different; I wouldn't have recognized it if I hadn't known. My aunt had her back to the window with the afternoon light behind her, framing her head and shoulders; her hair, still bleached and backcombed into a beehive, was thin and lifeless. I stared out into the park or at the television in the corner – on, but with the sound turned down – half listening as she complained about the other residents in the block, most of them women: the way they spoke, the way they treated her like dirt, 'as though having worked for a living was something to be ashamed of'. She didn't mention Jozef, which was only to be expected, or Nicholas, which surprised and disappointed me. Nicholas was the reason, I'd supposed, for her letter, which I had almost not opened, almost not read, almost refused to answer. It was half a page long, and told me she wanted to talk to me about what had happened. The words seemed to have nothing to do with my aunt, but to have been written by someone else entirely, someone who needed me. I'd come in the end, from Italy to this town I'd imagined I'd never see again, solely because I'd thought she might want to talk to me about Nicholas. Because I was curious. Because there were things I, too, wanted to say.

But once I was there, she didn't seem to want to talk about anything but herself. It was only when she paused to look at me properly, then mentioned my mother, that I gave her my full attention. 'You're nothing like her,' she said, and I wondered for a moment whom she meant. 'You were scrawny as a girl and you're no better now, skin and bone and no bosom to speak of. You're more like me when it comes to it, except that I've always known how to make the best of myself. I've always been admired. I've never worn *brown* in my life.' She lit a cigarette. 'She was the sexpot of the family, your mother was, like an actress. They used to say she looked like Margaret Lockwood when she was made up. I couldn't bring any boyfriend home without her swanning in and ruining everything. "Oh, hello," she'd say, and she'd practically wait to have her hand kissed while they drooled all over her.' She laughed. 'Not like you. You'd run a mile, you would, if anyone tried that game with you. Not that any-one'd bother. I used to wonder what that Teddy boy saw in you. I suppose you let him have you, didn't you? That's how you kept him sniffing round you like a dog on heat. You thought I didn't know what you were up to, but I'm not stupid. You couldn't keep your eyes off Joe either, even then. It's always the quiet ones, isn't it, in the end? They're the ones you need to watch.' Her tone, as she said these things, was equable, even amused. An observer, not hearing her words, seeing us together in the unlit room, would never have guessed that she was insulting me.

After an initial flush of embarrassment, then disgust, I found myself listening with the same detachment. Because this vulgar woman, with the sequins on her cardigan, the tight black leggings and the web of hair, no longer had any power to hurt me. I have always despised you, I thought, as she stood up and filled the kettle, then lit the gas and another cigarette from a single match. She made two cups of instant coffee and gave me one, already sugared, which I left to grow cold beside me, pleased to be given this final chance to reject what she had done for me.

'Why did you hate her so much?' I asked.

'Why did she hate me? That's the question.' She sounded proud, but also secretive, as though she intended to keep some truth hidden from me.

'I don't remember her ever talking about you,' I said, intending this to be cruel. 'She certainly never said anything about hating you. I don't expect she cared that much. She had her own life.'

'She didn't mind scrounging a bed for you both, though, did she, when no one else would have her? I was good enough for her then, wasn't I? When your father got rough.' She sipped her coffee, her eyes on the television. There was a children's programme on now, puppets, songs, a woman in dungarees. She gazed at the screen, apparently absorbed. She might as well have been alone in her room. I wondered if she had forgotten I was there. I would have left if I hadn't felt that she still had something to tell me.

'So why did she hate you, then?' I asked eventually. 'What did you do to her?'

'It's always the jealous ones that start slapping,' she said. 'If their wife so much as turns her head to look at another man, it's out with the belt, and them giving you what for. And yet they're the ones that play fast and loose with other women. It's one sauce for the goose and one for the gander.'

'You mean my father was unfaithful?'

'Yes, madam,' she said, in a voice that was clearly supposed to resemble mine, and filled with scorn. 'That's exactly what I mean. Your father was unfaithful. Like hell he was.'

'But why should that have made her hate *you*?' I insisted. 'If *he* was unfaithful?'

Margot laughed again, a tinkling cocktail-party sound that made her cough. 'You're not very bright, are you?' she said, when she'd got her breath back. 'I always knew you weren't.'

Thirty-Eight

Patricia wouldn't talk to me about Nicholas, except to say, with a teasing leer, that he was *very* passionate and that Maudie was a lucky girl to have such a *devoted* boyfriend. We had begun to see less of each other. We'd still go for a smoke together near the bins, but that was it. She had a boyfriend too, though she claimed not to like him because he had rubbery lips. 'It's like kissing one of those things you use to unblock the sink,' she'd say, with a shudder. 'He just clamps on and sucks. Even you're a better kisser than he is.' Those brief conversations were fun, if incomplete, because I never talked to her about Richie. But what I missed most was not Patricia so much as the chance to be in her house, to have a cup of tea at the kitchen table with her mother bustling around in the background. Richie never took me there, and I felt I had no other home to go to.

Patricia thought she knew everything about Nicholas, but she didn't know he'd be coming home for a week's leave after his first three months of basic training. She looked surprised when I told her, with an air of triumph, and then anxious. 'What's wrong?' I asked.

'Oh, nothing,' she said, then, uncharacteristically, added, 'I'd better tell Maudie. You know what she wrote on the envelope last time?'

'What?' I tried not to let her see how interested I was.

'SWALK.'

'What's swalk?'

Patricia groaned. 'Carol, you are so pathetic. Haven't you ever heard of anyone putting SWALK on their letters? It stands for "Sealed With A Loving Kiss". My mum used to put it on the flap when she wrote to my dad during the war.' She got up close to me and whispered, 'And you know what he wrote on the flap of his letters to her?'

'No.'

In an even quieter voice, which I could barely hear, she said: 'NORWICH.'

I was puzzled.

Patricia sighed.'"Knickers Off Ready When I Come Home",' she said wearily. 'You're so stupid, Carol, it's embarrassing.'

'But you don't spell "knickers" with an *n*,' I said. 'It ought to be Korwich, not Norwich.'

That set us both off giggling. When Patricia's boyfriend appeared from behind the bins, with a silly, hopeful grin, we collapsed against each other, floppy with laughter.

*

It was Aunt Margot who'd told me that Nicholas would be coming home. He hadn't written to me again after the second letter. I wasn't surprised: he was angry with me, I supposed, because he'd guessed I wasn't Maudie and that I'd told someone else about him. Although he must have been grateful too – he had a girlfriend now, who wrote him letters, which was what he'd wanted. At least the other soldiers would leave him alone.

'You make him welcome when he gets here,' Aunt Margot said. 'This is his home.' Not yours, her tone implied. She had rubbed her calves shiny smooth with the hair-removal glove and was lacquering her toenails white, one foot on the rung of the kitchen chair, her body hunched over to reach. I could see a few dark hairs she'd missed, behind her ankle, like a smudge of soot. It serves you right, I thought with satisfaction, hearing my mother's voice in my head. Now people will see you for what you are.

'Of course I will.'

'There's no "of course" about it with you,' she said, dipping the brush into the little bottle.

'I like Nicholas.'

'That's a new one to me, that is. Did you hear that, Joe? Madam's decided she likes Nicholas now.' My uncle didn't seem to hear. He was polishing his shoes, as he always did on Saturday mornings, two sheets of newspaper spread out before him, the brushes, cloths and polish arranged along one side. He gave his full attention to each shoe, applying the polish with one cloth and giving a final rub with the other. He had an oval brush that was too large for my hand, and almost too large for his. When my aunt wasn't there, when she had gone to town with one of the reps, he would clean my shoes and I would watch him.

'Carol won't hurt him,' Uncle Joey said, putting down one shoe and picking up another. He smiled at me. 'Will you?'

It was that weekend, late Sunday afternoon, after the club was closed, that Uncle Joey and I watched his glider hauled out from the hangar on a wheeled dolly. As soon as it was on the runway, Donald ran over and fixed a cable beneath it. Then Uncle Joey fetched a stepladder and climbed into the cockpit, which was barely large enough for him, easing himself into the seat. He was wearing a shirt and trousers and the lightest shoes he owned. Donald moved the ladder and took my hand. I let him, not caring, my eyes on my uncle as he fastened himself to his seat with a webbing belt I had helped him make. Then Donald and I began to run as fast as we could, gasping for breath, hearts pounding, to the far end of the runway. We didn't use the jeep – it made too much noise, Donald said, and Uncle Joey had agreed: 'No, no, the winch. I prefer the winch.'

It was locked inside a wooden case covered with tarpaulin to protect it from rain. 'It's more than my job's worth if we're caught,' Donald said, as he turned the key and put the padlock into his pocket, but I'd given him two bottles of whisky the day before; he wouldn't cause any trouble.

'Go on,' I said. 'He's waiting.'

As the winch turned, the cable tautened abruptly and the glider, which seemed so small, moved towards us, slowly and jerkily at first, then more smoothly as the momentum increased. I cheered when it lifted off the ground, then heard myself go, '*Oh*,' the breath scooped out of my mouth by the wind, the sound of blood in my ears and the whoosh of the cable snaking back on to its coil as the glider rose over our heads. We stared up into the darkening sky as it banked and turned towards the valley.

I didn't even care when Donald rested his heavy arm on my shoulders, and pulled me close. 'You're a grand lass,' he said.

Thirty-Nine

Flavio has made it clear that he will refuse to let me take Kakuna out of the camp another time, so I don't ask him. I simply pop her into the car and drive past the guards at the gate. I don't feel guilty about this. Nobody cares about Kakuna; nobody else, that is. The guards never ask if I have permission – they know me too well and assume it's all right. In any case, they barely glance up from their comic books or mobile phones to see whose car it is. And Kakuna adores the subterfuge, you can see that, keeping her head down as I wave, a grin on her face. She has changed so much in the last few weeks; I can't help but feel proud, of her, of course, but also of myself.

I don't always take her home. Sometimes we park in the town and go shopping, as I never went shopping with my aunt, or walk down towards the port to see the ships. Her English has improved so much we hardly ever speak Italian now and it's obvious she enjoys this, the way people turn in shops to look, unable to place us. She has a few clothes I have bought for her, which I keep in the boot of the car in a bag: it would be cruel to parade them in front of the other children in the camp, and Flavio might notice them and complain that I'm spoiling her. She has chosen them herself, and although I'm often surprised and slightly disappointed by her fondness for frills and watery pastels, I share her pleasure in them as she wriggles out of jeans and sweatshirts, then puts on skirts and skimpy tops. As soon as she's dressed again she clambers into the front of the car and sits beside me, transformed.

She loves to wander round the shopping streets, not buying necessarily but looking, repeating the names on the labels under her breath, like a chant, names I would never have known without her although I must have heard other girls mention them. Sometimes I follow her into the cubicle when she tries things on and see her smooth clean limbs and want to stroke them. She often declines offers I might make of one garment or another, accepting only what she really wants – a blouse, a pair of lacy white socks – with a fervent gratitude I'm unnerved by, a sign of power I'd rather not possess. And yet I am also grateful, touched to be allowed this grace. This is what I feel as the light goes out of the sky and we drift along streets filled with people and cars and motorbikes and the constant flashing of signs, all of which normally sets my teeth on edge. I am in a state of grace because I have Kakuna with me, her small cool hand in mine.

Of course, the other reason I don't always take her home is that Jozef doesn't want her there. He hasn't said this in so many words, but he doesn't believe me when I talk to him about Kakuna. He puts on the face I see when people talk to him about religion. He closes off, his lips set in a tight smile of refusal, as if to say: 'Nothing will make me change my mind.' When I told him that Magda had been transferred to another camp, he said how 'convenient' that was, which shocked me because Jozef is never cheap. He wants me to talk about Margot, I can tell, although I don't know why. He resents my curiosity when he would prefer to see me suffer, as he appears to be doing. He resents my cold blood almost as much as I begrudge what I see in him – his unexpected pity for the woman. And I am hurt by his grief, which seems to reduce me. But he seems hurt too.

'Why do you want to see the letters?' he asks.

'Because she didn't tell me everything,' I say. 'I want to see if there's anything about my parents.'

'There will be nothing in them that will make you any happier,' he says.

And I reply, my voice cold, 'How do you know what will make me happy?' Immediately I feel guilty, because Jozef has always known exactly what makes me happy. I touch his cheek to see what he'll do, but he only smiles and shakes his head, so that my hand feels awkward. I take it away.

He is working on the installation, which has doubled in size and now occupies much of the barn. The most recent sections are darker than those at the centre as the work grows concentrically, like an onion, the narrow gaps between the lacquered paper sheets increasingly opaque as Jozef fills them with objects he has made or found. I wander round and look for things I recognize, a newspaper cutting, a scarf I thought I'd lost. Sometimes whole figures seem to have coalesced in the papery envelopes. There is a part of it, one of the newer sections, that seems concerned with me as I am now, with things of mine, and this makes me uncomfortable, but I say nothing, my silence a further source of regret because I have never felt like this with Jozef. It is harder than it was to move around inside the barn; the sense of the work as a labyrinth is stronger each time I see it. It will be impossible to get it out of here. But then I think of the glider, how we assembled it in the hangar, and see how much this installation resembles a machine for flight.

'What was it like to fly?' I asked him that first time, when the glider had landed and I'd run across to it, shaking with excitement. I had to shout over the wind to be heard as his head emerged from the cockpit.

He couldn't answer at first, it took him a moment to get his breath, but then he laughed. 'It is very good,' he said finally. 'It is to be alive. To fly is to be alive.' He grinned, which made him look as young as I was. 'But then it is all over and you must come back to where you were before. Here,' he said, reaching down. 'Give me your hand.'

*

The strangest thing of all since Margot died is this. For the first time in our lives together, we have made love in a greedy, selfish way I'd never imagined possible with Jozef, as though we have been starved and are fighting over food. Or maybe not selfish, but self-centred, when we have always been so aware of the other, of the other's pleasure, even at the cost of our own. Now I find what we do both exciting and repellent and these are somehow the same feeling; there is no contrast between them, as there should be. But what I feel, when we have finished and turn our backs to each other to sleep, consumed, is loneliness. I feel I have never known him and will never understand him; that my love for him has been built on gratitude, because he was there when I needed him, and looked after me. And I wonder, with a resentment that borders on despair, why he has never told me the truth about his life.

It isn't my idea to go to the port but Kakuna's. I'm surprised when she suggests it: I think it will bring back unwanted memories of her arrival, her desperate swim to shore through all that darkness. The last thing I imagined was that she would seek out the water. We walk down the road to where the ferries dock, Kakuna tugging me behind her in a playful but determined way, as though afraid she might miss her boat.

Most of the sea is hidden from the road by buildings, warehouses, Customs and shipping offices, but we find a place where nothing but a metal railing stands between us and the water. Beneath it are rocks and concrete, and beyond that the sea, oil-slicked, grey and slow, plastic detergent bottles and water-rounded lumps of polystyrene bobbing, seagulls hovering. We watch as a rat emerges from the rocks and scurries beneath a washed-up sheet of plywood. Kakuna clambers on to the railing and points at the nearest ferry, about two hundred yards away from us. 'I want to see the people on the ship,' she says. 'Where are they from?'

'I don't know. Most of the ferries come from Greece.' She leans so far over I clutch at her sleeve. 'Be careful,' I say, with a nervous laugh. 'I'm scared you'll fall.'

'Don't be scared,' she says, the wind blowing her blue-black hair across her face. 'I'm fine. Look.' And she swings on the top rail, her legs flying up, her head dipping down until her hair almost touches the concrete. Upside-down, her manic smile is like that of someone unknown to me, and I cry out, oddly thrilled with apprehension.

Forty

I didn't recognize Nicholas when he got off the coach in his uniform, kicking his holdall down the steps in front of him – not until he glanced up from under his beret, saw us and waved. He was so thin he looked older, or ill, as though he'd caught TB or some wasting disease. Aunt Margot gave a gasp of shock behind me and I turned round – despite myself – with a sympathetic grimace. 'What in heaven's name have they done to him?' she murmured, as he walked across to us, hoisting his holdall on to his shoulder. 'Oh, my God, he looks as though he's on his last legs,' she said. His face was gaunt and pale; when he smiled, creases appeared at each side of his mouth; his eyes were twice the size they'd been when he went away.

Uncle Joey took the holdall from him. 'Welcome home,' he said, while Aunt Margot adjusted his beret and gave him a sharp kiss on the cheek.

'Thanks,' said Nicholas. He didn't say much else, just sat in the back of the car with me, staring out of the window, nodding, murmuring 'Yes' or 'No' each time we asked him anything. But nobody knew what to say and the questions dried up before we were out of the town.

We'd almost reached the pub when I couldn't bear the silence any longer. 'Those trousers must be really prickly on the inside,' I whispered to him, and he gave me a grateful smile.

'Yes,' he said, his voice so quiet I could barely hear it.

'Never mind, you can take them off when you get back. You can take it all off. We're nearly there now. You can put your jeans on.' But as soon as I'd said it, I thought, They'll fall off him. He's half what he was.

'What are you two muttering about in the back?' Aunt Margot asked, not moving her head; she'd had her hair done that morning and didn't want it ruined.

When Uncle Joey had parked, Nicholas got out of the car and picked up his holdall, then stood there, as if waiting to be told what to do. 'Come on,' I said. I could have cried.

It wasn't until after we'd had something to eat, with Aunt Margot heaping extra mashed potatoes on to his plate and Nicholas pushing them around with his fork as though something nasty were buried beneath them, that I dared ask him about Maudie. We were sitting together on the car-park railings, our backs to the pub, looking down towards the valley. It was August but the wind had come up and I was shivering, with just a cardigan on over my school blouse and the skirt I wore at weekends when it didn't matter who saw me. Nicholas had taken off his uniform trousers and cinched his jeans round him with a borrowed belt, but he'd kept on his khaki jacket and boots, which made him look odd. He didn't answer at first. Then he asked, 'Are you still going out with that Richard?'

'Yes,' I said.

'And does he fuck you?'

'Nicholas!' I was less offended than surprised. 'No, he doesn't.'

'Why not? Won't you let him?'

'I don't want to. That's why not. I'd do it if I wanted to.'

'Only if you did, would you say it? I mean, would you say "fuck" and all that? Or would you use different words?'

'I don't know. It'd depend on who I was talking to, I suppose. I mean, I wouldn't say "fuck" to Aunt Margot or one of the teachers.' And I wouldn't say it to you either, I thought. I'd be embarrassed.

'What if you were talking to him? To your boyfriend?'

'I wouldn't need to say anything to him,' I said. 'He'd know without my saying, wouldn't he? If he's my boyfriend. We wouldn't need to talk about it.'

'You'd just do it, wouldn't you?' Neither of us spoke for a few moments, until Nicholas pointed down to the road that ran through the valley. 'Look,' he said, 'bloody army trucks.'

'Is it terrible?' I asked. He bit his lip and I thought, My God, he's going to cry.

Then he nodded. 'They don't believe me, you see,' he said. 'They think I've made her up.'

'But what about the letters?' I said. 'Why didn't you show them the letters?'

'I did,' he said, 'but they think I'm having them on. No girl'd ever write that sort of filth, they said.'

'But how could you be having them on?'

'Well, I am, aren't I?' he said. 'I am having them on. There isn't any Maudie, is there?' He looked at me. 'Who's writing them anyway? You aren't, I know that.' He sounded . . . not angry exactly . . . resentful, as though he'd been found out doing something wrong and didn't know who to blame.

'I tried, Nicholas,' I said. 'Honestly, I did. I wrote you a letter only I never sent it. It sounded silly, what I'd written. They'd never have believed it, and it would have been worse than nothing.'

'I doubt that,' he said. He pulled his jacket tighter round him. 'You could have tried a bit harder, though, couldn't you? You didn't have to tell anyone else. You could have kept it to yourself.'

'I'm sorry,' I said. To my surprise he pulled a packet of ten Park Drives out of his breast pocket and lit one, flicking the match down the hill before the flame was out. I'd never seen him smoke before. After a couple of greedy drags he offered the cigarette to me. I took it, glancing behind me out of habit to the bedroom windows, not really caring who was there.

'They think I got a mate to write them,' he said.

I didn't know how to answer but I almost wanted to giggle as I thought of what Patricia would say when I told her. 'They think you must be a bloke, you're so foul-mouthed; I told you no decent girl would ever say those things.' I wondered how much worse the letters had become. The first had been bad enough.

'But what did *you* write?' I asked.

'I never said nothing like what she did. I never used that kind of language. So who was it?' He faced me again, his eyes damp with tears. 'It wasn't you, was it? Pretending?'

'No.'

'Bloody *Maudie*,' he said, with contempt. He lifted one side of his jacket, pulling his shirt with it. 'I've got Maudie to thank for this,' he said, as he showed me a ragged bruise, the skin broken in a thin line through the middle. It started at his lowest rib and continued below the belt I'd lent him. 'This is Maudie's doing, this is.'

'Does it hurt?' I asked.

He snorted ribbons of smoke from his nostrils, then threw the half-smoked cigarette away from him. 'I thought it was our Maudie here at first,' he said, 'after I'd realized it wasn't you. I thought it might be true, you know, that she really fancied me. She tried to kiss me once, only I wasn't having it, not with all that chip fat on her hands and her being older as well. But Maudie'd never say the things them letters said.'

'How did they get to see them? I thought that friend of yours told you to keep them to yourself.'

'It was all right till Johnny went,' he said. 'They'd leave me alone, because he looked after me. But then he had to go because his dad got ill with cancer and they started again. They took all the letters from my locker when I was in the toilet and read them out and they wouldn't give them back. They said I was too young to have them. They kept asking me questions about what the words meant, you know, and what we did. "Did you do this? Did you do that?" They said she was a right scrubber. I tried to write to her, to tell her to stop it, but they threw it away and made me write what they wanted. I didn't understand half of it, only they'd hit me if I didn't. Then what she wrote back got worse, it was really filthy, not just the words but what it said she'd like to do to me. So then they thought it was a mate of mine who was writing them, because one of them said it had to be because no girl swears like that and the others started calling me a pansy again, like they had done at the start, because if it was a bloke I'd have to be.' He gulped back tears. 'Only it was a lot worse this time. They wouldn't leave me alone. They'd keep teasing me and thumping me and making me do things.'

'Couldn't you tell anyone?'

'Don't be daft,' he said. 'If I'd gone and told tales I'd have had it from the sergeant as well. That's the worst thing you can do in the army, snitch on your mates.'

'But they weren't your mates,' I said. 'You can't call people who beat you up your mates.'

He shrugged. He'd pulled his jacket down but I

couldn't get the bruise out of my head. We were both silent. Then I said: 'It was Patricia. Patricia wrote them. She's Maudie. Maudie was my idea, but that's all. Only the name.'

'Patricia? Your Richard's sister?'

'Yes. I didn't want her to send you the letters, honestly. I only saw the first one – she wouldn't show me the others. I tried to stop her, but she wouldn't listen. She only did it because she was jealous of me, because I'd got a boyfriend and she hadn't, not a proper one.'

Nicholas lit another cigarette. When he offered it to me and I reached over to take it, he grabbed my wrist so hard it hurt. 'Perhaps I'll see if she'll let me,' he said. 'Then I'll know what to say.'

'Let you?' I didn't understand what he meant.

'You know, let me do her.'

'Oh, no,' I said.

'No?' He let my wrist go. I didn't know what to say. I shivered and moved a bit closer to him until my shoulder was against his.

He looked at me shyly. 'Does that Richie kiss you?'

'Sometimes.'

'And does he touch your – you know – down there?'

'Nicholas,' I said, embarrassed.

'I'm not a pansy,' he said, with sudden fury. 'I'm not a pansy.'

'Do you want to kiss me?' I asked. I felt so sorry for him.

He blushed immediately. Even the back of his neck went red. 'You're my cousin. It wouldn't be right.'

'A kiss doesn't count. I wouldn't let you do anything else. It'd just be so that you know what it's like. Then you wouldn't have to pretend with the others.'

'What – now?' He turned his head to see if anyone was looking from the windows.

'Or we could walk up to the pool,' I said. 'Come on, I haven't been there for ages.'

He thought about it. Then, 'No,' he said, jumping off the railings. 'Let's go over to the gliders.'

'I'll show you Uncle Joey's glider,' I said, following him. 'He took it up last week, when the club was closed. It was wonderful, Nicholas, you should have seen. I thought he was never coming back. I helped Donald with the winch, the way you used to before you left. He tried to kiss me too.'

'Did you let him?'

We walked across the car park and a few seconds later we were climbing over the stone wall on the other side of the road, taking the short-cut across the fields. This was the way we had come, Uncle Joey, Nicholas and I, when we carried the glider in pieces from the cellar to the club. I didn't answer him until we were walking across the first field and I was a step or two in front of him, so he couldn't see my smile.

'Of course I didn't. I don't just kiss anyone, you know.'

But I kissed Nicholas. We were sitting on the wall by the club, the stones digging into my thighs where my skirt had ridden up. Then his funny soft lips were touching mine, which made me ticklish at first, because he was afraid to press too hard; and then he did press against me, with a little moan deep in his throat, and I could feel his teeth behind his lips, which he held tight shut. He wouldn't open his mouth the way Richie did, I could tell that, not unless I encouraged him, so I gave him the tiniest prod with my tongue, more out of curiosity than anything, which made him jump and then suddenly his hand was fumbling at my cardigan. I twisted away from him and slipped off the wall, scraping the back of my legs on the coping. It hurt but I started to giggle; I couldn't help myself.

'You see?' he said. 'I'm useless.'

'Show me what else they did to you.' He looked at me, distrustful, then took off his jacket, draping it on the wall, and began to unbutton his shirt; he had his head down, watching his hands, perhaps so he wouldn't see me standing in front of him, so he could pretend to be alone. 'You'll get cold,' I said, wishing I'd never asked, but he shook his head, as if to say it didn't matter, and carried on, half folding his shirt and putting it next to the jacket because Nicholas was always neat. He had a green vest on underneath, which must have been army issue as well, but even before he'd pulled it over his head, which he did with a low groan and a wince, I could see the bruises.

They covered his shoulders and the upper part of his back, blue and black and yellow and purple, so many colours they were almost beautiful except where the skin had been broken and there were crusts of blood and scabs. You could see his ribcage too, the white bone under the livid flesh of his back. I wanted to touch him but I didn't dare; I didn't want to make things worse. And I thought of the letter Patricia had shown me, the one where Nicholas had written 'I LOVE YOU' over and over again.

Forty-One

They don't send me just Margot's letters. The parcel – which has to be collected from the post office – contains two A4 box files of assorted papers and three photograph albums. My hands shake as I open the first album, but both this one and the second are full of cuttings from newspapers and magazines about her favourite actors and singers, dating back to the 1950s. The third album is different, but I'm prepared, I think: I've been reminded of the woman's shallowness and can't be hurt.

The album itself looks fairly new, with transparent plastic over sticky white cardboard pages, and I suppose she sat in her living room, with the television on, and took the pictures out of a tin or chocolate box to put them in, one after another as they came to hand, without any attempt to organize them, because there seems to be no order, chronological or otherwise, in their arrangement. Nicholas is on the third page, plump in his new suit on the day he left for the army, with his holdall beside him. There's a photograph of the Mermaid, with people standing around the door, lined up and staring towards the camera as people do, tiny and unrecognizable because the aim had clearly been to get the whole pub into the picture. I continue to thumb through, scanning the rest of the album for faces or scenes I'm familiar with, half knowing what I'm looking for. So I'm not surprised, except in the dulled way that signals the return of an ache, when I turn a page and see my parents.

They are sitting at a table with other people, but I recognize them at once. Like most of the others, my mother is laughing, her head thrown back. My father is gazing at a woman further down the table and I see immediately that it's Margot, although she seems much younger than when I knew her. Her hair is in a bob and she's wearing a round-necked jumper without jewellery. She's smiling, but there's an intensity in the look between her and my father that has nothing to do with the rest of the table, bright-eyed with expectation; so obvious it's extraordinary the other diners haven't noticed and become embarrassed for them. But what they think wouldn't matter; the expressions on the faces of my father and aunt utterly exclude everyone else, as though they are the only ones alive in a room full of mannequins.

I study the picture for Jozef, but he isn't there, so either he was behind the camera or the meal dates back to before their marriage, which is also possible and would explain the unusual freshness of my aunt's appearance. It's odd to see how young she seems beside my mother, who has never grown old for me as her sister did, so that I always think of her as the younger of the two; odd to see my mother looking flushed, even blowsy, in her amusement. She would hate this photograph, I think, and not only because her husband is openly ignoring her in favour of her sister.

There are no more pictures of my parents, either alone or together. The last half of the album is empty, as though she had run out of photographs or exhausted the desire to stick them in. I put it to one side and pick up the first box file.

It takes me a quarter of an hour to find my father's letters. I suppose I've known since my final visit to my aunt that she and my father were lovers at some stage, and now the photograph has confirmed it. I sift through the contents of the file – birthday cards, bank statements, beauty tips cut from newspapers, now brown and fragile, correspondence from the brewery – and find nine letters tied together with a scrap of ribbon and addressed in my father's handwriting. According to the postmarks, the first six were sent the year before I was born, when Nicholas was still a baby, and the other three much later, at different dates. Trembling, I start to read them in the order they were written, but after the second I put them down and sit with my hands in my lap, overwhelmed by disappointment and a sort of anger. I don't know what I expected, but not this: they're so *typical*, so hackneyed and unimagined, I can't bear to read on. Eventually I force myself to open the last one, but the tone's the same. I love you, I miss you, I want to put my arms round you. Not a word about me.

Are all love letters so banal? I wonder, and see Nicholas suddenly as he was when he left for the army, in his stiff new suit, before his own love letters began. And I think: You fool, Margot. He was playing you along – surely you must have seen? You, with your experience of men?

Though maybe that wasn't true, not then: when she wore her hair in a bob and was in love. And more and more it occurs to me that I know nothing of my aunt and have no idea of her except the one I formed as a desperate child, which is hardly likely to reflect the truth. With a rush of something that is almost sympathy, I imagine her opening each of these letters and reading it, in secret surely, away from everyone else; I imagine her rereading it a dozen times, lingering over certain phrases, then slipping it into her pocket, patting it a hundred times a day to check that it was there.

When Jozef comes into my study I flinch and am about to hide the letters, just as Margot must have done. Overcoming my instinct, I leave them on the floor beside me, where they can be seen. He kisses the back of my neck, then picks up one of the envelopes and reads out the name in a low voice. 'So they've arrived.'

'Did you know?' I ask. 'About my father and Margot?'

'I knew there was someone she'd loved – and still loved – because she told me from the beginning that I would never be more than a companion to her. For a long time

I thought she was still in love with her first husband, with Nicholas's father. But then I saw from the way she spoke about him that there was someone else. Her secret.'

I pick up the envelopes and cradle them in my hand. 'These letters were written before I was born, Jozef, before my parents were even married. She told me once that my father had married my mother because she was expecting me, not because he loved her. And I believed her. I remember that perfectly. She called my mother a whore and I wasn't shocked. It was as though I'd known.' I turn to look at Jozef, to see his face. He seems pale and tired. 'Did she ever say that to you?'

'Can't you leave things as they are, Carol? What good does it do to try to understand all this?' His tone is pleading. 'They are all dead.'

But I won't be put off. 'Did she?'

He sighs. 'Yes, in her own way. It was after your mother had died. When she heard what your father had done, she was strange. I couldn't understand her reaction to the murder. I knew, of course, that Margot and your mother weren't close but she didn't seem upset – shocked, certainly, but not upset. She even seemed glad, but in a bitter and angry way. As though she'd been proved right. She was mostly upset about your father. How odd, I thought at the time. It's as though she's trying to hide her real feelings. And that was when I realized that she loved your father.'

'What did she say about him? She must have said something.'

He strokes my hand, taking the envelopes away from me. 'She told me your mother had stolen him from her, out of spite and greed. She and your mother were living together then; they kept each other company. Your mother must have helped with Nicholas. She was working for your father, I think, and I suppose he met Margot through her. They must have had friends in common.'

I think of the photograph again. When exactly was it taken? It might have been before my parents were married. What was the event? A business outing of some kind, the meeting of a club they all belonged to? As I remember it, my parents had no friends. 'But my mother had no idea they were in love? She wasn't jealous?' My tone is harsher than I intend and Jozef withdraws his hand with a pained expression, as though I've accused him of something.

'You must understand that when I married Margot I had never met your mother or father. I had no idea what happened before. I had never seen you.' You don't need to excuse yourself, I think, and I want to tell him to stop, but he continues, his voice more doubtful now. 'I think your mother was not aware that there was still a feeling between Margot and your father. Margot said she never noticed other people, and I suppose she meant she never noticed her sister. Perhaps at the end your mother understood what she'd done, what they'd all done. I sometimes wonder if that was what the last fight was about.'

'She can't have known,' I say, because I want this to

be so. 'We hid from him at Margot's house. She took us in. My father came for us and had to wait outside in the car. Why would my mother have gone to her if she'd known?' But that last time, I think, we went to a hotel.

'It might not have been so difficult for her,' Jozef says, suddenly calm and even relieved, as though on surer ground, and I realize that he isn't talking about my mother, whom he never really knew, but defending Margot. 'She was still your mother's sister, whatever your mother might have done.' I turn away, but he brushes my hair from my face and I can feel him studying me, and I wish he would stop; I wish he would leave me alone now, to think about what I know. 'Don't simplify them, Carol. It is too easy. People are not simple.'

I refuse to meet his gaze. 'You never knew my father?'

'I met him once or twice, in the beginning, before we were given the Mermaid. We spent an evening together, the four of us, but it wasn't easy. There was tension between your mother and Margot. Besides, your father found me boring. I didn't drink with him, not as he wanted . . . not as much as he wanted. Then, when we had the pub, we stopped going out.

'That was how I heard about you first, when your mother spoke about you that evening. I never met you, you see, until you came to live with us. I thought it odd they hadn't brought you with them, you were still so small, but your father said they'd left you with a babysitter. Of course, your father knew how painful it might have been for Margot to see you – I saw that later. Then, after the murder, you were the first thing I thought of, I don't know why. I suppose because you had no one. I said to Margot that we must give you a home. She didn't want to at first – that was when she told me about your parents' marriage, about your father – but then she agreed. I was surprised: I thought she would refuse to take you. I wouldn't have blamed her in a way. It must have been hard for her. In one sense, you ruined her life.'

'So I have you to thank,' I said.

At lunch, neither of us talks. We're cautious, as though we'd argued, and over-polite. As soon as we've finished eating, Jozef stands up and leaves the kitchen and I want to call him back and ask him so many other questions, but all I do is tell him I'm going to the camp that afternoon.

He stops by the door. 'Tuesday isn't one of your days.'

'I know that.' I sound tetchy to myself and, apparently, to Jozef as well, because he pauses before he speaks. I stare at him, my eyes unexpectedly damp, as he holds out his hands towards me but doesn't approach.

'We can be happy now, if we choose, Carol. We have been, surely, these years we've spent together.' He sounds hopeless, as though he fears I'll disagree. His hands fall to his side. 'All this is bad for you, for both of us. This thinking about the past.'

When I don't answer him – I'm at a loss for words – he goes to the barn. It takes me a minute or two to decide, but then I follow him out, breaking into a run as I cross the drive.

He's already at work, bent over a cardboard box near the door.

'And what's all this?' I say, sweeping my hand around the installation. 'Isn't this the past? Isn't this dwelling in the past? It's like a mausoleum in here. Why can't you face up to it? What gives you the right to tell me what to do? Because you took me in? Because you saved my life? And that makes me beholden to you for ever? You can't even tell me the truth about yourself.'

His shoulders are set, stubborn; I can't see his face. Before he can answer – although I think I know already that he won't, because I have hurt him too deeply – I leave the barn and drive off.

Kakuna's nowhere to be seen. I drop in at the office, but Flavio's out and Salvo, playing solitaire on the computer, barely looks at me when I speak to him. The other girls haven't seen her, or say they haven't, although two or three giggle together as I walk away. I wander from barracks to barracks, glancing in – I don't want to seem intrusive – but most are empty, the women preferring to sit in the sun and talk, the men to gather in little huddles around the outer fence. I realize I'm walking more quickly, as though I'm afraid I'll lose her if I delay. By the time I see her standing alone near the gate, I'm breathless and almost running. I call her name and she sees me and smiles, waving as I cross the empty space between us, more slowly now.

When I get back Jozef is still in the barn. I tell him I want to take Kakuna away from the camp and have her live with us. No one else cares about her. She will never be claimed.

'You know they won't let us,' he says. His voice is unsympathetic.

Us? I wonder, but don't comment.

'You know we're too old to foster,' he continues, 'let alone adopt. We've been through this before, Carol. You know they will say no.'

'In that case,' I say, 'I'll take her without asking. One missing child more or less will make no difference.'

He shows his anger then, which frightens me but gives me strength. 'You condemn her to a life of subterfuge if you do that,' he says.

'Isn't that what all of us are condemned to?' I ask. 'One way or another? A life of lies and subterfuge. At least she will have a life.'

Abruptly Jozef pushes past me to leave the barn. Some impulse brings him back as I stand there, feeling free and lost at the same time. I let him take my shoulders in his hands and grip them until it hurts, but I don't flinch. I don't let him see I'm scared.

'Oh, Carol,' he says. 'Can't you see what you're doing? She already has a life, but you refuse to recognize it. You think she is a slate to be wiped clean, that you can wipe her clean and start again with her. But she will never be clean.'

'Leave me alone,' I snap.

'Is that what you want?'

I don't know what I want. 'Yes,' I say, defiantly.

He nods. 'Very well.'

I'm sitting in the car when the taxi arrives. Cocoa barks frantically from inside the house as Jozef walks down the drive to the gate, a suitcase in his hand. It's only a small case, I notice, and I wonder if this means he'll soon be back. I've been crying for more than an hour, but I can't leave the car and catch him up. Not now. He doesn't turn to look at me, but he stands with his hand on the car door before opening it and my heart leaps, because I think he has changed his mind and will stay. And then he climbs in and the taxi draws away.

Forty-Two

'I'm not going back,' Nicholas said. 'They'll have to kill me if they want to take me because I'm not going back alive.'

'Don't be silly,' I said, surprised by his rebelliousness, but excited too.

'You'll help me, won't you?'

'Are you going to tell Aunt Margot?'

'Don't be daft. What could she do?'

'Couldn't she buy you out?' I asked.

'What with? Peanuts? She hasn't got any money. She wouldn't do it anyway. She wants me to be a soldier like my dad was.'

'What about Uncle Joey?' I said. 'You could talk to him. He'd understand.'

'I want *you* to help me,' he said, stubborn, shaking his head with frustration. 'I don't want anyone else. You did before, with the application, when I didn't know what to write. You helped me then. You could have helped me with the letters from my girlfriend, but you didn't.' He let this sink in, then turned his eyes towards me. 'You will, won't you?'

'I will if I can,' I said. But I didn't know how; I couldn't imagine what he would do. I suppose I thought that when the time came he would lose his nerve and return without complaint. And somehow I must have made myself forget the state of his arms and shoulders, the bruises that covered his back.

'What'll I do?' He was desperate.

'I'll ask Richie,' I said. 'He might help.'

'He doesn't know about the letters?' Nicholas sounded anxious now.

'Of course not. I haven't told anyone, only Patricia, right at the start. And I'm sure she'd never have told him. Not with the things she wrote to you in them. She'd have been too ashamed.'

'But what could he do?'

'I don't know.' I thought for a moment. 'He's got his motorbike. He could take you somewhere you could hide.'

'But where?'

'I could talk to Patricia, if you wanted,' I said. 'She might know someone.'

'I'll kill that Patricia if I get my hands on her, after what she's done to me,' he said, with unexpected fervour. And then he reproached me, for the final time. 'I asked *you* to write those letters, Carol. You should have written them. You wouldn't have done them like she did. They'd have believed me then.'

*

I spoke to Richie one evening after school, when all he wanted was to kiss me and I had to keep pushing him away, but not too forcefully because I needed him to help us. Finally he gave up and listened.

'They'll come and get him if he doesn't go back of his own accord,' he explained, and I knew he was right. Then he said, quite out of the blue, 'Our mum thinks the world of you, you know. You'd be better off with us than getting involved in all their business. They're nothing to you.'

'But they're my family,' I said, and immediately wished I could retract the words because, of course, I'd never admitted this to anyone, not even Richie.

But: 'Our mum loves you,' he said again, as if he hadn't heard.

I didn't tell Nicholas this. All I said, when he asked if I had spoken to Richie, was that we would think of something, which seemed to calm him. We went for walks together, wrapped in our windcheaters, watching the land get dark before we headed back to the pub. He stole cigarettes from behind the bar and if Aunt Margot noticed she didn't say anything; she would have guessed it was Nicholas. Perhaps she thought that was the least she could do for him, to keep him in cigarettes. We'd stop and smoke together, sitting on a wall until the stones bit into our bottoms, often silent because there was nothing to say that hadn't been said. Sometimes, though, as if we were talking about someone else, we imagined what Nicholas might do, as though his flight had been accomplished.

When I asked him where he would most like to go he said Canada and began to talk about the Rocky Mountains and grizzly bears and living on salmon. 'They have the oldest and biggest trees in the world,' he said.

'How did you find out all that?' I asked, surprised.

He didn't know. 'And I'll live in a cabin,' he said, 'and wear skins.'

'All you need to do is get to a boat,' I said, excited. 'There must be thousands to Canada. You could be a stowaway. Even if they find you, you can always say you're someone else – how would they know who you were?'

'But where can I get a boat from?' he asked, the fun ebbing out of his voice.

'I don't know. London?'

'But London's so far away.'

'Liverpool, then. Why not? It's nearer and I know there are docks. There's bound to be a boat for Canada. It might be a foreign boat and they won't even speak English, so how could they find out who you are? Perhaps they'll let you work your passage.'

We talked like this until everything seemed possible, and Nicholas was flushed with excitement again, escape as real and solid as the wall we sat on. And then it was too cold to stay outside any longer without moving and we headed back to the pub, where no one asked us anything, not even Uncle Joey, so that I felt as though neither the real Nicholas nor I existed – which was another kind of escape entirely.

Forty-Three

Jozef has been away for two days now; I've had no news of him apart from a message on the answerphone to say that he is well and will be in touch because we must talk; I cancelled it at once, my hand shaking as I pressed the button. As if there hadn't been opportunity enough for talk in the past thirty years, I thought.

Last night I lay in bed alone, unable to sleep, and found myself thinking about my parents, about that last time in the hotel. We could have stayed away, my mother and I; we could have made a new life for ourselves without him. I know that now. Escape is not so difficult. And so, this morning, with Jozef gone, I decide to take Kakuna from the camp.

My final lesson is interrupted by another volunteer. In a loud voice that amuses the children – because there is no need to shout, we are all silent and curious – she tells me to go to Flavio's office at once. She is the kind of woman whom unobtainable men like him attract. She loves to give me what she sees as orders for, of course, anything Flavio might want is instantly an order and treated accordingly; and she shivers, offended, when I fail to obey. I tell her I'll drop by when the lesson's over.

'He's a very busy man,' she says.

'And I am a very busy woman,' I say, in English, to the giggling class.

'Just listen to what our Internet genius has discovered about your favourite girl,' Flavio cries, gesturing towards Salvo at the other desk, when I walk into the office. The woman volunteer is washing cups in the corner of the room, but I ignore her. It's a moment before the words sink in. They have found her family, I think. She's been claimed. She's going to be taken away from me. I feel physically sick with trepidation.

'Which favourite girl?' I ask.

Salvo grins and points to whatever is on the screen. 'Kakuna, of course. Who else? Don't tell me you haven't got a teacher's pet.' He glances at Flavio and I understand at once that everything is known to them, the shopping afternoons in town, our jaunts to the port. Everything has been mulled over and allowed. We have no secrets. I wonder if they know that Jozef has left me.

Salvo continues: 'Do you remember, ages ago, we wondered where her name had come from? How it didn't ring true? We were right. I thought I'd type it into Google and see what popped up and – would you believe it? – it isn't a Kurdish name at all. It's the name of a Pokémon, one of those cartoon characters the kids collect the cards for. And I'm pretty sure it's the one she's always got in her hand. In Japanese, her name's Kokoon. She's some kind of bug, it says here, or a poison, it isn't very clear. I suppose you need to know all about them to understand and I'm no expert. She's what they call stage one, because she's evolved from something called Weedle, which is a kind of fat worm with a spike on its head, very unpleasant. Then she turns into something else called Beedrill, a sort of killer bee apparently, and that's stage two. It doesn't look like there is any stage three. She seems to be about as unattractive as you can get if you're a Pokémon, a very low life form, and she's not much use either. Listen: "Almost incapable of moving, this Pokémon can only harden its shell to protect itself from predators." There's a sort of picture of her too. Look.'

My hands are shaking as I walk across to the desk and look at the image on the screen. I see a yellow larval form that is identical to the toy that Kakuna – but now what shall I call her? What name shall I use? – brought with her. Its eyes are black and slit-like in the way that alien eyes are always represented, unblinking and incapable of emotion. I skim the text. I see the words 'must evolve quickly or perish'. What shall I call her? I think again. My alien child.

'We shall have to speak to her about this,' I hear Flavio saying at my side, his voice amused and distant, 'though there's not much we can do if she doesn't want to tell us what her real name is. I must say, it's the first time we've had a cartoon character in the camp. I wonder which came first, the name or the toy.'

'Do you need to say anything?' I ask. 'Surely it won't do her much good to let her know we've found her out. We'll simply damage any self-esteem she's managed to develop since she arrived.'

'I knew she was a liar,' the woman volunteer remarks. She has been listening to this conversation with unconcealed delight. 'She has a dishonest face.'

'It isn't your job to make psychological profiles of the refugees,' I snap. 'That's clearly outside your competence.'

'And it isn't yours to act as their advocate,' she snaps back. 'Or nursemaid, for that matter.'

'Ladies, ladies,' says Flavio. Unusually, he has his dog collar on. I wonder if he's expecting visitors – perhaps the bishop who thinks refugees are bad publicity.

She is waiting outside the office for me. I can see from her wary smile that she must have sensed we were talking about her and been anxious, and now I understand why. So many subterfuges, so many secrets; she must have flinched inside each time her name was called. I grab her by the hand. 'We're going,' I say. 'Before they even realize.' She may not have grasped the second part, but she certainly understands the first. I feel her fingers tighten round mine and briefly she is in front of me as we hurry off, so that I am following her. By the time we reach the car, we are laughing. Moments later, we are through the camp gates, with Kakuna waving at the startled guards. I shall always call you Kakuna, I decide. I shall never question you or pester you about the lies you've told in the past. The past is over. From today, with me at least, there will be no need to lie. And I will also tell you the truth.

I drive as fast as I dare, taking the road to the sea as if by instinct, while Kakuna, beside me, bends to pick up a scrap of paper from the floor. She holds it out to me with a pleading expression on her face. It's the flyer the woman from the circus gave us, with Circo Paradiso written on it and the garish image of a lion tamer cracking his whip. Yes, I think, why not? And I say, 'My father took me to the circus once, when I was younger than you are now. We sat in the front row and when the clowns came near I hid my face. I don't know where my mother was,' I add, and my heart is beating in my chest because I'd forgotten that trip to the circus, just the two of us, and I wonder now if the memory is true.

'Oh, yes.' Kakuna sighs, sinking back in her seat, exhausted with joy.

Forty-Four

Neither Aunt Margot nor Uncle Joey seemed to notice as the day approached for Nicholas to return to the barracks: on the morning itself, nobody laid out his uniform or told him to pack his holdall; nobody gave him money or made sandwiches for the journey. Even Nicholas seemed to be holding his breath while I had breakfast and prepared for school. Because that was what our planning had come to: holding our breath and waiting.

Then, just as I was about to leave to catch the school bus, Aunt Margot spoke: 'Aren't you supposed to be reporting back today?' she asked.

And Nicholas said, 'No, it's the day after tomorrow. It's Friday.'

'Are you sure?' she asked, taking a sip of her tea, not really listening.

'Of course I am.' He brazened it out with a laugh. 'I'd be in real trouble if I got that wrong.'

'You'd be a deserter,' she murmured vaguely, as if the word had just occurred to her.

I should have been happy she'd lost track of the days so easily, but I despised her all the more for her indifference – although what she had done, of course, was solve what we had seen as our biggest problem, that of timing his escape. Too soon, and he would draw attention to himself before he had to; too late, and Nicholas was convinced Aunt Margot herself would hand him over to the army. This way, she and Nicholas's lie had given us two full days, as long as the army didn't react before that.

When I came home from school that afternoon, Nicholas was waiting where the bus set me down, sitting on the wall with the hood of his windcheater pulled over his head. He took my satchel from me, as a boyfriend would, and offered me the rest of his cigarette. We didn't go into the pub immediately, but headed towards the pool. I wanted to ask him if anything had happened, but what could have happened in a day? He was here beside me, wasn't he? In his own clothes, his face a little rounder than when he had arrived, his cheeks flushed from the wind. We walked as close to the brink of the pool as we could get, then sat on the grass with the hill behind us and the valley in front; as it got dark and the valley disappeared, the only sign of the road between Leek and Buxton was the lights of passing cars.

'That's where they'll come from,' Nicholas said. 'We'll be able to see them from here. They'll come from the north.'

I wondered what he imagined, his mind still fed by comics. A fleet of army trucks, a squadron of police?

'Surely there won't be that many of them?' I asked, half amused.

He faced me, his eyes in the shadow of his hood. 'It's the worst thing you can do, desert,' he said, voice trembling. 'It's treason. They used to shoot you in the war.'

'They wouldn't shoot you now, though,' I said, not because I knew this for sure but to comfort him. I had no idea what they might do; it seemed quite likely that deserters should be shot. Otherwise nobody would ever stay.

'I'll go to Liverpool tomorrow morning,' he said. 'I'll say I've got to pick something up from school. I'll come into town with you on the bus. Then I'll hitch to the station in Stoke. I've got some money saved. Only I don't know how much I'll need.'

'I've got some you can have.'

He nodded his thanks. 'I saw Donald today,' he said. 'He came in for a drink at lunchtime. He says I can have a job at the club when I leave the army. I wish he'd said it before I joined up.'

'It wouldn't have made any difference,' I said. 'You'd still have done it. You didn't know what it was going to be like then.'

Nicholas shrugged. 'We went over to the club. He showed me how the new winch worked. He'd have taken me for a flight, but there wasn't time. Anyway, with the wind like this, we'd have been mad.'

'Did he show you Uncle Joey's glider?'

'He did,' Nicholas said. 'He said it was like a dream,

how it went up and stayed. He said it was like watching a seagull.'

I was doing my history homework in the kitchen, with Maudie making chips behind me, when Nicholas burst in, white in the face, as though his blood had been drained from him. He mouthed something at me, which I didn't understand, then tugged at my arm until I let him drag me from the room.

'They're here,' he hissed, as soon as we were out of Maudie's hearing.

'Where?'

'In the bar. Two of them. And there's a jeep outside in the car park. They've come for me.'

I darted down the corridor and squinted through the half-open door into the pub. There were a dozen people sitting at the tables, waiting for their food, and two men in army uniform leaning against the bar, being served by Aunt Margot. She was laughing at something one of them had said, her right hand lifted to the nape of her neck to make sure her hair was in place. There was no sign of Uncle Joey.

'They've not come here for you,' I whispered to Nicholas. 'She wouldn't be behaving like that if they were. She'd be screaming mad. They're here for a drink, like everyone else.'

'They must be here for me,' he said. 'They're having her on, trying to find out if she knows where I am.' He glanced at the bare walls either side of us. He looked like a trapped rat, shaking, his forehead damp with sweat. I'd never seen fear before, what it did to you. 'I've got to get out of here,' he said.

I nodded. 'Go and get your stuff. Take the money you've got and I'll get mine. I'll see you back here.'

We ran upstairs together, banging into each other in our haste, then into our separate rooms. I kept what I thought of as my escape money hidden beneath my knickers in a drawer and I scooped it up quickly – some ten-shilling notes, a few coins; how ludicrous to think that someone could escape with so little, barely enough for a meal or two, a train fare – and shoved it into my pocket. I was hurrying downstairs as Maudie came out of the kitchen with baskets of scampi and chips on a large tray. 'I've put a couple of nice fat ones on a plate for you,' she said, with a wink, as she went into the bar.

Moments later Nicholas appeared, wearing his wind-cheater and army boots, a duffel bag over his shoulder. He'd reached the bottom step when Aunt Margot stuck her head round the door and saw me. 'Tell Nicholas to get in here a minute. There's someone who wants to meet him.'

'All right,' I said. I didn't want her to follow my eyes, so I kept my face turned towards hers, her drunken smile, as Nicholas froze against the wall, his hands flapping at the periphery of my vision. 'I think he's in his room.' I edged past the door as she went back into the bar and let it close behind her. 'I'll go and see.'

Seconds later, we were in the car park. Nicholas

ducked down. ‘There’s someone in the jeep,’ he hissed. ‘I told you they’d come for me.’ I looked across to where it was parked. He was right; I could make out two heads, both wearing berets, through the transparent flap at the back. They were facing the road, though; they hadn’t seen us.

‘We can go the other way,’ I said. Nicholas was paralysed with fright so I grabbed his arm and pulled him behind me, turning right and following the wall until we were at the rear of the pub. Nobody ever came round here: there was no paving, just rubble and earth, and we stumbled in the dark, Nicholas bumping into me when I lost my footing. I hadn’t had time to put on my coat and I shivered as the wind whipped round the building. Then we emerged on the other side of the house, where there was nothing but a narrow path flanked by a stone wall and, beyond that, a field. We climbed over the wall and sank down, breathing hard. Nicholas began to cry.

‘Don’t worry,’ I said, impatient with him now. ‘You’ll have to hitch, that’s all.’

‘But I don’t know which way they’ll go,’ he said, gulping back tears. ‘They might take the same road and catch me. They’ll have guns. I’m a deserter now – I should have been back by two o’clock. They can shoot me if they want.’

‘We can stay here till they’ve gone,’ I suggested. But he shook his head violently. ‘I’m not staying here. What if they’ve got dogs?’

‘Well, we’ve got to do something. We can’t just hide

behind a wall all night.' My thoughts raced. 'They won't be driving back into town, will they? Didn't you say they'd be coming from the north? That means they'll take the road past the pool. If we go the other way, towards the town, you could be miles from here before the two in the pub have even finished their beer.'

He gaped at me, his face a mixture of gratitude and doubt. 'Do you think so?'

'I'm sure,' I said. 'And I'll come with you. The first bit anyway, to where the road starts going down.' I took the money out of my pocket. 'Here, take this. You'll need it when you get to Liverpool.'

We had to cross the road and climb the stone wall on the opposite side to be sure of getting past the pub without being seen. Nicholas seemed hardly aware of what was happening, stumbling blindly in my wake; I think if I had heaved him back on to the road and sent him towards the jeep he would have gone there like a beaten dog, without resistance, almost relieved it was over. But I wasn't having that.

'We can get across now,' I said.

'No, not yet.'

'But they're miles back.'

'I'm too scared,' he whispered, and I thought – oh, God, forgive me – You'll never make a soldier, you're a snivelling coward.

That's when I had the idea.

'You could fly away if you wanted. You could take Uncle Joey's glider. They'd never catch you then.'

Forty-Five

The first thing we do, still flushed with laughter from our escape, is park in town to buy clothes for Kakuna, because she has nothing apart from the few things left in the car and what she is wearing, a Bugs Bunny sweatshirt and some faded jeans with over-elaborate stitching that even I recognize as unfashionable; everything she owns has been left behind, to be picked over and possessed by others. I glance down once, almost grudgingly, at her hands while we are in the car, to see if she has the Pokémon, but they are empty, palm-up and open on her lap. I think, relieved, Even this has come to an end, the final link.

This time, as we rush from shop to shop, it is different. Whatever she wants, I buy. I watch her preen and twirl in front of a series of mirrors and a picture comes into my head of Patricia's jewellery box, a musical box with a spinning dancer mounted in the middle and fillets of mirror in the lid that reflected her as, jerkily poised on her single leg, she turned, independently of the music.

We are in a shoe shop when it occurs to me, with a

rush of panic, that Kakuna's abduction might be reported. I make myself stand still on the pavement to breathe, to wait for the moment to pass – as it does – and try to be rational: Why should it be reported? And even if it is? What importance does one child have? No one will care where she is or who she's with. Later, when Kakuna calls me into a changing room and I see her, naked apart from the pale blue briefs and bra she has chosen, I'm entranced. How graceful she is! She hugs me and her skin beneath my hands is smooth and warm; I hug her back, not wanting to let her go.

We stop to buy some pizza and as soon as we are home I take it out of the box and put it on to the best plates, to celebrate, while Kakuna drops her bags in a heap by the kitchen door and runs outside, calling for Cocoa, her voice high-pitched with excitement. I set Kakuna's plate, glass and napkin in the place I would normally lay Jozef's, and I do this deliberately so that, should he choose to enter while we are eating, he will know at once I have not been bluffing: that space will be made for her. When Kakuna comes in, alone, I tell her that maybe Cocoa and Jozef are out together, perhaps they have gone for a walk along the beach. Privately, though, I wonder where the dog can be; even worse, I wonder why I've lied to her after I'd promised myself there would be no more deceit. I shall tell her as soon as we have eaten, I decide.

'Did you look in the workshop?' I ask, and Kakuna nods. She is sitting and eating, hasn't waited for me to join her. I find this impulsiveness, this disregard even, touching.

After lunch, I show her to the smaller guest room, suggesting that she rest or hang her new clothes in the wardrobe. I have to work on a report, already overdue, so I go to my study and turn on the computer, but the words are meaningless to me and I know that anything I do today will have to be repeated tomorrow. Mostly I stare in front of me at my noticeboard, at pictures from magazines and photographs I have pinned up: a woman sitting beneath a tree in Gabon, which I cut out of a travel brochure, two dogs asleep in an abandoned tyre, Jozef and me some years ago at a Chinese restaurant in London, self-conscious because we asked a man at the next table to take our picture, which is focused not on us but on the wall behind, on the series of mass-produced Chinese landscapes in gold and crimson. We are staring at the camera with blurred expressions of apology, Jozef looking small beside me because I had put on weight then, for a while, almost without noticing, weight that I have since lost in the same way. Now I am almost as thin as Margot was.

When the telephone on my desk rings, I am startled out of my daydream, and almost don't answer; the possibility that it might be Jozef, wanting to talk, unnerves me. Finally, when I think it is about to ring for the last time, I pick up the receiver. It is Flavio. He sounds worried, almost reproachful, as he asks me where the girl is.

'Which girl?'

'For the love of God, Carol, you know perfectly well which girl,' he says. 'The Pokémon girl. Kakuna.'

'What do you mean, where is she?' I'm elated, despite my unease. 'You don't mean you've lost her?'

'She hasn't been seen since this morning. Since you left, as a matter of fact. One of the guards is convinced he saw someone with you in the car. He says it looked like a girl. I know how much she means to you, Carol. You needn't feel alarmed.'

'Are you accusing me of abducting her, Flavio?' I ask, my voice perfectly calm. I'm ready for this. 'That's a very serious charge.'

'Don't be dramatic. Naturally I assumed if the girl wasn't here she'd be with you.'

'I've no idea where she is,' I say, my heart beating hard with excitement. 'I really think you should be more careful, though, Flavio, about people wandering in and out of the camp. You can't just lose a child, you know.' I realize that I'm using his first name as he uses mine, to pin him down. I know your game.

'Of course we haven't lost her,' he snaps. 'She's bound to be in the camp somewhere. She's probably hiding on purpose. In large measure this is your fault, Carol, and I hope you realize that. Your favouritism has made her uncontrollable.'

'Whatever my favouritism may have done to her, you still don't seem to know where she is,' I insist, enjoying myself now. I relish the word *lose* and the effect it seems to have on Flavio; I can't resist repeating it. 'It looks rather careless, to say the least, to lose a child.'

He puts the phone down on me. I sit there, flushed

with joy, then lay the receiver in the cradle. Two or three seconds later, the phone rings again. I pick it up.

'I think,' says Flavio, in a tremulous voice, 'it would be better for everyone if we interrupted your English lessons.'

'It would be better for *you*, Flavio,' I say. This time I end the conversation.

I start to rush through to tell Kakuna, but in the corridor I decide against it. When I enter her room, without knocking, because it doesn't occur to me to knock, I find her standing in front of the mirror in her new underwear. She sees me, reflected, and blushes, as though I have caught her out, and I stand at the door, awkwardly. Seeing her there, both in the flesh and framed by the mirror, her head turned to face me, her slender body twisted round in the pale blue bra and briefs, I have the strangest sensation that she is no longer Kakuna but someone else, Kakuna's older sister, perhaps. She looks more like a woman than a girl.

She giggles and walks across to me and I notice she's wearing shoes with stiletto heels I don't remember buying, although everything she possesses has been bought by me. It occurs to me that she must have stolen them. Speechless, I watch this woman-child sway towards me and I can see at once that she isn't used to heels. She puts her arms round my neck, our eyes almost level. She gives me a delicate kiss on my cheek, almost my mouth, grazing the corner with her lips and there is lipstick on them. I can taste it.

'Thank you,' she says. Then, 'I am beautiful, yes?'

We are standing together in this half-embrace when car tyres crunch on the gravel outside. She darts away from me, stooped, and reaches towards the bed for something to cover herself, while I cross to the window. There is a police car in the drive. Kakuna, in a dressing-gown, shivers behind me.

'Don't worry,' I say. 'Nobody knows you're here. I'll tell them to go.'

They ring the doorbell a moment before I get there to open it, so I pause and take a deep breath. It is impossible that they know she is here, I think. Even Flavio had his doubts. In any case, he would never send the police, he'd come himself. By the time I open the door, my heart has stopped pumping so frantically and I feel almost calm.

There are two, in uniform, a man and a woman, neither much older than twenty-five. Both have sunglasses and long hair, the woman's falling in heavy waves to her shoulders, the man's swept back and stiff with gel. In their perfectly pressed uniforms, they look more like models than police officers.

'Signora Foxe?' the man enquires. I can tell they are wondering if I speak Italian, so I put them at their ease and ask what they want. The woman smiles in a sympathetic way that frightens me immediately – I recognize the smile intended to sweeten bad news. Jozef is dead, I think, and a wave of nausea sweeps over me, so strong I feel I am going to faint. I lean against the doorpost.

'*Lei ha un cane?*' the woman says. '*Un Labrador?*'

'*Si, un Labrador nero,*' I say, ashamed that I feel weak with relief. '*Si chiama Cocoa.*'

'*Mi dispiace molto, Signora, ma è morto,*' the policewoman says, laying her hand on my arm to comfort me as her colleague steps back. Death is women's business. '*È stato investito da un'automobile. Non c'era niente da fare.*'

I ask her what has to be done and she tells me I have to collect his body, either this afternoon or tomorrow. He died immediately, she says, there was no pain: he was struck on the head by the car as it sped past, but the driver, unusually, stopped and called the police from his mobile before driving on. They have a contact number if I would like to ask him anything. She seems to be talking now to stop me thinking, perhaps hoping to cosset me with details. I was wise to put my name and number on his tag, she says; if everyone cared for their dogs as I did how much easier their work would be. So many dogs are killed on the roads and never identified, so many dogs abandoned, it's a terrible thing, people don't think. That's when it hits me that Cocoa is dead. I stand and wait for them to leave. I have to tell Kakuna what has happened.

But when I look for her, she isn't there. Nothing remains of the purchases we made – no shoes, blouses or underwear, no dressing-gown or jumpers. Only the clothes she had on this morning, the cheap jeans and the faded sweatshirt, screwed into a bundle and left in the corner of her room.

Forty-Six

It must have taken us twenty minutes to get to the club, staggering across the rough ground in the dark, with Nicholas constantly looking over his shoulder as if he expected the jeep to be bouncing across the fields in pursuit of us, like something out of a dream. I tripped once and landed with my knees in pellets of sheep shit, but I didn't care: I'd never felt better or freer in my life. The wind dropped a little, but not before it had shifted a cover of cloud from the moon, the pale stone of the walls glinting in the light. By the time we got to the club, my eyes had adjusted and I ran to the doors of the hangar, barely aware of Nicholas, panting and stumbling behind me. I might have been alone. I felt like a runaway myself, the cold air scraping my throat as I gulped it in, burning my lungs.

I didn't expect the doors to be open but that didn't worry me. I knew where the key was kept because Donald had shown me one afternoon when he thought I might be available, when he dreamt I'd slip over the fields one night to meet him there. As it turned out, though, the sliding doors had been pulled shut but not locked. The padlock slipped through the loops like a charm on a bracelet.

After that it was easy – we had done it dozens of times before. We pushed the wheels under the glider and rolled it out of the hangar on to the runway, then hooked it up to the cable. While Nicholas watched me, his mouth hanging open as though he had only just grasped what he would have to do, I dragged the ladder over and gestured to him to climb into the cockpit. 'Come on,' I urged, as he put his foot on the first rung. Thank goodness he's lost weight, I thought; the glider would never have held him as he was before. Once he was inside and seated, with his hands on the controls, I moved the ladder and ran down the strip towards the winch. I didn't look back. I didn't want to see his face or hear him if he called my name to say he'd changed his mind. I wanted him gone.

As soon as the winch began to turn, the cable tautened and the glider jerked forward. It swung slightly from one side to the other. Then, abruptly, it was in the air, lifted by a buffeting wind. It was over my head when Nicholas released the cable.

I didn't hear Uncle Joey approach. It wasn't until he touched my shoulder and I spun round, not frightened but hot-cheeked with exhilaration, expecting to see soldiers, that I realized anyone was behind me. How long he'd been there I didn't know, not long enough to have intervened, to have stopped Nicholas taking off into the dark, that much was certain.

'What have you done?' he cried. 'Oh, Carol, what have you done?'

'He won't go back to the barracks,' I said. 'No one can make him go back.' I stared out into the sky but there was no longer any sign of the glider. The wind had risen again, a warmer, blustery wind. He'll die, I thought suddenly. He won't escape at all. I trembled and Uncle Joey put his arm round my shoulders and pulled me tightly towards him until my face was pressed against his coat and I could hardly breathe.

'Now what shall we do?' he said. 'The two of us.'

After that events had their own momentum. All I could do was stand and watch as one thing followed another, and that was all I seemed to be expected to do: stand and watch, alternately furious and numb and scared as people I had never seen before, police and men in other uniforms, gathered to speak above and around and across me – never, or rarely, *to* me because by then I'd already said all I could say. Only Aunt Margot tried to blame me, crying and beating the wall with her hands, lunging at me with her painted nails; but Uncle Joey put a stop to that, the way a man might interpose himself between a dog and a child, allowing himself to be bitten in the child's stead.

They found the glider the following morning, with Nicholas still in the cockpit, although the safety harness was unbuckled. His face was calm. They said he'd died at once, on impact, but I didn't believe them. I don't know why. Perhaps because none of his injuries was visible. My aunt made sure I saw him in his pasteboard cubicle at the undertaker's, the coffin on trestles and a cross on the bare wall; his was the first corpse I'd ever seen and she was right to force me to stand there and gaze at him, his made-up face and Brylcreemed hair. They had dressed him in his uniform, which was almost unbearable.

The glider had crashed in a shallow valley five or six miles beyond the pool, its nose crumpled into the rocky bed of a stream. Other than that, and a split along the underside of the fuselage, it was pretty much intact. Nicholas had covered a fair distance, Donald said, given the bad weather, all that wind and the wrong sort too – no wonder he came down. He was a grand lad. It was a shocking waste.

I ran away from home two weeks after the accident, when Uncle Joey had been charged with criminal negligence and manslaughter and I was left alone with Aunt Margot, who simply ignored me in her state of shock. I walked into town, but I had no escape money any more because I had given it to Nicholas. I was found almost immediately. I fought like a cat, though, when the policewoman came for me. 'I won't go back,' I cried. '*I won't go back.*' But they didn't try to take me back; she wouldn't have me, I found out later. At the time they said it was for my own good, which I suppose was also true: I think she might have killed me in the end. Instead, I was fostered by Patricia's mother. I lived with them for four years, until I went to university, sharing a bedroom with Patricia, although we were never really friends again; I blamed her in part, because of the letters, but I never said this to her or anyone else.

So I know what it's like. That was what I wanted to say to Kakuna. I know what it's like not to be wanted, to be hounded and hunted down. If she had given me the chance, I would have told her everything. But now all I do is hunt her down myself.

Forty-Seven

I expected to lie awake all night but I fell asleep almost immediately, a dead sleep that has left me groggy and headachy this morning. As I shower, snatches of dream come back to me, less images than moods, a sense of anguish primarily, although there is also an image, of Kakuna walking towards me in her underwear, her arms outstretched, hair hanging damply round her shoulders. And all the time I have the sense that I must behave normally – wash my hair, floss my teeth – despite the effort. I must take off my dressing-gown, choose what to wear today and wear it, eat my usual yoghurt with honey while I wait for the coffee to rise in the pot. More than anything, I must decide what to do.

She'll come back, I thought, at first, as I searched the empty rooms of the house; she panicked, that's all. It's only natural for a child like her, a refugee, to run at the sight of police, to want to flee. But when she didn't return I checked the house again and found that she'd taken a suitcase of mine. Articles were gone from the bathroom as well, soaps and cosmetics, my hair-dryer, two small towels, a sponge, a pair of scissors, an unopened bottle of Madame Rochas; probably other things that I haven't noticed yet. The window was open and there was water on the sill. I thought for a moment she must have climbed out, but it's far too high for that. Perhaps she leant there, her elbows wet, to try to hear what the police were saying. She must have had everything ready, I realize now; she must have found and prepared the case while I was talking to Flavio. And then I remember the suitcase that was packed for me after my mother's death, with those clothes I would never have chosen myself. I remember arriving at the Mermaid and how abjectly I sat in silence on the narrow bed in that bedroom over the kitchen, with the muffled noise of the pub below, a convivial noise, I think, now that the emptiness of the house oppresses me.

Eventually I go to my study and call the camp because Flavio is the only person who can help me, but when he answers and I hear his voice, unctuous and alert, I find I can't say anything, not even my name, and I put the phone down at once. I must tell him to his face, I decide. I go downstairs and pick up my bag. Ashamed of myself, I check my wallet and find it empty. I have no reason to be ashamed.

I am getting out of the car to close the gate behind me when it crosses my mind that it must have been left open yesterday, when we arrived from town, or Cocoa would never have been able to run off. I must have neglected to close it – or Kakuna must. Because, of course, it was

Kakuna who had dashed across to lift the metal clasp from the post while I sat in the car, watching her as she swung the gate in a wide arc, then grinned at me as I drove past and parked, expecting her to follow on foot because the distance from gate to house is no more than twenty yards.

Flavio isn't pleased to see me.

'Well, there's no sign of the girl,' he says, as I walk though the door.

'That's what I'm here about.'

But before I can continue, he interrupts, 'And please don't start blaming it on me. It isn't our job to police the place – you know that as well as I do. Of course I'm responsible on paper, but what does that mean? I can't keep an eye on every single child in the camp. Even if I could, it would be inappropriate. I'm supposed to be here to meet their needs, nourish them materially and spiritually, not act as an armed guard. I'm sure Jozef would agree. Or does he take your side in this?'

'Please, Flavio,' I say. 'Let me explain.'

'I've been asking round, though.' He's deliberately talking over me to shut me up. He isn't normally so rude. 'And I don't much like what I hear. That other girl, Magda, she left because she was being threatened. Did you know that? We all assumed it, but now I've spoken to one of the others from that little group and she confirms it. They all have things to say about her now she's gone, terrible things some of them. She told Magda she'd have her kidnapped, apparently, and put on the streets if she talked, God knows what about, some tale about a dog . . .' And now he gapes at me. 'It was your dog, wasn't it? Didn't something happen to your dog on that picnic?'

'Please let me talk to you.' Flavio is finally silent.

'I think she may have gone to join a circus,' I say. 'Circo Paradiso. We saw some camels once, two in a trailer. She couldn't leave them alone. Perhaps she had camels around her where she lived. The circus flyer was in my car and it's disappeared. She must have taken it.' This sounds so lame that I wonder if the alarmed expression on Flavio's face might not be justified; now that I've lost everything else – Kakuna, my husband, my dog – perhaps I'm also losing my reason. I find the notion almost amusing, which is surely a confirmation of its truth. 'I'm sure we can find her if we locate the circus,' I continue. 'It was here not so long ago. They can't move that fast surely, with all those animals and the tent to put up and take down?'

'What are you saying, Carol?' he asks. 'You want me to find a circus?'

By the time we reach the circus ground it is dark and I don't know why we have come. We have driven almost two hundred miles along the coast, with Flavio hunched beside me in a wordless rage far worse than anything he could say, his jacket pulled around him as if to keep out the cold. We sit in the car outside the ticket office, a brightly painted wooden caravan, the skin on my hands stained lurid violet by the lights strung from tree to tree, creating an impression that strikes me as unbearably sad and tawdry. Flavio's face is much the same colour as I turn to look, reluctant, because it's obvious he's waiting for me to admit I'm wrong. 'Have you spoken to Jozef?' he asks eventually, in an irritated way, to break my silence.

'No,' I say. 'Jozef appears to have left me as well.'

Later, as we drive back, Flavio talks to me about Salvo. 'He thinks I should give up the Church, you know,' he says, his chin pushed down into his jacket so that he seems to be speaking to himself; even his face is turned away from me towards the window. I have to strain to hear. 'He has that kind of fundamentalism the young have, everything black or white. He can't bear it when I say something *depends* on something – I don't know, on what someone else might think, on circumstances. And here I am, a servant of the One True Church, constantly insisting things are relative, contingent. Heaven knows what the Pope would say if he could hear me. Salvo thinks I should come out – that's what he says, "come out". Out of what, I say, into what? And what earthly good would it do? He's a missionary, all that zeal, and for what? To make a priest who's almost old enough to be his father give up his dog collar and cease to be useful to anyone. What he doesn't say is that I should give it up for him, which is the only argument that might persuade me, however absurd that might sound. And it's quite deliberate,

I'm sure, that he's never said, "Do it for me." Because he doesn't want my resignation on his conscience. I know he'll leave me eventually, it's only a matter of time. I suppose I should respect that, the fact he's never made any promises he couldn't keep, even if it's only a matter of principle that stops him. He really does love me, I'm sure of that; he isn't lying when he tells me he loves me.' He pauses. 'Or perhaps I'm not so sure, perhaps I'd rather not know if he's lying. It's just that it isn't always so simple, is it? I mean, look at you, Carol. Who'd ever have imagined that Jozef would leave you?'

We get back well after midnight and, following Flavio's instructions, I drive through the outskirts of the town to see if Kakuna is among the girls at work. We cruise around the streets that lead down towards the harbour and its dark, still water. Mine is one of many cars, I discover, my heart in my mouth, one of many cars looking for some girl or other. Flavio knows the area better than I do – he has worked with these women in the past. He tells me which stretch of pavement is reserved for Albanian prostitutes, which for Nigerian and Somali women, which patch belongs to transsexuals from Brazil; he points out the small park used by gays. Finally he takes me to the area occupied by Kurdish girls – a pornographic geography offered up without comment, as drily as any other set of directions. When he tells me to stop, two teenage girls run across and the second is so like Kakuna I could weep and almost tell myself that I'll take her on in Kakuna's place. He asks them if they have seen a new girl out that night, describes her briefly, and they stare with interest into the car. Perhaps they think we're clients after all and this is the game that must be played, to tease them and titillate ourselves. They don't seem concerned that I'm a woman.

'No,' they say. Then the taller one pushes her hips against the car. 'Won't we do?'

We're almost at the camp when I say to Flavio, 'My father was a murderer.' He is quiet for a moment, as I think, *I have never said this to anyone*, and listen to the silence because there is nothing more to be said.

'Yes?' he asks finally. And then, 'I see.'

'Yes. He killed my mother in a rage. I've never really understood. He was drunk. He'd been unfaithful. She may have been unfaithful too. I saw it happen. I blame myself.'

Flavio reaches out to touch my hand, but thinks better of it. In a way, I'm sorry. I wouldn't have minded a little comfort. 'You've never mentioned it.'

And now I have. I've found the words, simple words, really, to say what happened. And yet nothing is changed.

Forty-Eight

There are lights on in the barn. My first thought is that Kakuna has come back, found the house closed, and let herself into the workshop, which is often shut but not locked. I am about to break into a run when I hear hammering and it strikes me that it can't be Kakuna after all.

I pass through a narrow opening and walk from section to section of the work, my hands raised in front of me as though to ward off something. The structure is more of a labyrinth than ever, a series of cubicles and corridors, into which Jozef has begun to incorporate sheets of mirrored plastic, thin as cellophane, that reflect my presence but not the detail of me, so that I seem a ghostly indefinite figure surrounded by solid objects. Everything that was light and airy about the work, everything that gave it charm, has disappeared and been replaced by darkness, despite a string of lights that runs through the lower part of the panels.

There is no hammering now, and the barn is so silent I wonder if I imagined it; it's hard to believe I'm not alone in here. Some sort of fabric, something coarse and woollen, like white tweed, has been laid on the floor, muffling my steps. Each cubicle has become a cocoon, I think, in an enormous hive. When I find myself faced by the outer wall of the barn and see that the panels have been woven into it, so the structure is no longer independent of the barn but integral to it, I'm not surprised. It has taken root. I was wrong when I thought the work was a machine for flight: nothing could shift it now. I walk back towards what I think is the centre, uncertain where I am.

It takes me a minute or two to find Jozef. He is sitting on a small chair, a hammer in his hand.

'Do you remember,' he asks, 'how some winter mornings when there was frost, the valley below the Mermaid used to fill with cloud, so white and firm you felt you could walk right across it to the hills on the other side? And the way we used to hold our breath as the van went downhill because we thought it would be like going under water? But the boundary wasn't clear when we arrived; there wasn't a clean break. There was a sense of the cloud that gathered around you and of the light fading, but it was not dramatic. And then we were surrounded and had to turn on the fog-lights and I would drive as slowly as I could.

'Up there, though, was another world. It felt that way too, for good and bad, another world, with its own laws. Do you remember the way the gliders would pass overhead and if you didn't look up you wouldn't know?

Sometimes a shadow moved across the land and that was the only sign. Or you would stand and wait in the car park until you saw one and waved. It didn't matter whether they saw you or not. The important thing was to wave. Sometimes we would stand there for half an hour or more to watch them complete their circuit and come back. And sometimes they didn't come back and you were scared. And I would reassure you. Do you remember?'

'Yes,' I say, my voice sounding strange to me. 'I remember.'

'I spent six months in the same prison as your father,' Jozef says, his voice low and soft, a wry smile on his lips. 'I never told you. This is another of my secrets. He wasn't a dangerous man. By then he was treated like someone who had committed a small crime, that is the value of contrition, so I had the opportunity to speak to him sometimes. And, of course, Margot would visit him and talk about you and he would tell me. So I knew that you were happy with your foster-family, that you were working hard at school, that you had left the boy – what was his name? Richie? Yes, Richie. I knew this also from your letters, which I treasured. They were fine letters, from the heart. Nobody knew about those letters, Carol. This is the truth. I kept them to myself, I read them many times, many times, until they came to pieces in my hands. I thought of you very often. How could I not love you? I was proud that you had let me protect you. Does that sound strange? I made things for you out of bread and paper and scraps of cardboard I was able to collect while

I was at work, my first small pieces. Lovely things. There are copies of some inside these panels, you will come across them if you look, by chance, because sooner or later everything will find its place in here, everything will come to hand. You have to be patient sometimes, Carol. You have to let things come to you.'

'Where have you been?' I ask. I could tell him about Kakuna now, but don't. There will be time for that. 'I've missed you.'

'I have been to Poland. There were things I had to do. I should have spoken to you, I know that. I have been weak with you, I have always had a streak of cowardice in me. I have pushed things away, pretended. But there were things I had to find out finally. And now I have. I have been to find my family, Carol. It wasn't difficult. There is so much information.' He plays with the hammer, lifting it, letting it fall back into his hand. 'My father and mother died in separate camps. It seems that my father was shot almost immediately, no more than a few miles from the house. My mother died later, towards the end of the war, in a place called Sobibor. Only my sister is missing. I have found no record of her.' He pauses. 'I wonder sometimes if I have invented her, to make their crime more unpardonable.' He lifts his face. 'Forgive me, Carol. Forgive my silence. There are so many things that must be said.'

I walk across and take the hammer from his hand. For a moment I don't know what to do with it, whether to use it as a weapon or a tool. I weigh it in my left hand while he watches me. Then, with a sigh that startles me, I crouch in front of him and lay it on the floor and use my two bare hands, palms down, to cup his knees. How frail his legs feel beneath the fabric, nothing but bone and sinew, the legs of an old man. This work will never be finished, I think. No barn will hold it.

Acknowledgements

I'd like to thank my sister, Jane Lambert, and my friends, Clarissa Botsford, Flora Botsford, Peter Douglas, Wayne Harper, Joanna Leyland, Sally MacLaren, Jutta Schettler, Jane Stevenson and Phyllida White, for casting a critical and affectionate eye over earlier drafts of this novel.

I'd like to thank my agent, Isobel Dixon, for her commitment and faith, and my editor, Sam Humphreys, for her invaluably creative pedantry (her word, not mine!).

I'd like to thank Giuseppe for everything else.